James Patterson is one of the best-known and biggest-selling writers of all time. He is the author of some of the most popular series of the past decade — including the Alex Cross and Women's Murder Club novels — and he has written many other number one best-sellers including romance novels and standalone thrillers. He lives in Florida with his wife and son.

James is passionate about encouraging children to read. Inspired by his own son who was a reluctant reader, he also writes a range of books specifically for young readers. James has formed a partnership with the National Literacy Trust, an independent, UK-based charity that changes lives through literacy. In 2010, he was voted Author of the Year at the Children's Choice Book Awards in New York.

I, ALEX CROSS

Detective Alex Cross is pulled out of a family celebration and given the devastating news that his niece, Caroline, has been found brutally murdered. Cross vows to hunt down the killer and soon learns that Caroline was mixed up in one of Washington's wildest scenes. And she was not this killer's only victim. The search leads Cross to a place where every fantasy is possible, if you have the credentials to get in. Alex is soon facing down some very important, very protected, very dangerous people in levels of society where only one thing is certain — they will do anything to keep their secrets safe. As Cross closes in on the killer, he discovers evidence that points to the unimaginable — a revelation that could rock the entire world.

JAMES PATTERSON

I, ALEX CROSS

Complete and Unabridged

CHARNWOOD
Leicester

First published in Great Britain in 2010 by
Arrow Books
The Random House Group Limited, London

First Charnwood Edition
published 2012
by arrangement with
The Random House Group Limited, London

The moral right of the author has been asserted

This novel is a work of fiction. Names and characters are the product of the author's imagination and any resemblance to actual persons, living or dead, is entirely coincidental.

British Library CIP Data

Patterson, James, *1947 –*
   I, Alex Cross.
   1. Cross, Alex (Fictitious character)- -Fiction.
   2. Police- -Washington (D.C.)- -Fiction.
   3. Prostitutes- -Crimes against- -Fiction.
   4. Suspense fiction. 5. Large type books.
   I. Title
   813.6–dc23

   ISBN 978–1–4448–1157–5

Published by
F. A. Thorpe (Publishing)
Anstey, Leicestershire

Set by Words & Graphics Ltd.
Anstey, Leicestershire
Printed and bound in Great Britain by
T. J. International Ltd., Padstow, Cornwall

This book is printed on acid-free paper

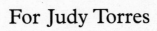

For Judy Torres

Prologue

FIRE AND WATER

1

Hannah Willis was a second-year law student at Virginia, and everything that lay ahead of her seemed bright and promising — except, of course, that she was about to die in these dark, gloomy, dismal woods.

Go, Hannah, she told herself. *Just go. Stop thinking. Whining and crying won't help you now. Running just might.*

Hannah stumbled and staggered forward until her hands found another tree trunk to hold on to. She leaned her aching body into it, waiting for the strength to take another breath. And then to move another burst of steps forward.

Keep going, or you'll die right here in these woods. It's that simple.

The bullet lodged somewhere in her lower back made every movement, every breath an agony, more pain than Hannah had ever known was possible. It was only the threat of a *second* bullet, or maybe worse, that kept her on her feet and going at all.

God, the woods were almost pitch-black back in here. A quarter moon drooping over the thick forest canopy did little to light the ground below. Trees were shadows. Thorns and brambles were invisible in the underbrush; they pierced and raked her legs bloody as she pushed through. What little she'd been wearing to begin with — just an expensive black lace teddy — now

3

hung in shreds off her shoulders.

None of that mattered, though, or even registered with Hannah anymore. The only clear thought that cut through the pain, and the panic, was *Go, girl*. The rest was a wordless, directionless nightmare.

Finally, and very suddenly — had it been an hour? more? — the low canopy of trees opened up around her. 'What the . . . ' Dirt turned to gravel underfoot, and Hannah stumbled to her knees with nothing to hang on to.

In the hazy moonlight, she could make out the ghost of a double line, showing the curve of a country road. It was like a miracle to her. Half of one, anyway; she knew she wasn't out of this mess yet.

When a motor sounded in the distance, Hannah leaned on her hands and pushed up off the gravel. Summoning strength she didn't know she still had, she stood again, then staggered into the middle of the road. Her world blurred through sweat and fresh tears.

Please, dear God, don't let this be them. This can't be those two bastards.

You can't be so cruel, can you?

A red truck careened around the bend then, coming at her fast. Too fast! Suddenly, she was just as blind as she'd been before, in the woods, but from the truck's headlights.

'Stop! Please stop! Pleee-ase!' she screamed. '*Stop, you sonofabitch!*'

At the last possible second, the tires squealed on the pavement. The red pickup skidded into full view and stopped just short of flattening her right there into roadkill. She could feel heat coming off the engine through the grille.

'Hey, sweetheart, nice outfit! All you had to do was stick out your thumb.'

The voice was unfamiliar — which was good, really good. Loud country music was blasting from the cab too — *Charlie Daniels Band*, her mind vaguely registered, just before Hannah collapsed onto the pavement.

The driver was down there on the road a second later as she regained consciousness. 'Oh, my God, I didn't . . . What happened to you? Are you — *what happened to you?*'

'Please.' She barely mustered the word. 'If they find me here, they'll kill us both.'

The man's strong hands wrapped around her, grazing the dime-sized hole in her back as he picked her up. She only exhaled, too weak to scream now. A cluster of gray and indistinct moments later, they were inside the truck and moving really fast down the two-lane highway.

'Hang in there, darlin'.' The driver's voice was shaky now. 'Tell me who did this to you.'

Hannah could feel her consciousness slipping away again. 'The men . . . '

'The men? *What men*, sweetheart? Who are you talking about?'

An answer floated vaguely through Hannah's mind, and she wasn't sure if she said it out loud or maybe just thought it before everything went away.

The men from the White House.

2

His name was Johnny Tucci, but the boys back in his South Philadelphia neighborhood all called him Johnny Twitchy, on account of the way his eyes jumped around when he was nervous, which was most of the time.

Of course, after tonight, the boys in Philly could go screw themselves. This was the night Johnny got into the game for real. This was man time. He had 'the package,' didn't he?

It was a simple job but a real goody, because he was alone and had to take full responsibility. He'd already picked up the package. Scared him, but he'd done just fine.

No one ever said so, but once you started making deliveries like this, it meant you had something on the Family, and they had something on you. In other words, there was a relationship. After tonight, there'd be no more running numbers for Johnny, no more scrapping for crumbs in southside neighborhoods. It was like the bumper sticker that said, *Today is the first day of the rest of your life*.

So naturally, he was pumped — and just a little bit nervous.

His uncle Eddie's warning kept playing like a tape in his mind. *Don't blow this opportunity, Twitchy*, Eddie had said. *I'm way out on a limb here for you*. Like he was doing him some kind of big favor with this job, which Johnny supposed

6

maybe he was, but still. His own uncle didn't have to rub his face in it, did he?

He reached over and turned up the radio. Even the country music they played down here was better than listening to Eddie's nagging in his head all night long. Turned out, it was an old Charlie Daniels Band tune, 'The Devil Went Down to Georgia.' He even knew some of the words. But the familiar lyrics couldn't keep Eddie's voice out of Johnny's head.

Don't blow this opportunity, Twitchy.

I'm way out on a limb for you.

Oh, fuck!

Blue flashers danced off his rearview mirror — coming out of nowhere. Two, three seconds ago, he could have sworn he had I-95 all to himself.

Apparently not.

Johnny felt the corner of his right eye start to twitch.

He goosed the gas; maybe he could make a run for it. Then he remembered the piece-of-shit Dodge he was driving, lifted out of a Motel 6 parking lot back in Essington. *Goddamnit! Should have gone to the Marriott. Got a Jap car.*

Still, it was possible the stolen Dodge hadn't been flagged yet. Whoever owned it was probably sleeping back at that motel. With any luck, Johnny could just eat the ticket and no one would ever have to know.

But that was the kind of luck other people had, not him.

It took the cops forever and a day to get out of their cruiser, which was a bad sign — the worst.

7

They were checking the make and the plates. By the time they came up on either side of the Dodge, Johnny's eyes were going like a couple of Mexican jumping beans.

He tried to be cool. 'Evening, officers. What seems to be — '

The one on his side, a tall dude with a redneck accent, opened the driver's door. 'Just keep your mouth shut tight. Step out of the vehicle.'

It didn't take them any time at all to find the package. After they checked the front and back seats, they popped the trunk, pulled the spare-tire cover, and that was that.

'Holy mother of God!' One of the troopers shone his light down on it. The other one gagged at the sight. '*What the hell did you do?*'

Johnny didn't stick around to answer the question. He was already running for his life.

3

Nobody had ever been any deader, or dumber, than he was right now. Johnny Tucci knew that, even as he broke across the tree line and started slip-sliding down a ravine at the side of the highway.

He could hide from these cops, maybe, but not from the Family. Not in jail, not anywhere. It was a fact of life. You didn't lose a 'package' like this without becoming one yourself.

Voices came from up the slope, and then dancing flashlight beams. Johnny dropped down low and threw himself under a clump of bushes. He was trembling all over, his heart was going so fast it hurt, and his lungs were heaving from too many cigarettes. It was almost impossible to keep still and keep quiet.

Oh shit, I am so dead. I am so, so dead.

'You see anything? See that little bastard? That freak?'

'Nothing yet. We'll get him. He's down here somewhere. Can't be far.'

The troopers fanned out on either side of him, working their way down. Very deliberate and efficient.

Even as he caught his breath now, the trembling only got worse, and not just because of the cops. It was because he'd started to figure out what he had to do next. Strictly speaking, there were only two real options. One involved

9

the .38 he had holstered to his ankle. The other, the package — and who owned it. It was only a question of which way he wanted to die.

And in that cold moonlight, it didn't really seem like much of a question at all.

Moving as slowly as he could, he reached down and pulled the .38. With a badly shaking hand, he fitted the barrel in his mouth. The damn metal clacked hard against his teeth and tasted sour on his tongue. He was ashamed of the tears coming down his face, but that couldn't be helped, and who would ever know but him anyway?

Jesus, was it really going down this way? Crying like a punk, all alone in the woods? What a crummy world this was.

He could just hear the boys now. *Sure wouldn't want to go out the way Johnny did.* Johnny Twitchy. They'd put it on his gravestone — just for spite. Those heathen bastards!

The whole time, Johnny's brain was saying *pull*, but his trigger finger wouldn't do it. He tried again, both hands on the grip this time, but it was no go. He couldn't even do this right.

He finally spit the gun barrel out, still crying like a little kid. Somehow, knowing he was going to live another day didn't do a thing to stop the tears. He just lay there, biting his lips, feeling sorry for himself, until the cops got as far as the stream at the bottom of the ravine.

Then Johnny Twitchy crawled real fast back up the way he'd come, ran across the interstate, and dropped into the woods on the other side — wondering how in Christ he was going to make himself disappear off the face of the earth, knowing that it just wasn't going to happen.

He'd *looked*. He'd seen what was in 'the package.'

Part One

FIRESTORM

1

I celebrated my birthday with a small, very exclusive, very festive and fun party on Fifth Street. It was just the way I wanted it.

Damon had come home from boarding school in Massachusetts as a special surprise. Nana was there, acting large and in charge of the festivities, along with my babies, Jannie and Ali. Sampson and his family were on hand; and of course Bree was there.

Only the people I loved most in the world were invited. Who else would you want to celebrate another year older and wiser with?

I even made a little speech that night, most of which I forgot immediately, but not the opening few words. 'I, Alex Cross,' I began, 'do solemnly promise — to all those present at this birthday party — to do my best to balance my life at home with my work life, and not to go over to the dark side ever again.'

Nana raised her coffee cup in salute, but then she said, 'Too late for that,' which got a laugh.

Then, to a person, everybody did their best to make sure I was aging with a little humility but also a smile on my face.

'Remember the time at Redskin stadium?' Damon cackled. 'When dad locked the keys in the old car?'

I tried cutting in. 'To be fair — '

'Called me out of bed past midnight,'

15

Sampson said, and growled.

'Only after he tried breaking in for an hour because he didn't want to admit he couldn't do it,' Nana said.

Jannie cupped a hand around her ear. '''Cause he's what?' And everyone chorused back, 'America's Sherlock Holmes!' It was a reference to a national-magazine piece from a few years ago that I will apparently never live down.

I swigged my beer. 'Brilliant career — or so they say — dozens of big cases solved, and what am I remembered for? Seems to me, someone was supposed to have a happy birthday tonight.'

'Which reminds me,' Nana said, somehow taking the bait and cutting me off at the same time. 'We've got a piece of unfinished business here. *Children?*'

Jannie and Ali jumped up, more excited than anyone. Apparently, there was a Big Surprise coming for me now. No one was saying what it was, but I'd already opened a pair of Serengetis from Bree, a loud shirt and two minis of tequila from Sampson, and a stack of books from the kids that included the latest George Pelecanos and a biography of Keith Richards.

Another *clue*, if I can call it that, was the fact that Bree and I had become notorious plan cancelers, with one long weekend after another falling by the wayside since we'd met. You might think that working in the same department, same division — Homicide — would make it easier for us to coordinate our schedules, but it was just the opposite most of the time.

16

So I had some idea, but nothing really specific, about what might be coming.

'Alex, you stay put,' said Ali. He'd started calling me Alex lately, which I thought was all right but for some reason gave Nana the creeps.

Bree said she'd keep an eye on me and stayed back while everyone else snuck off to the kitchen.

'The plot thickens,' I muttered.

'Even as we speak,' said Bree with a smile and a wink. 'Just the way you like it.'

She was on the couch, across from where I sat in one of the old club chairs. Bree always looked good, but I preferred her like this, casual and comfortable in jeans and bare feet. Her eyes started on the floor and worked their way up to mine.

'Come here often?' she asked.

'Once in a while, yeah. You?'

She sipped her beer and casually cocked her head. 'Want to get out of here?'

'Sure thing.' I jerked my thumb toward the kitchen door. 'Just as soon as I get rid of those pesky, um — '

'Beloved family members?'

I couldn't help thinking that this birthday was getting better and better. Now I had two big surprises coming up.

Make that three.

The phone rang in the hall. It was our home line, not my cell, which everyone knew to use for work. I also had a pager up on the dresser where I could hear it. So it seemed safe to go ahead and

17

answer. I even thought it might be some friendly soul calling to wish me a happy birthday, or at the very worst, someone trying to sell me a satellite dish.

Will I ever learn? Probably not in this lifetime.

2

'Alex, it's Davies. I'm sorry to bother you at home.' Ramon Davies was superintendent of detectives with Metro, and also my boss, and he was on the line.

'It's my birthday. Who died?' I asked. I was ticked off, mostly at myself for answering the phone in the first place.

'Caroline Cross,' he said, and my heart nearly stopped. At that very moment, the kitchen door swung open and the family came out singing. Nana had an elaborate pink-and-red birthday cake on a tray, with an American Airlines travel folio clipped on top.

'Happy Birthday to you . . . '

Bree held up a hand to quiet them. My posture and my face must have said something. They all stopped right where they were. The joyful singing ended almost midnote. My family remembered whose birthday this was: *Detective Alex Cross's.*

Caroline was my niece, my brother's only daughter. I hadn't seen her in twenty years; not since just after Blake died. That would have made her twenty-four now.

At the time of her death.

The floor under my feet felt like it was gone. Part of me wanted to call Davies a liar. The other part, the cop, spoke up. 'Where is she now?'

'I just got off the phone with Virginia State

19

Police. The remains are at the ME's office in Richmond. I'm sorry, Alex. I hate to be the one to tell you this.'

'Remains?' I muttered. It was such a cold word, but I appreciated Davies not over-handling me. I walked out of the room, sorry I'd said even that much in front of my family.

'Are we talking homicide here? I assume that we are.'

'I'm afraid so.'

'What happened?' My heart was thudding dangerously. I almost didn't want to know.

'I don't have a lot of details,' he told me, in a way that instantly gave me a hint — *he was holding something back.*

'Ramon, what's going on here? Tell me. What do you know about Caroline?'

'Just take one thing at a time, Alex. If you leave now, you can probably be there in about two hours. I'll ask for one of the responding officers to meet you.'

'I'm on my way.'

'And Alex?'

I'd almost hung up the phone, my mind in splinters. 'What is it?'

'I don't think you should go alone.'

3

Running hard, and using my siren most of the way, it took less than an hour and a half to get down to Richmond.

The Department of Forensic Science was housed in a new building on Marshall Street. Davies had arranged for Detective George Trumbull from the State Police CI Bureau to meet us there — Bree and me.

'The car's been towed to our lot up at division headquarters on Route One,' Trumbull told us. 'Otherwise, everything's here. The remains are downstairs in the morgue. All the obvious evidentiary material is in the lab on this level.'

There was that terrible word again. *Remains*.

'What did you bag?' Bree asked him.

'Troopers found some women's clothing and a small black purse wrapped in a mover's blanket in the trunk. Here. I pulled this to show you.'

He handed me a Rhode Island driver's license in a plastic sleeve. The only thing I recognized at first was Caroline's name. The girl in the photo looked quite beautiful to me, like a dancer, with her hair pulled back from her face and a high forehead. And the big eyes — I remembered those, too.

Eyes as big as the sky. That's what my older brother Blake had always said. I could see him now, rocking her on the old porch glider on Fifth Street and laughing every time she blinked up at

21

him. He was in love with that baby girl. We all were. Sweet Caroline.

Now both of them were gone. My brother to drugs. And Caroline? What had happened to her?

I handed the driver's license back to Detective Trumbull and asked him to point us toward the investigating ME's office. If I was going to get through this at all, I had to keep moving.

The medical examiner, Dr. Amy Carbondale, met us downstairs. When we shook hands, hers was still a little cool from the latex gloves she'd been wearing. She seemed awfully young for this kind of work, maybe early thirties, and a little unsure of what to do with me, what to say.

'Dr. Cross, I've followed your work. I'm very, very sorry for your loss,' she said in a near whisper that carried sympathy and respect.

'If you could just give me the facts of the case, I'd appreciate it,' I told her.

She adjusted her glasses, silver wire rims, working up to it. 'Based on the samples I took, there was apparently a ninety-six percent morselization of the body. A few digits did survive, and we were able to get a print match to the name on the license that was found.'

'Excuse me — *morselization?*' I'd never heard the word before in my life.

To her credit, Dr. Carbondale looked me right in the eye. 'There's every reason to believe a grinder of some sort was used — likely a wood chipper.'

Her words took my breath away. I felt them in my chest. *A wood chipper?* Then I was thinking: *Why keep her clothes and driver's license?* As

22

proof of Caroline's identity? A souvenir for the killer?

Dr. Carbondale was still talking. 'I'll do a full tox screen, run a DNA profile, and of course we'll sieve for bullet fragments or other metals, but actual cause of death is going to be hard to prove here, if not impossible.'

'Where is she?' I asked, just trying to focus. *Where were Caroline's remains?*

'Dr. Cross, are you sure right now is the time — '

'He's sure,' Bree said. She knew what I needed, and she gestured toward the lab. 'Let's get on with it. Please, Doctor. We're all professionals here.'

We followed Dr. Carbondale through two sets of swinging doors into an examination room that resembled a bunker. It had a gray concrete floor and a high tiled ceiling, mounted with cameras and umbrella lights. There were the usual sinks and stainless steel everywhere, and a single white body bag on one of the narrow silver tables.

Right away, I could see something was very strange. Wrong. *Both.*

The body bag bulged in the middle and lay flat against the table at the ends. I was dreading this in a way I couldn't have imagined beforehand.

The remains.

Dr. Carbondale stood across from us and pulled back the zipper. 'The heat sealing is ours,' she said. 'I closed it back up after my initial exam earlier.'

Inside the body bag *there was a second bag.*

23

This one looked like some kind of industrial plastic. It was a frosted white translucent material, just clear enough to show the color of meat and blood and bone inside.

I felt like my mind shut down for a few seconds, which was as long as I could deny what I was seeing. It was a dead person in that bag but not a body.

Caroline but not Caroline.

4

The drive back to Washington was like a bad dream that might never end. When Bree and I finally got home, the house was starkly quiet and still. I thought about waking Nana, but the fact that she didn't get up on her own told me she was out cold and needed the rest. All of this bad news could wait until later in the morning.

My birthday cake sat untouched in the refrigerator, and someone had left the American Airlines folio on the counter. I glanced at it long enough to see two tickets for Saint John, an island I'd always wanted to visit in the Caribbean. It didn't matter; all of that was on hold now. Everything was. I felt as though I was moving in slow motion; certain details had an eerie clarity.

'You have got to go to bed.' Bree took me by the hand and led me out of the kitchen. 'If for no other reason than so you can think clearly about this tomorrow.'

'You mean today,' I said.

'I mean tomorrow. After you rest.'

I noticed she hadn't said *sleep*. We dragged ourselves upstairs, took off our clothes, and fell into bed. Bree held my hand and wouldn't let go.

An hour or so later, I was still staring at the ceiling, hung up on the question that had been dogging me ever since we left Richmond: Why?

Why had this happened? Why to Caroline?

25

Why a goddamn wood chipper? Why remains instead of a body?

As a detective, I should have been thinking about the physical evidence and where it could lead me, but I didn't exactly feel like a detective, lying there in the dark. I felt like an uncle, and a brother.

In a way, we'd lost Caroline once before. After Blake died, her mother didn't want anything more to do with the family. She'd moved away without so much as a parting word. Phone numbers were changed. Birthday presents were returned. At the time, it seemed like the saddest possible thing, but since then, I'd learned — over and over — what a staggering capacity the world has for misery and self-inflicted wounds.

Somewhere around four thirty, I swung my legs over the edge of the bed and sat up. My heart and mind were not to be eased.

Bree's voice stopped me. 'Where are you going? It's still night.'

'I don't know, Bree,' I said. 'Maybe the office. Try and get something done. You should go back to sleep.'

'I haven't been asleep.' She sat up behind me and put her arms around my shoulders. 'You're not alone on this. Whatever's happening to you is happening to me.'

I let my head hang and just listened to her soothing voice. She was right — we were in this together. It had been like that ever since we'd met, and that was a good thing.

'I'm going to do anything it takes for you and for this whole family to get through this,' she said. 'And tomorrow, you and I are going to go out there and we're going to start to find out who did this terrible thing. You hear me?'

For the first time since Davies's phone call, I felt a warm spot in my chest — nothing like happiness or even relief, but gratitude, anyway. Something to be glad for. I'd lived most of my life without Bree, and now I couldn't imagine how.

'How did I find you?' I asked her. 'How did I get so lucky?'

'It's not luck.' She held on to me even tighter. 'It's love, Alex.'

5

It seemed both appropriate and ironic to Gabriel Reese that this odd, almost unprecedented middle-of-the-night meeting take place in a building originally built for the State, Navy, and War Departments. Reese lived by a deep sense of the historic in everything he did. Washington, you could say, was in his blood, in his family's blood for three generations.

The vice president himself had called Reese, sounding more than a little tense, and Walter Tillman had run two Fortune 100 companies, so he knew a thing or two about pressure. He hadn't given details, just told Reese to be at the Eisenhower Executive Office Building, *now*. Technically, this was the VP's ceremonial office, the same one where veeps from Johnson through Cheney had welcomed leaders from every quadrant of the globe.

More apt and to the point, it was away from the West Wing and whatever eyes and ears this secret meeting was clearly designed to avoid.

The doors to the inner office were closed when Reese got there. Dan Cormorant, head of the White House's Secret Service detail, was stationed outside with two other agents farther down the hall in either direction.

Reese let himself in. Cormorant followed and closed the heavy wood doors behind them.

'Sir?' said Reese.

Vice President Tillman stood with his back to them at the far end of the room. A row of windows reflected the glow of half-lit globes on an elaborate gasolier overhead, a reproduction. Several glass-encased ship models gave a more specific reference to the building's history. This office had been General Pershing's during World War Two.

Tillman turned and spoke. 'We've got a situation, Gabe. Come and sit down. This is not good. Hard to imagine how it could be much worse.'

6

Agent Cormorant walked forward and took a standing position next to the vice president. It was an odd move, and Reese's gut tightened another notch. He was chief of staff — there was very little that the Secret Service should know about ahead of him. But they clearly did in this case. What in the name of God had happened? To whom had it happened?

The vice president nodded for Cormorant to go ahead and speak.

'Thank you, sir. Gabe, keeping what I'm about to tell you to yourself probably constitutes a felony. You need to know that before I — '

'Just spit it out, Dan.'

Gabe Reese liked Cormorant well enough, just not the way he pushed the bounds of his position. Tillman had brought both of them along, all the way up from the old days of Philadelphia politics, so there was some leeway to be expected here. It was just that Cormorant always seemed to make a little more of it than Reese thought he should. Then again, Cormorant probably thought Reese lived with a stick up his ass.

'Have you ever heard the name Zeus mentioned in any work-related context?' the agent asked. 'Zeus, as in the Greek god.'

Reese thought for a moment. Secret Service had revolving code names for all protectees, but that certainly wasn't a familiar one, and, of course, it would have to be a higher-up. He shook his head. 'I don't think so. Should I have?'

Cormorant didn't answer the question, merely continued. 'Over the past six months, there have been a series of missing-persons cases, all over the mid-Atlantic region. Mostly women, but a few men too, and all of them in a certain profession, if you follow me, which I'm sure you do. So far, nothing's connected them.'

'Until now,' Reese inferred aloud. 'What the hell is going on?'

'Our intel division has three separate communications intercepts linking this tag, *Zeus*, to three separate cases. Last night, it came up again, but on a known homicide this time.' He paused for emphasis. 'All of this is classified, of course.'

Reese felt his patience slipping fast. 'What does this have to do with the vice president? Or the president — since you've called me in? I'm not even sure we should be having this conversation.'

Tillman spoke up then, cutting through the bullshit as usual. 'This Zeus, whoever it is, has some kind of connection to the White House, Gabe.'

'*What?*' Suddenly Reese was up and out of his chair. 'What kind of connection? What are you saying — exactly? What the hell is going on here?'

'We don't know,' Cormorant said. 'That's the first part of the fucking problem. The second is shielding the administration from *whatever* this is going to be.'

'Your job is covering the president and vice president, not the entire administration,' Reese shot back, his voice rising.

Cormorant stood firm, both arms folded across his chest. 'My job is to investigate and prevent any potential threat — '

'Both of you, please shut it!' Tillman's voice rose to a shout. 'We're all together on this or the meeting is terminated right now. You got that? *Both of you?*'

They answered in unison. 'Yes, sir.'

'Dan, I already know what you think. Gabe, I want your honest opinion. I'm not at all sure we should keep this quiet. It could very easily come back to bite us, and we're not talking about censure or a slap on the wrist here. Not with this Congress. Not with the press either. And surely not if this actually involves murder.'

Murder? Dear God, Reese thought.

He ran a hand through his hair, which had been silver since his midtwenties. 'Sir, I'm not sure that an off-the-cuff answer to a question like this is in your best interests, or the president's. Is this a rumor? Are there hard facts to substantiate it? What facts? *Does the president know yet?*'

'The problem is that we know very little at this juncture. Goddamnit, Gabe, what does your gut tell you? I know you have an opinion. And *no*, the president doesn't know. We know.'

Tillman was big on gut, and he was right; Reese did already have an opinion.

'Going public is a bell that can't be unrung. We should find out what we can, within a very limited time frame. Say two or three days. Or

32

until you specify otherwise, sir,' he added for Agent Cormorant's benefit. 'And we'll need an exit strategy. Something to distance ourselves when and if any story comes out before we want it to.'

'I agree, sir,' Cormorant put in. 'We're way too much in the dark right now, and that is unacceptable.'

Tillman took a deep breath that Reese read as both resignation and assent. 'I want you two working together on this. No phone calls, though, and for God's sake, no e-mails. Dan, can you assure me that absolutely none of this goes through the Crisis Center?'

'I can, sir. I'll have to speak to a few of my men. But it can be contained. For a while.'

'Gabe, you mentioned exit strategies?'

'Yes, sir.'

'Think dimensionally here, all possible scenarios. Anticipate everything. And I mean *everything*.'

'I will, sir. My mind is going at about a million miles an hour right now.'

'Good man. Any other questions?'

Reese had already started scanning his memory for historical or legal precedent, more out of habit than anything. There were no questions of loyalty here. His only reservation was situational. Good God Almighty — *if there was a serial killer connected to the White House? Any kind of killer?*

'Sir, if there's word out on this, what's to keep anyone else — God forbid a reporter — from picking up on it?'

33

Cormorant looked offended, but he let the vice president answer.

'It's the Secret Service, Gabe. We're not talking about an open-source intelligence here.' Cormorant stood down and Reese tensed.

'But that's not the kind of insurance I'm going to depend on either. I want this done fast, gentlemen. Fast and clean and thorough. We need some real facts. *And clarity.* We need to find out who the hell Zeus is and what he's done, and then we have to deal with it *like it never happened.*'

7

The punches kept coming, hard ones. Despite the Rhode Island driver's license, Caroline had been living in Washington for the last six months, but she'd never tried to make contact with me. She had an English-style basement apartment on C near Seward Square — less than a mile from our house on Fifth Street. I'd jogged by her building dozens of times.

'She had nice taste,' Bree said, looking around the small but stylish living room.

The furniture and decor had an Asian influence, lots of dark wood, bamboo, and healthy-looking plants. A lacquered table by the front door held three river stones, one of them carved with the word *Serenity*.

I didn't know if that felt more like a taunt or a reminder. Caroline's apartment was nowhere that I wanted to be right now. I wasn't ready for it.

'Let's split up,' I told Bree. 'We'll cover the apartment faster that way.'

I started with the bedroom, forcing myself to keep going. *Who were you, Caroline? What happened to you? How could you die the way you did?*

One of the first things that caught my attention was a small brown leather date book on a desk near her bed. When I grabbed it, a couple of business cards fluttered out and onto the floor.

I picked them up and saw they were both for Capitol Hill lobbyists — though I didn't recognize the names, just the firms.

Half of Caroline's date book pages were blank; the others had strings of letters written on them, starting at the beginning of the year and going about two months ahead. Each string was ten letters, I noticed right off. The most recent, from almost two weeks before Caroline had died, was SODBBLZHII. With ten letters.

The first thing I thought of was phone numbers, presumably coded or scrambled for privacy.

And if I asked myself *why* at that point, it was only because I was putting off an inevitable conclusion. By the time I'd gone through the big rosewood dresser in her walk-in closet, there was little doubt left about how my niece had been affording this beautiful apartment and everything in it.

The top drawers were filled with every kind of lingerie I could imagine, and I have a good imagination. There was the more expected lacy and satin stuff, but also leather, with and without studs, latex, rubber — all of it neatly folded and arranged. Probably the way her mother had taught her to organize her clothing as a kid.

The bottom drawers held a collection of restraints, insertive objects, toys, and contraptions, some of which I could only guess about and shake my head over.

Separately, everything I'd found was no more than circumstantial. All together, it got me very depressed, very quickly.

Was this why Caroline had moved to DC? And was it the reason she'd died the way she did?

I came out to the living room in a fog, not even sure I could talk yet. Bree was down on the floor with an open box and several photos spread in front of her.

She held one up for me to see. 'I'd recognize you anywhere,' she said.

It was a snapshot of Nana, Blake, and me. I even knew the date — July 4, 1976, the summer of the Bicentennial. In the picture, my brother and I were wearing plastic boaters with red, white, and blue bands around them. Nana looked impossibly young and so pretty.

Bree stood up next to me, still looking at the photo. 'She didn't forget you, Alex. One way or another, Caroline knew who you were. It makes me wonder why she didn't try to contact you after she came to DC.'

The picture of Nana, my brother, and me wasn't mine to take, but I put it in my jacket pocket anyway. 'I don't think she wanted to be found,' I said. 'Not by me. Not by anybody she knew. She was an escort, Bree. High-end. Anything goes.'

8

Back at the office, which was buzzing with activity and noise, I got word from Detective Trumbull down in Virginia. Prints on the stolen car matched up to a John Tucci of Philadelphia, now at large.

I played some fast connect-the-dots — from Trumbull in Virginia, to a friend at the FBI in Washington, to their field office in Philly and an agent, Cass Murdoch, who threw down another piece of the puzzle for me: Tucci was a known but small-time cog in the Martino crime family organization.

That information cut both ways. It was a specific lead early in the case. But it also suggested that the driver and the killer might not be the same person. Tucci was probably part of something bigger than himself.

'Any guesses what Tucci was doing all the way down here?' I asked Agent Murdoch. Bree and I had her on speakerphone.

'I'd say he was either reassigned or else moving up in the organization. Taking on bigger jobs, more responsibility. He'd been arrested but never served time.'

'The car was stolen in Philadelphia,' Bree said.

'So then, yeah, he was working from home, emphasis on the *was*. My guess is he's probably dead by now, after a screwup like that, *whatever* the hell happened out there on I-95.'

'How about possible clients in Washington?' I asked. 'Does the Martino family have any regular business down here?'

'Nothing I know of,' Murdoch said. 'But there's obviously someone. John Tucci was too small-time to have drummed this up on his own. He probably thought he was lucky to get the assignment. What an asshole.'

I hung up with Murdoch and took a few minutes to scribble some notes and synthesize what she'd told us. Unfortunately, every new answer suggested a new question.

One thing seemed pretty clear to me, though. This wasn't just a homicide anymore, and it was no individual act. Maybe it involved a sex-and-violence creep — but maybe it was a cover-up? Or both?

9

There was more, of course, lots more, the kind of upsetting detail that keeps certain stories in the news for months, and some of it came right away for a change. Dr. Carbondale reached me in my car on the way home. Bree was driving her own car. 'Toxicology shows no known poisons in Caroline's system,' Carbondale told me. 'No drugs of any kind, other than a .07 blood alcohol level. She couldn't have been more than tipsy at the time of death.'

So Caroline hadn't been on drugs, and she hadn't been poisoned. That wasn't much of a surprise to me. 'What about other causes?' I asked Carbondale.

'I'm more and more certain that's going to be an unanswerable question. All I can do is rule out certain possibilities. There's no way of determining, for example, if she was beaten or strangled or — '

She stopped short.

The words came out of me like bile. 'Or put right into that machine.'

'Yes,' she said tightly. 'But there is one other thing to tell you.'

I gritted my teeth and wanted to hit something with my fist. But I had to listen.

'We've isolated the remaining fragments. There's some indication of antemortem bite marks.'

40

'Bite marks?' I looked around for a place to pull over. '*Human* bite marks?'

'I think so, yes, but I can't be certain at this point. Biting can look almost identical to bruising, even under the best of circumstances. That's why I'm bringing in a forensic odontologist to consult. What we're working with is bone fragments where some of the tissue survived, so I can only see — '

'I'm going to have to call you back,' I said.

I pulled to the side of Pennsylvania Avenue and just let people honk their horns and go around me. This was too much — the unfairness, the cruelty, the violence, all those things I'm usually so good at dealing with.

I threw back my head and cursed at the car ceiling, or God, or both. *How could this be allowed to happen?* Then I laid my head against the steering wheel and I started to tear up. And while I was there, I said a prayer for Caroline, who didn't have anyone with her when she needed it most.

10

Eddie Tucci knew he had screwed up really bad this time. *Unbelievable!* It was a terrible mistake to give that job — or any job — to his nephew Johnny. Not for nothing did they call the kid Twitchy. Now he'd gone AWOL and Eddie had spent the past three days waiting for the rest of the shitstorm to hit the fan.

Even so, when the lights in his bar went out just after closing on Wednesday night, Eddie didn't think too much about it. The building was going to shit, the whole neighborhood. Breakers popped all the time.

He slid closed the register drawer and walked out from behind the bar in the dark. Through the swinging door to the back room. If he could manage to find it, there was an electrical box on the wall.

Eddie didn't get that far.

Out of nowhere, a bag came down over his head. At the same time, something hit his right knee from the side, hard. Eddie heard the joint pop just before he went down, moaning from the pain.

His moans didn't stop them. Somebody put him in a powerful headlock, while someone else tied his ankles. He couldn't even get off a punch, a kick, nothing. He'd just been hog-tied.

'You fuckers! I'm going to kill you. You hear me? *You hear me?*'

Apparently not. They hoisted him up onto the big table in back and cuffed each hand to the wooden legs underneath. Eddie yanked at the cuffs, but they only cut into his wrists. Even if he could get up, his knee felt like it was never going to work right again. He'd be a cripple now.

Then a faucet was turned on — full force.

What was that about?

11

When they pulled the bag off his head, the lights were back on. That was good, right?

Well, not exactly. Eddie saw two upside-down faces looking at him, a white guy and a brown one, maybe Puerto Rican. They were dressed right for the neighborhood, but their short haircuts and the way they operated marked them as suits or military, maybe both.

And Eddie knew right then just how scared he ought to be. This thing, his nephew's screwup, had obviously gotten way out of hand.

'We're looking for Johnny,' the white guy said. 'Any idea where he is?'

'I haven't heard from him!' It was the God's honest truth. These were not people to screw around with. He was sure of that much.

'That's not what I asked you, Ed. I asked if you knew where he was.' The voice was cool, the two of them watching him like he was a specimen in a lab.

'Hand to God, I don't know where Johnny is. You gotta believe me on that.'

'Okay, I hear you.' The dark one nodded. 'I believe you, Ed. Let's just be sure, though.'

Eddie's heart jumped into his throat before they even moved on him. The white one put him in another powerful headlock, grabbed his jaw, and forced the handle of a screwdriver into his mouth. Then he pinched Eddie's nose closed with two fingers.

The other dude came back into view, holding the running end of a green rubber hose. He held it over Eddie's face and let the water pour into his mouth.

Eddie gagged hard. This was bad! The water was coming too fast to swallow. He couldn't breathe; he nearly bit through the screwdriver handle trying to spit it out.

Pretty soon, his chest began to burn and his lungs were pulling for air. He bucked on the table, but the cuffs yanked him right back down. Pressure was building behind his eyes and nose, and he realized suddenly that he was going to die.

That's when the panic really took over. There was no pain anymore, no sound of him choking — just overwhelming fear. It was worse than any nightmare he could imagine, because this was real. It was happening in the back room of his own gin mill in Philly.

Eddie didn't even know that the water had stopped at first. The white guy tilted his head to the side, pulled out the screwdriver, and let him hack it out for a minute. It felt as if he were going to cough up a lung.

'Most people last a couple of minutes before they cave. Of course, these are soldiers I'm talking about.' One of them patted him on the belly. 'That doesn't quite describe you, Ed. So let me ask you again. *Do you know where Johnny is?*'

Eddie could barely talk, but he choked out a fast answer. 'I'll find him. I swear to God I will!'

45

'See, this is what I hate about the mob.' The voice came a little closer to his left ear. 'You people just say whatever you need to say, whenever you need to say it. There's no integrity. Nothing you can depend on.'

'Give me a chance! I'm begging you!'

'You don't get it, Ed. This *is* your chance. You either know where Johnny is or you don't. Now, which is it?'

'I don't know!' He was blubbering, half out of his mind. 'Please . . . *I don't know.*'

They broke a couple of teeth getting the screwdriver back in his mouth. Eddie clenched his jaw and thrashed and begged for his life, but only until the torrent of water cut him off again. It didn't take long before he was right back where he'd been a minute ago, absolutely convinced he was about to die.

And this time he was right.

12

The bizarre murder case was spreading out like spidery legs around me, but one question hung over the rest: *Were there others who had died like Caroline? Was that a possibility? A probability?*

Obtaining a credible account of missing persons in DC is harder than it might seem. After speaking with someone at the Youth Investigations Bureau, which has a centralized database, I had to go district by district, personally talking with detectives all over the city. Incident reports are public information, but what I needed were PD252s, which are private case notes.

That's where I could start to filter for students, runaways, and above all, anyone with a known or suspected history of prostitution.

I brought home the files I'd gathered and took them to my office in the attic after dinner. I cleared off one entire wall and started tacking up everything — pictures of the missing, index cards with case vitals that I'd written up. Plus a DC street map, flagged everywhere that victims had last been seen.

When all that was done, I stood back and stared, looking for some kind of pattern to reveal itself.

There was Jasmine Arenas, nineteen, two priors for solicitation. She worked Fourth and K, where she'd last been seen getting into a blue Beemer around two a.m. on October 12 of last year.

Becca York was just sixteen, very pretty, an

47

honor student. She'd left Dunbar High School on the afternoon of December 21 and hadn't been seen or heard from since. Her foster parents suspected she'd run away to New York or the West Coast.

Timothy O'Neill was a twenty-three-year-old call boy who had been living with his parents in Spring Valley at the time of his disappearance. He drove away from the house around ten p.m. on May 29 and never came home again.

It wasn't like I actually expected any kind of connect-the-dots pattern to jump out at me. This was more like *building the haystack*. Tomorrow, we'd start looking for the needle.

That meant fieldwork, and lots of it, following up on every one of these tawdry files. If just one of them showed a connection to Caroline, it could be huge. This was the kind of homicide that used to make me wonder why I keep coming back for more, year after year. I knew that on some level I was addicted to the chase, but I used to think that if I figured out why, then I'd stop needing it so much, maybe even turn in my badge. That hadn't happened. Just the opposite.

Even if Caroline hadn't been my niece, I still would have been standing in my attic at two in the morning, staring at that terrible board, as determined as ever to find out who had killed her and maybe these other young people — and why.

Remains.

That was the single word, or maybe the concept, that I couldn't get out of my head, couldn't shake if I wanted to.

13

I fell asleep hard that night and woke up the same way, diving into sleep and having to be ripped out of it. I ate breakfast with Nana, Bree, and the kids, but when I left the house I still wasn't completely awake. It didn't augur well, if you believe in auguring.

The one appointment I needed to keep that day was my meeting with Marcella Weaver. Three years earlier, the breakup of her high-priced escort service had made national headlines and earned her the nickname 'Madam of the Beltway.' An alleged client list had never surfaced but still had power brokers all over town shaking in their Florsheims.

Since then, she'd bounced back Heidi Fleiss-style, with a syndicated radio show, a couple of lingerie boutiques, and a speaking fee reported to be five thousand. *An hour*, ironically enough.

I didn't care about any of that. I just wanted her insight into the possible murders of escorts. Once I'd agreed to have her lawyer present, she said she'd meet with me at her apartment.

The place was a gorgeous duplex not far from Dupont Circle. She answered the door herself, looking casual and refined in jeans and a black cashmere sweater. She also wore diamond earrings and a diamond-studded cross.

'Is it Detective or Dr. Cross?' she asked.

'Detective, but I'm impressed that you asked.'

'Old habits die hard, I guess. I'm careful. I do my research.' She smiled easily, way more laid back than I'd expected her to be. 'Come on in, Detective.'

In the living room, she introduced me to the lawyer, David Shupike. I recognized him from a couple of high-profile cases around town. He was a dour, balding stereotype of a lonely guy; it was easy to imagine how he and Marcella might have met.

She poured me a tall glass of Pellegrino, and we sat down on a leather couch with a view of the city.

'Let me get this out of the way.' I slid a picture of Caroline across the coffee table. 'Have you ever seen her before?'

'Don't answer that, Marcella.' Shupike started to push the picture back, but Ms. Weaver stopped him. She stared at it, then whispered something in his ear until he nodded.

'I don't recognize her,' she said to me. 'And for whatever it's worth, if I had, I wouldn't have taken David's advice. I really do want to help if I can.'

She seemed sincere to me, and I chose to believe her.

'I've been trying to figure out who Caroline was working for when she was killed. I wonder if you could point me in any direction,' I said.

She pulled her small bare feet up onto the couch while she thought about it.

'How much rent was she paying?'

'About three thousand a month.'

50

'Well, she certainly wasn't making that on the street. If you haven't already, you should check and see if she had a profile with any of the services. Almost all of them are posted online now. Although, if she was truly higher end, it will be that much harder.'

'Why is that?'

She smiled, not impolitely. 'Because not everyone caters to the kind of clientele who use Google to find their girls.'

'Point taken. I've checked out the services already, though.' I liked this woman, in spite of her job history. 'What else?'

'It would help to know if she was working in-call, out-call, or maybe both. Also, if there was any kind of specialty that she had. Dominant, submissive, girl on girl, massage, group parties, that sort of thing.'

I nodded, but this wasn't easy for me, and it was getting worse. Every turn of the case reminded me of something else I didn't want to know about Caroline. I took a sip of mineral water.

'What about the girls themselves? Where are they coming from?'

'I'll tell you this — college newspapers were my gold mine. These kids think they can handle anything. A lot of them already despise men. Some just want an adventure. I advertised in a lot of places, but you'd be surprised.' She pointed at the pocket where I'd put away Caroline's picture. 'She might have been paying her way through law school. Even medical school, believe it or not. I had a future surgeon as one of my very best girls.'

She stopped then and leaned toward me to see into my eyes. 'I'm sorry, but . . . did this girl mean something to you? If you don't mind my asking. You seem . . . sad.'

Normally, I might have minded, but Marcella Weaver had been nothing but helpful and open with me so far.

'Caroline was my niece,' I told her.

She sat back again with a manicured hand over her mouth. 'I never even saw the slightest violence against any of my girls. Whoever did this deserves to die a painful death, if you ask me.'

It seemed like I'd said enough already, but if that lawyer hadn't been sitting there, I probably would have told Marcella Weaver that I felt exactly the same way.

14

I could feel some positive movement on the case, but the rest of the day was all dreaded missing-persons follow-up. Sampson hooked up with me for the afternoon, and we interviewed one distraught family member after another.

By the time we got to Timothy O'Neill's parents, the only thing I felt we'd accomplished for sure was stirring up bad feelings.

The O'Neills lived in a brick-and-stone colonial in Spring Valley. It was modest for the neighborhood but still seven figures, I was pretty sure. Like a lot of people up here, the O'Neills were part of the Washington machinery. They struck me as a 'good' Irish Catholic family, and I wondered how that jibed with the story of their missing son.

'We love Timothy very much' was Mrs. O'Neill's first response to my questioning. 'I know what his file says, and I'm sure you'll think we're naive, but our love for Timmy is unconditional.'

We were standing in their living room, next to a baby grand with family photos spread out over the top. Mrs. O'Neill held on to one of Timothy, a larger version of the same picture I had on my bulletin board at home. I hoped for their sake he had just moved away from Washington.

'You said he was working as a bartender?' Sampson asked.

'As far as we knew,' Mr. O'Neill said. 'Tim was saving up for his own place.'

'And where was that job?'

Their eyes went to each other first. Mrs. O'Neill was already in tears. 'That's what's so very hard,' she said. 'We don't even know. It was some kind of private club. Timothy had to sign a confidentiality agreement. He said he couldn't tell us anything about it — for his own protection.'

Mr. O'Neill picked up for his wife. 'We thought he was being a little grandiose at the time, but . . . now I don't know what to believe.'

I think he did know what to believe, but it wasn't my job to convince the O'Neills either way. These people were desperate to have their son back. I wasn't going to begrudge them whatever it took to get through a difficult interview with two police detectives.

Finally, I asked to see Timothy's room.

We followed the two of them back through the kitchen and attached laundry room to what I assumed had once been a maid's quarters. There was a separate entrance from the back hall and a bedroom with its own bathroom — small but with lots of privacy.

'We haven't touched anything,' Mr. O'Neill said, and then he added almost affectionately, 'You can see what a slob he was.'

My first reaction was that messes are good for hiding things in. The room had as much strewn on the floor as anywhere else. Timothy had never really grown up, had he?

There were clothes piled everywhere — on the

bed, over the easy chair, on top of the desk. Some of it was just jeans and T-shirts, but there was a lot of expensive-looking stuff, too. The one thing he seemed to keep hung up was a collection of suits and jackets, and three leather coats. Two of them were Polo, one Hermès.

That's where I found the haystack needle. Sampson and I had been sifting for about fifteen minutes when I pulled a piece of paper out of one of the blazer pockets.

It had a string of ten letters written on it — like the ones from Caroline's date book. This one said AFIOZMBHCP.

I held it up for Sampson to see. 'Check this out, John.'

Mrs. O'Neill stepped back into the room. She'd been waiting outside the door. 'What is it? Please tell us.'

'Could be a phone number, but I'm not sure,' I said. 'I don't suppose Timothy left his cell phone behind.'

'No. He was attached to that thing twenty-four/seven. I mean, who isn't these days?'

She tried a weak smile, and I tried one back, but it was hard. All I could think about was how much more likely it had just gotten that she would never see Timothy again.

15

Johnny Tucci had stuck to a rigid system for survival since the trooper car stopped him on I-95. For starters, he never traveled in the same direction for two days in a row and never spent more than twenty-four hours in any one place. In fact, if the skinny girl working the register at the 7-Eleven in Cuttingsville hadn't been such an easy, willing young thing, or if he could even remember the last time he'd gotten laid, he probably would have been long gone by now.

Woulda, coulda, shoulda, he was thinking.

He was in the middle of his second time around with the register girl when the flimsy door to room 5 at the Park-It Motel opened. Two men in gray suits strolled in like they had a key or something. How the hell had they gotten in the door? Whatever. They were in.

Johnny jumped about three feet off the bed and pulled the sheet up to cover himself. So did the girl. Liz? Lisl?

'Johnny Tucci? *The* Johnny Tucci?'

One intruder — the speaker — was a white guy, the other Hispanic. Maybe Brazilian? Johnny had no clue who they were, but he sure knew why they'd come to the motel. All the same, he gave it his best. 'You got the wrong room, man. Never heard of John whatever-you-said. Now, please get out!'

The Hispanic guy fired before Johnny even

56

saw he had a gun in his hand. He flinched hard and almost had a heart attack on the spot. When he looked, the girl, Liz/Lisl, was sitting cockeyed against the headboard with a hole in her forehead and blood seeping down to the tip of her nose, then onto her breasts.

'Jesus Christ!' Johnny fell off the bed more than got off, and then crab-walked himself back into a corner. He'd never actually been shot at before.

'Let's try this again. Johnny Tucci?' said the white dude. '*The* Johnny Tucci?'

'Yeah, yeah, *okay!*' He kept his hands up, one of them at the side of his face so he wouldn't have to see the girl lying there dead and leaking blood. 'How'd you find me? What do you want? Why'd you hurt her?'

The two guys looked at each other and laughed at his expense.

These guys obviously weren't Family. They were too 'white' for that, even the dark one. 'What the hell are you? CIA or something?'

'Worse for you, John. We're *former* DEA. Less paperwork, if you know what I mean.'

Johnny was pretty sure he did. They weren't going to write up what had happened to poor Liz or Lisl. What — like she'd tried to pull a gun on them from her pussy?

The white guy crossed the floor in a couple of fast steps and kicked him a swift one in the groin. 'That doesn't mean we like wasting our time running after pathetic garbage like you, though. Let's go. Get your pants on.'

'I . . . can't. Where are we going?' Johnny was

57

doubled over, with his hands on his crotch, only wishing he could hurl. It felt like his stomach had turned inside out. 'Just . . . shoot me and get it over with.'

'Yeah, you'd like that, wouldn't you? Join your little girlfriend in the everlasting. Afraid it's not going to be that easy, my friend.'

The two guys leaned over and started wrapping him in the motel bedsheet. They pulled the corners up all around, tied them tight. Johnny couldn't even take his hands off his meat to do anything. Then they dragged him out the door like he was a bag of dirty laundry.

That's when he would have started screaming, if he'd had the air for it, because Johnny Tucci had just figured out where they were going, and what was going to happen next.

16

When Caroline's mother pulled the black Chevy Suburban into the parking area at Rock Creek Cemetery, it was the first time I'd seen her in over twenty years. We'd spoken on the phone about funeral arrangements, but now that it was here, I didn't know what to expect or really what to say to her.

I opened the car door myself. 'Michelle, hi.'

She looked the same to me, still pretty, with the same long wild hair, shot through with gray now, half-tamed in a braid twisting down her back.

It was her eyes that were different. They'd always been so alive. I could see she'd been crying, but they were dry now. Dry, red around the rims, and so very tired.

'I forgot how much you looked like him,' she said.

She meant Blake; he and I had always been unmistakably brothers, at least physically, especially in the face. Blake was buried here at Rock Creek too.

I held out my arm and was a little surprised that she took it. We started walking toward St. Paul's, with the rest of the family not far behind.

'Michelle, I want you to know that I'm handling Caroline's case myself. If there's anything you need from me — '

'There's not, Alex.'

It came out quickly, a simple statement of fact. When she spoke again, her voice started to shake. 'I'm going to lay my baby to rest . . . ' She stopped to take a steadying breath. 'And then I'm going to go back home to Providence. That's as much as I can handle right now.'

'You don't have to go through this alone. You can come stay at the house. Nana and I would like that. I know it's been a long time — '

'A long time since you turned your back on your brother.'

So there it was. Twenty years of misunderstanding coming out, just like that.

Blake's addiction had done a lot of the talking for him near the end. He'd cut me out when I got aggressive about rehab, but that was obviously not what he told Michelle, who was using heroin at the time too, even while she was pregnant with Caroline.

'It was actually the other way around,' I said to her as gently as I could.

For the first time, her voice rose. 'I can't, Alex! I can't go back to that house, so don't ask me to.'

'Of course you can.'

We both turned around. It was Nana who'd spoken. Bree, Jannie, and Ali were there too, coming up on either side of Nana, her honor guard, her protectors.

Then she walked right up to Michelle and put her arms around her.

'We lost sight of you and Caroline a long time ago, and now we've lost her for good. But you are *still* a part of our family. You always will be.'

Nana stepped back and put a hand on Jannie's

shoulder. 'Janelle, Ali, this is your aunt Michelle.'

'I'm very sorry for your loss,' Jannie said.

Nana went on. 'Whatever happened before today, or whatever happens tomorrow, doesn't mean a thing right now.' Her voice was filling with emotion, and I could hear shades of the southern Baptist heritage coming through. 'We're here to remember Caroline with all the love we have in our hearts. When those good-byes are over, then we'll worry about what comes next.'

Michelle seemed conflicted. She looked around at each of us, not speaking a word.

'So all right, then,' Nana said. She patted her chest a few times. 'Lord, all this grief has given me an awful feeling. Michelle, take my arm, would you?'

I knew Nana's heart was breaking too. Caroline was her granddaughter, though she never really got to know her, and gone forever now. Meanwhile, there was someone else here who needed her help. *Maybe that's where I get it*, I thought. Sometimes the best, or only, way to take care of the dead is to take care of the living.

17

Michelle did go back to her home in Rhode Island that night. I put her on a plane to Providence myself, but I made sure she had my numbers and told her that I hoped we'd hear from her — when she was ready.

The next morning, I was right back at it, the investigation of her daughter's awful murder, and possibly the murders of others.

The first thing I tackled at the office were the phone numbers we'd found at Caroline's apartment and in Timothy O'Neill's bedroom.

My backup plan was to hit up the Bureau for help, but I had a feeling about these numbers. If there was a key to unlocking them, it was probably something that Caroline or Timothy O'Neill could use on a regular basis. I was betting I could do this myself.

I started by writing out all the lettered strings I had on a piece of paper, just to get them rolling around in my head.

A simple A-to-Z, one-through-twenty-six substitution didn't seem right, since anything above J, or 10, wouldn't apply to a phone keypad.

But what if it came off the keypad itself?

I opened my cell on the desk and wrote down what I saw.

ABC — 2
DEF — 3

GHI — 4 (I=1?)
JKL — 5
MNO — 6 (O=0?)
PQRS — 7
TUV — 8
WXYZ — 9

The one and the zero keys didn't have any letters of their own, of course, but the I and O seemed like intuitive substitutions.

That still left G and H for number four, and M and N for number six.

When I used that logic to translate the first string, BGEOGZAPMO, it gave me 2430492760. Then I took the first three digits and Googled them as an area code. But 243 came up invalid.

It felt too soon to abandon the idea, so I kept going with it. I translated the rest of my list into numbers and lined them all up in a column on the page to see if anything jumped out at me.

It sure did. Nearly half the numbers started with a *two*.

It didn't take long from there to see that all of those numbers had a zero in the fourth position and another two in the seventh.

202 is Washington's area code.

I went back to the first number and underlined.

2<u>43</u>04<u>9</u>2760

Things were starting to come together. When I looked at the same positions in the non-202 numbers, all but three gave me either 703 or 301, which are for areas of Virginia and Maryland close to DC.

The final three codes turned out to be from Florida, South Carolina, and Illinois — out-of-town customers, presumably.

Again, I went back to the first string. If positions one, four, and seven were an area code, didn't it make sense to look at positions two, five, and eight for the exchange? I started scribbling again.

2430492760=202
2430492760=447
2430492760=3960
202-447-3960

Next question — was 447 an actual DC exchange? I grabbed the phone book and found out that it was.

This was starting to feel like the first good day of my investigation. A very good day.

Once I'd deciphered everything I had so far, I called a good friend at the phone company, Esperanza Cruz. I knew that the reverse directories we used at work were only good for listed numbers. It took Esperanza maybe fifteen seconds to find the first listing.

'Okay, now you've got me curious,' she said. 'This one is for Ryan Willoughby, unlisted. What's *he* done? Other than being a walking, talking stiff.'

I was surprised but not shocked. Ryan Willoughby was the six o'clock anchor for a network TV affiliate here in the Washington area.

'Esperanza, if you and I were actually having this conversation, I could tell you, but given as how we never spoke today — '

'Yeah, yeah, story of my life, Alex. What's the next number?'

In a few minutes, I had a list of fifteen names. Six of them were familiar to me, including a sitting congressman, a professional football player, and the CEO of a high-profile energy-consulting firm in town. This thing was starting to bubble over, and not in a good way. When I thought about how these men knew Caroline, it made me sick, physically ill.

My next call was to Bree. She recognized two more of the names. One was a partner at Brainard & Truss, a political PR firm on the Hill; and it turned out that Randy Varrick, who was the mayor's press secretary, was a woman.

'Things are about to get real nasty around here,' Bree said. 'These are high-resource people, and I'm afraid they're going to push back hard.'

'Let them push,' I said. 'We'll be ready for them. In fact, I'm going to make my first call right now. In person.'

18

High-resource people, and apparently a lot of them were involved. What was this about, and how had it led to the death of Caroline Cross? Where else would it lead?

It took me less than fifteen minutes to get from the Daly Building on Indiana up to Channel Nine's offices on Wisconsin. By the time I got there, I hadn't cooled down one bit. My badge got me past the guard in the lobby, then up to a receptionist on the third floor. A big number 9 hung on the wall behind her, along with postersized head shots of their news team.

I showed my badge and pointed at the wall. 'I'm looking for *him*.'

She pushed a button without taking her eyes off me. 'Judy? I've got a police officer out here for Ryan?'

She covered the receiver and spoke to me. 'What is this regarding?'

'Tell him I'll be happy to share that information with anyone who wants to listen if he and I aren't face-to-face in the next two minutes.'

About ninety seconds later, I was ushered past reception, past the news studio entrance, and into a hall of windowed offices someplace in the back. Ryan Willoughby was waiting for me, looking like his tie was a little too tight. I'd seen him dozens of times delivering the news, but now all that polished blond congeniality of his was nowhere in sight.

'What the hell is this about?' he asked me, after he closed the door. 'You come barging in here like Eliot Ness, or Rudolph Giuliani back in his prosecutor days.'

I held up a picture of Caroline. 'It's about her,' I said in the quietest voice I could manage.

It took him a second, but I saw a flash of recognition on his face, then a fast recovery. He was brighter than he seemed.

'Pretty girl. Who is she?'

'Are you saying you've never seen her before?'

He laughed defensively, and a little more of the anchorspeak came into his voice. 'Do I need a lawyer here?'

'We found your phone number in her apartment. She was murdered.'

'I'm sorry about that, the girl's murder. A lot of people have my number. Or they can get it.'

'A lot of call girls?' I asked.

'Listen, I don't know what you want with me, but this is obviously some kind of mistake.'

Whatever he was publicly, this guy was nothing but a scumbag to me now. It was clear he didn't care about Caroline and what had happened to her.

'She was twenty-four,' I said.

I held up the picture again.

'Someone took bites out of her. Probably raped her before they killed her. Then they put her body through a wood chipper. We found what was left of her — the remains — in a plastic bag being transported by a mob guy.'

'What are you . . . Why are you telling me this?

67

I don't know the girl.'

I looked at my watch. 'I'm going to offer you a deal, Ryan. The terms are good for the next thirty seconds. You tell me how you found out about her, right now, and I leave your name out of my investigation. Unless, of course, you're guilty of something a lot more damaging than procuring.'

'Is that a threat?'

'Twenty seconds.'

'Even if I had any idea what you were talking about, how do I know you are who you say you are?'

'You don't. Fifteen seconds.'

'Excuse me, Detective, but you can go to hell.'

My hand was cocked, but I caught myself. Willoughby flinched and took a step back.

'Get out of my office, unless you want me to have you thrown out.'

I waited until the full thirty seconds were up.

'I'll see you on the news,' I said. 'Trust me, you won't be the one delivering it.'

19

Twenty miles of thick, old-growth Virginia forest separated Remy Williams's cabin from pretty much everything else in the world. It was a pristine bit of wilderness with all the privacy he could ever want. A person could scream all night long out here and never be heard.

Not that there ever was much screaming or carrying on out here. Remy appreciated efficiency, and he was good at what he did.

Disposal.

The thing he didn't like was surprises — like the bright headlights that raked back and forth over his cabin window just after darkness fell that night.

In a few seconds, he was out the back door with one of the three Remington 870 shotguns he kept around for exactly this reason — uninvited visitors. He hustled over to the side of the cabin and took up a position with a perfect view of the dark-colored sedan that was just coming to a stop out front.

He saw that the vehicle was a Pontiac sedan, either black or dark blue.

Two men got out. 'Anybody home?' one of them called. The voice was familiar, but Remy kept the Remington on his hip anyway.

'What are you doing out here?' he yelled to them. 'Nobody called ahead.'

Their shadows turned toward him in the dark.

'Relax, Remy. We found him.'

'Alive?'

'At the moment.'

Remy slowly came around to the porch and traded the shotgun for a battery-powered lantern, which he lit.

'What about the other one? The girl who run off?'

'Still working on it,' said the cocky one, the white guy. Remy didn't know either of their names and didn't want to. He knew the spic was the smart one, though, and the most dangerous. Silent but deadly all the way.

He walked to the back of the car and thumped on the trunk with his lantern.

'Pop it.'

20

The young punk inside was naked as a newborn, half-wrapped in a soiled bedsheet with a double dose of duct tape twisted across his mouth. As soon he as laid eyes on Remy, he started scrambling around like there was somewhere inside that trunk he could go and hide.

'Why in hell's he not wearing anything? What's the point in that?'

'He was banging some girl when we found him.'

'And she's — ?'

'Been taken care of.'

'Awww, you should have brought her to me for safekeeping too.'

Remy turned back to the kid, who'd gone still again — except for the eyes. Those never stopped moving.

'He's a funny little gerbil, isn't he?'

He reached down and pulled the boy up, then spun him around so the punk could see the twenty-year-old wood chipper in the car's headlights.

'Now, you know why you're here, so I won't quibble on the details,' he said. 'I just need to know one thing from you, and I want you to think real careful about this. You ever tell anyone about this place? Anyone a'tall?'

The kid shook his head way more than he needed to — *no, no, no, no, no.*

'You're real sure about that, son? You wouldn't lie to me? 'Specially now?'

The head changed direction and went *yes, yes, yes.*

Remy laughed out loud. 'You see that? He looks like one of those stupid bobbleheads. For your dashboard?' He bent his knees to be face-to-face with the kid, and palmed his skull. Then he started rocking it up and down and side to side, laughing the whole time.

'Yes, yes, yes . . . no, no, no . . . yes, yes, yes . . . '

Then, just as fast, he twisted the head halfway around with a crisp snap and let the boy fall to the ground like a broken toy.

'That's it? Break his neck?' one of the other two asked. 'That's what we wanted him alive for?'

'Oh, it's jus' fine,' Remy told them, pushing the accent a little. 'I got an intuition about this stuff.' They both shook their heads like he was some ignorant redneck, which Remy took as a compliment to his acting abilities.

'Hey, you fellas want to stick around for a drink? I've got some good stuff out back.'

'We've got to keep moving,' said the dark-skinned ghost. 'Thanks for the offer. Maybe some other time, Remy.'

'Suit yourself. No problema.'

In truth, there wasn't a drop of alcohol anywhere on the property. The only thing Remy drank besides bottled water, which he bought by the case, was the sun-brewed iced tea he sometimes made from it. Alcohol was poison to

72

the system. He just liked letting these sanctimonious pricks think what they wanted to think about him anyway.

They were typical government issue, those two, the way they saw everything and nothing at the same time. If they looked a little closer, they'd know when they were being tested, and what they were up against.

'One other thing,' he added. 'No more pickups.' He prodded the dead boy with his foot. 'That part ain't been working out so well, you know? I'll do the disposals, starting with him.'

'Agreed. He's all yours.'

They drove off without even a good-bye wave. Remy waved, then he waited until he couldn't hear the car anymore, and got to work.

The kid was just skin and bones, and it didn't take any more cutting to get him ready than it would have for a girl. Two at the knees, two at the hips, two at the shoulders, one at the neck. Then one long swipe down the middle of his skinny little torso. It was messier with the knife than it might have been with a chainsaw or an axe, but Remy liked wet work, always had.

Once that was done, it took only about ten minutes to get the Philly Flash through the machine and into a plastic bag. It was amazing how light the bags always felt — as if it was something more than just foam and residue that got left behind inside the chipper.

He took a shovel and a flashlight from the cabin and threw the bag into a wheelbarrow. Then he started walking into the woods. It didn't matter which way. Wherever this kid landed, he was going to disappear forever.

'Never to be seen or heard from again,' Remy muttered to himself. He bobbled his head up and down and side to side as he walked, and started to laugh. 'No. No. No. No. Never. No. No. No. No.'

21

A loud noise woke me in the middle of the night. Something had fallen and broken downstairs. I was almost sure of it.

I looked at the clock. Saw it was just after four thirty. 'Did you hear that?'

Bree raised her head off the pillow. 'Hear what? I just woke up. If I'm awake.'

I was already out of bed and pulling on a pair of sweats.

'Alex, what is it?'

'I don't know yet. I'll go see. I'll be right back.'

Everything seemed quiet from where I stopped to listen in the middle of the stairs. I could just see the sky going to blue outside, but it was still dark in the house.

'Nana?' I called in a voice barely louder than a whisper.

There was no answer.

Bree was up now too, and at the top of the stairs, only a few feet away. 'I'm right here.'

When I came down into the front hallway, I could see straight back to the kitchen.

The refrigerator door was open, and there was just enough light from it that I could see Nana lying on the floor. She wasn't moving.

'Bree! Call 911!'

22

Nana lay there on her side, in her favorite old robe and slippers. The pieces of a mixing bowl were on the floor around her, and her face was contorted, as if she'd been in terrible pain when she fell.

'Nana! Can you hear me?' I said as I hurried into the kitchen.

I knelt down and felt for her pulse.

It was weak, but it was there. My own was spiking like crazy.

Please, no. Not now. Not like this.

'Alex, here!' Bree ran in and handed me the phone.

'Nine-one-one, what is your emergency?'

'My grandmother has just collapsed. I found her unconscious on the floor.' My eyes scanned her face, her arms, her legs. 'There's no sign of injury, but I don't know what happened before her fall. Her pulse is very weak.'

Bree started timing Nana's pulse off the kitchen clock while the operator took my name and address.

'Sir, I'm dispatching an ambulance to your house right now. The first thing you want to do is make sure she's still breathing, but try not to move her. It's possible she injured her spine when she fell.'

'I understand. I won't move her. Let me check.'

Nana's face was angled toward the floor. I leaned down and held the back of my hand to her mouth. At first — it seemed like forever — there was nothing, but then I felt a faint movement of air.

'She's breathing, but barely,' I said into the phone.

A soft rattle came from Nana's chest.

'Please hurry. I think she's dying!'

23

Dispatch talked me through something called a 'modified jaw thrust' to help open Nana's airway. It was all nightmarish and surreal, in the worst way I could imagine. I took hold of the curved part of her jaw and pushed it forward and up, using my thumb to keep her lips open.

Her breathing picked up, but only slightly, and not a regular cadence.

Then Ali's voice came from behind me, soft and scared. 'Why is Nana on the ground like that? Daddy, what happened to her?'

He was standing in the kitchen door, holding on to the frame as if he didn't want to be pushed any farther into the room than that.

Bree put a hand over mine on Nana's cheek.

'I've got her,' she said, and I went to talk to Ali.

'Nana's sick and she fell down. That's all it is,' I told him. 'An ambulance is going to come and take her to the hospital.'

'Is she going to die?' Ali asked, and tears flooded his gentle eyes.

I didn't answer, but I kept my arms around him, and we stood in the doorway to the kitchen. The one thing I couldn't do right now was leave Nana. 'We're going to stay right here, and we're going to think about how much we love Nana. Okay?'

Ali nodded slowly without taking his eyes off her.

'Daddy?'

I turned and saw Jannie in the hall. She was even more shocked and wide-eyed than her brother. I motioned her over, and we all waited together for the ambulance to arrive.

Finally, we heard a low siren outside. In a strange way, it seemed to make everything worse.

Once the EMTs got there, they took Nana's vitals and started her on oxygen.

'What's her name?' one of them asked.

'Regina.' The word almost stuck in my throat.

Nana's name means queen, of course, and that's what she is to us.

'Regina! Can you hear me?' The tech pushed a knuckle into her sternum, and she didn't move. 'No pain response. Let's get a heart rhythm.'

They asked me a few more questions while they worked. Was she on medication? Had her condition changed since we called 911? Was there any history of heart trouble with her or in the family?

I kept a hand on Ali the whole time, to let him know I was there, but vice versa too. Jannie stayed right by my side as well.

Within minutes, the EMTs had started a saline lock. Then they slid a collar around Nana's neck and put a backboard under her. Jannie finally buried her face in my side, sobbing quietly.

That got Ali crying again. And Bree too.

'We're a mess,' I finally managed. 'That's why she can't leave us.'

They lifted Nana's tiny body onto a stretcher, and we followed them through the dining and living rooms, then out the front door. The familiarity of the surroundings seemed both sad and scary.

Bree had disappeared for a minute, and now she came up from behind, handing me my cell, a shirt, and a pair of shoes. Then she took Ali from me and put an arm around Jannie. Their faces were like mirrors of everything I was feeling.

'Go with Nana, Alex. We'll follow you in the car.'

24

Gabe Reese was pacing with his arms folded tightly, just inside the West Wing lobby doors. He wasn't used to this kind of uncertainty, the total lack of information, the fucking mystery of it all. He had plenty of resources at his disposal — he just couldn't use most of them on this. Not until he was sure what they were dealing with.

He was waiting for the vice president, and the subject was Zeus, of course, and what had been found out so far, and what kind of unprecedented scandal this could turn out to be. Tillman was scheduled to address the National Association of Small Business Owners from 12:30 to 1:00 at the Convention Center. It was less than a mile and a half away, which meant maybe five minutes in the car. Reese was going to need every second.

At exactly 12:20, the vice president strode into the lobby with the Secret Service's Dan Cormorant on one side and a deputy director of communications on the other.

Two scheduling assistants and another Secret Service agent trailed behind. The usual kind of entourage, trappings of power and arrogance.

Tillman looked surprised to see Reese standing there, holding his trademark fedora in one hand.

'Gabe, you're coming to this thing?'

'Yes, sir. Wouldn't miss it. Not a word. Not an arching eyebrow.'

'Okay. Okay. Let's go, then.'

They continued outside, where the vice president's Cadillac limo, two black Suburbans, and three motorcycle police waited with motors running. As the vice president stepped into his car, Reese put a hand on Cormorant's shoulder.

'We need some privacy, Dan.'

The senior agent squinted in annoyance, then turned to his number two. 'Bender, take the staff car. I've got this covered.'

'Yes, sir.'

'You know that has to go into the log,' Cormorant said as soon as the other agent was out of earshot.

'No, it doesn't,' Reese told him. There was more than enough precedent for this kind of request, even from Reese himself. Once Reese and the vice president were in the car, Cormorant got in. Then he radioed the go-ahead, and the motorcade pulled out toward 15th Street.

25

With the partition up and tinted bullet- and soundproof glass on all sides, this was as private a meeting as they were going to get today, given the vice president's busy schedule.

Reese took a quick breath, then he started right in on what he'd found out. For one thing, the FBI and Metro police were both pursuing the case — at least as a murder investigation. Apparently prostitutes were involved, male and female. Zeus hadn't been indentified yet. *If* there actually was a Zeus.

'I just heard that we've got another problem.' He turned to face the Secret Service agent on the jump seat. 'Dan, do you know who Alex Cross is?'

'MPD detective, specializes in major cases — homicides, serials. He's working on a certain murder in question?' Cormorant hadn't missed a beat. 'We're aware of Cross's involvement. We're watching him.'

'And I'm finding out about this on my own, *why?*'

Cormorant ticked off the vice president's wishes on two fingers. 'No phone, no e-mail, remember? I'll get information to you when I can get it to you, Gabe. We're talking about one homicide detective here.'

'Hang on,' the vice president cut in. 'Where are we on Zeus, Dan?'

'Quickly, please,' Reese added. They were already coming up on K Street, which was less crowded than usual — unfortunately.

'It's complicated. There are a lot of avenues to go down. We've had some SIGINT on a private club out in Virginia. Very discreet place for meetings. It's a sex club, sir. It's possible that Zeus has been there. It's likely he has. The White House, actually the Cabinet, keeps coming up, but that might be because of the code name, *Zeus*. I hope it's no more than that.'

Tillman's expression darkened as he leaned in toward the Secret Service man. 'And that's it? That's all you have?'

'This is a murder investigation. They usually don't solve themselves. The club is called Blacksmith Farms. We have the names of several clients. The owners are mob.'

Tillman snapped. 'Why can't we find out who Zeus is?'

'I'm sorry, sir, but I can't turn over too many rocks without attracting more attention than we want. We're not even sure if Zeus actually used the club in question. There are all these swirling rumors but nothing solid.'

Reese didn't like Cormorant's tone with the vice president any more than he did with himself. 'Swirling rumors. Who else knows about this?' he asked.

'Two senior agents in the Joint Operations Center, one intelligence officer, but it's all being contained. No links to the OVP at all.'

Cormorant gave Reese another one of his squints. 'You need to calm down. It's not helping. We're moving as fast as we can and there's lots to check. The circumstances couldn't be worse.'

The words *fuck you* ran through Reese's mind, but he was too savvy to lose it in front of Tillman. Still, this situation had the makings of one of the biggest bombshells to hit Washington in years. A serial killer involved with the Cabinet — or attached to the White House?

'Sir, I'm going to recommend you designate all Secret Service logs from your detail as sensitive compartmented information — until further notice.'

'Sir, any SCI order puts your thumbprint right where you don't want it,' Cormorant interjected.

'But simultaneously puts that information completely out of reach,' Reese answered back. Tillman had the authority to bypass not just the White House Security Office on this one, but the Freedom of Information Act.

'Okay.' Tillman nodded agreement with the chief of staff. It was done. Then he asked, 'What about this detective, Cross? How worried do we need to be about him?'

Cormorant thought for a moment. 'It's hard to know until he turns something up. *If* he does. I'm keeping my eye on it, and if anything changes at all, I'll update you — '

'*Not me.*' Tillman said firmly. 'Go through Gabe. Everything goes through Gabe from now on.'

'Of course.'

Reese found he was repeatedly running a hand through his hair without even realizing it. They were just arriving at the Convention Center; the pressure was on to wrap this discussion up somehow.

Quickly he said, 'Anything else I should know? Anything else that you've been keeping to yourself? *Like who the hell Zeus is?*'

Cormorant's face reddened, but all he said was 'We're here, sir.'

26

Nana was alive. That's what mattered; it was all I cared about right now. But I did wonder why it was that when you lose someone, or are about to lose someone important to you, they become more precious than ever.

It was hell waiting for her to come back from tests at the hospital. I had to sit for hours in a sterile, fluorescent-lit corridor, while my mind ran through every possible worst-case scenario, a bad habit of mine from work. I tried to fill my head with memories of Nana, going all the way back to when I was ten and she had replaced my parents in life.

When they finally wheeled her out, it was a gift just to look into her eyes. She'd been unconscious when we arrived, and there had been no guarantee I would ever see her alive again.

But here she was, and she was talking.

'Gave you a little scare there, did I?' Her voice was weak and wheezy, and she looked even tinier than usual sitting up on the gurney, but she was alert.

'More than a little scare,' I said. It was all I could do to keep from squeezing the life right back out of her. I settled for a lingering kiss on the cheek.

'Welcome back, old woman,' I whispered in her ear — just to make her smile, which it did.

'Good to be back. Now, let's get out of here!'

27

Once we got Nana settled — *in a hospital bed* — the cardiologist on call came in to meet with us. Her name was Dr. Englefield, and she looked about fifty, with a compassionate face but also the kind of professional detachment I've seen with a lot of specialists.

She worked off Nana's chart while she spoke. 'Mrs. Cross, your general diagnosis is congestive heart failure. Specifically, your heart isn't pumping enough blood into your system. That means you're not getting enough oxygen or nutrients, and that's most likely why you collapsed this morning.'

Nana nodded, not showing any emotion. The first thing she asked was 'How soon can I leave the hospital?'

'The average stay for something like this is four or five days. I'd like to adjust your blood pressure medication and see where we are in a few days.'

'Oh, I'll be at home, Doctor. Where will you be?'

Englefield laughed politely, as if she thought Nana was joking. As soon as she was gone, though, Nana turned to me.

'You need to speak with someone else, Alex. I'm ready to go home.'

'Is that so?' I asked, trying to keep it light.

'Yes, that's so.' She wagged her hand, trying to

shoo me out of the room. 'Go on. Make it happen.'

This was starting to get uncomfortable for me. I'd never called any shots for Nana before, and now, suddenly, I had to do just that.

'I think we should go with the doctor on this one,' I said. 'If a few nights in the hospital means we don't have to repeat this morning, then I'm all for it.'

'You're not listening to me, Alex.' Her voice had changed in a beat, and she grabbed my wrist. 'I am not going to spend another day in a hospital bed, do you hear me? I *refuse*. It's my right to do so.'

'Nana — '

'No!' She let go and pointed at me with a shaking finger. 'I will not have that tone, either. Now, are you going to respect my wishes or not? I'll get right up and do it myself if I have to. You know I will, Alex.'

It was an awful feeling, standing there on the other end of that finger of hers. Nana was insisting, but she was also pleading with me to listen to her wishes.

I sat down on the edge of the bed and leaned in so that my head was right next to hers. When I spoke, it was with my eyes closed.

'Nana, I need for you to get serious about this recovery. Slow down a few miles an hour here and let this happen. You must. So be smart.' The latter was something that Nana had been saying to me since I was ten years old. *Be smart.*

It was totally quiet in the room except the sound of her leaning back against the pillow.

89

When I opened my eyes, there were tears on her cheeks. 'That's it, then? This is where I die?'

I pulled up a chair and sat down next to the bed. Later, I'd sleep in that same chair. 'Nobody's dying in here tonight,' I said.

Part Two

FIRE WITH FIRE

28

Tony Nicholson was already anxious enough, *crazed* actually, and now he was running late, thanks to an overturned tractor-trailer on the way out of the city. By the time he reached Blacksmith Farms, it was just after 9:30 and his important guests were due in less than half an hour. Including a very special guest.

He stayed in his car and buzzed.

'Yes?' a woman's voice answered. Cultured. British. His assistant, Mary Claire.

'It's me, M.C.'

'Good evening, Mr. Nicholson. You're a bit late.' *No shit, Sherlock*, Nicholson thought but didn't say out loud.

The gate swung open and closed again behind his Cayman S as he pulled in.

The long driveway cut across nearly a mile of open field, then through a swath of forest, mostly hickory and oak, before coming out in view of the main house. Nicholson parked his Cayman in the old carriage barn and came in through the patio French doors.

'I'm here, I'm here. Sorry.'

His hostess for the evening, a Trinidadian beauty by the name of Esther, was arranging leather guest folios on a Chippendale table in the foyer.

'Any issues for me?' he asked. 'Any unanticipated problems for tonight?'

'None, Mr. Nicholson. Everything is perfect.' Esther had a wonderfully serene manner that Nicholson loved. It slowed him down right away. 'The Bollinger is iced, we have the Flor de Farach coronas in the humidors, the girls are all beautiful and properly briefed, and you have' — she pulled a watch out of her pocket; there were no clocks in the house — 'at least twenty minutes before our first guests are scheduled to arrive. They called ahead. They are right on time. They sound very . . . *enthusiastic.*'

'Right, then. Excellent job. You know where to find me if you need me.'

Nicholson made a quick pass through the first floor before heading upstairs. The foyer and lounges on this level evoked an English gentlemen's club more than anything, with their mahogany paneling, brass fixtures on the bars, and lots of ridiculously expensive antiques. It looked like the kind of place his father could have only dreamed of joining, given England's obscene class system. Nicholson was a working-class Brighton boy by birth, but he'd left all of that dreary shit behind long ago. Here, he was king. Or at least a crown prince.

He took the main stairs up to the second floor, where several of the girls were already dressed and waiting for the first rush of guests, the 'early buggers.'

Stunningly beautiful girls, elegant *and* sexy, they sat chatting on the low sofas in the mezzanine, which also had comfortable floor cushions all around and layers of soft drapes that could be pulled for more or less privacy,

94

depending on the desires of the party.

'Evening, ladies,' he said, looking them over with an expert eye. 'Yes, yes, very nice. You're all gorgeous. Perfect, every one of you, in every way.'

'Thank you, Tony,' one of them said a little louder than the others. This was Katherine, of course, whose gray blue eyes always lingered over his Nordic features a little longer than the others. She would have loved to have a go at the boss, and for all the wrong reasons, he understood. *Like replacing his wife in his life.*

Nicholson leaned down to whisper in her ear, fingering the hem of her white lace mini as he did. 'A different dress, though, I think, Kat. Can't have the whores looking like whores, now, can we?'

He watched the beautiful girl struggle to keep the brilliant smile on her face — as if he'd just said something charming and sweet. Without another word, she got up and left the room. 'I have to use the little girls' room,' she whispered.

Once he'd been satisfied that everything else was in superb working order, Nicholson continued up to his locked office on the third floor. This was the one area of the house he kept off limits to both the guests and the help.

Inside, he poured a glass of seven-hundred-dollar-a-bottle Bollinger — a gift to himself from the client's stock — and sat down. It had been a hectic day; now he could finally relax.

Well, not really relax, but at least there was the Bollinger.

Two large flat-screen monitors dominated the

desk in front of him. He powered up the system and typed in a long password.

Rows of thumbnail images tiled open like dominos across one of the two screens.

At first glance, they looked like miniature still lifes, each one from a different area of the house — foyer, mezzanine, guest suites, massage rooms, dungeon, screening rooms. There were thirty-six in all.

Nicholson stopped for just a moment to watch the duplicitous Katherine in one of the changing rooms, wearing just a thong, breasts heaving, fussing at her runny eye makeup in the mirror. Beautiful though she might be, Katherine was a mistake — too ambitious, too cunning — but she was not his real priority right now.

He clicked on an image of the driveway in front of the house and dragged it so that it jumped screens to open full-size on the other monitor. A time signature began to count out at the bottom.

He clicked once more, on a red triangular button in the border, for 'record.'

The first cars were just pulling in. The party was about to start.

'Let the fucking begin — mind and otherwise. Whatever their little hard-ons desire.'

29

By eleven thirty, the very expensive and exclusive Blacksmith Farms was in full swing. Each of the guest suites was occupied, the massage rooms, the dungeon, even the mezzanine was hopping with hot sex and related shenanigans — girl-boy, girl-girl, boy-boy, girl-boy-girl, whatever the customer wished.

The entire house had been booked for a bachelor party that evening: five pretty-boy escorts, thirty-four girls, twenty-one very horny guests, a hundred-and-fifty-thousand-dollar fee, already transferred into the club's numbered account.

The host — and best man — was well known to Nicholson: he was Temple Suiter, a partner with one of DC's most prestigious and well-connected law firms, with clients including the Family Research Council and the royal family of Saudi Arabia, as well as members of the former White House administration.

Nicholson had done his homework, as always.

Benjamin Painter, the bachelor of honor, was about to marry into one of Washington's dynasty families. Next week, he'd be calling the senior senator from Virginia Dad, and one of DC's most beloved plastic-surgery victims Mom. He was also widely believed to be gearing up for a Senate run of his own, all of which made Mr. Painter quite valuable — in Nicholson's way of viewing the world, anyway.

Right now, the future groom and senator was sprawled on a club chair in suite A. Two of the youngest, prettiest, and least threatening girls, Sasha and Liz, were slowly undressing each other on the bed while a new one, Ana, worked him over through the cotton of his yuppie boxers. The threesome looked to be in their midteens, but all were of legal age. Nineteen, to be exact. Barely legal.

Nicholson ran a finger across his touchpad to adjust the image. The cameras were wireless, pantilt-zoom units the size of pencil erasers. This particular one was embedded in the room's smoke detector.

A microphone, no bigger than a match head, was hardwired through the ceiling and into the chandelier directly over the king-size bed, where Sasha was just sitting up, smiling blithely, *cooing*.

She straddled Liz, both of them naked now except for expensive-looking costume jewelry, their slinky black cocktail dresses in tiny heaps on the floor.

Sasha reached across to the nightstand, opened the drawer, and pulled out a thick flesh-colored phallus. She held it up and waggled it for Benjamin Painter to see. His eyes widened appropriately.

'Would you like me to do Liz?' she asked, smiling demurely. 'I'd *like* to do Liz. I'd really like to do Liz.'

'That's great,' Ben said, as if praising a useful underling at his father's firm. 'Get her ready for me, Sasha. And you — ' He put his hand on the top of Ana's head as she knelt in front of him.

'You just take your time, Ana. Slow and steady wins the race, am I right?'

'Oh, I wouldn't have it any other way, Benjamin. I'm enjoying this too.'

If Mr. Painter was busy giving Nicholson excellent video material to work with, his good friend from their days together at NYU Law, Mr. Suiter, was all but writing a blank check.

Suiter had two of the prettiest Asian girls, Maya and Justine, in the spa. Maya was lying across the tiled soaking-tub platform, on her back, with her small, shapely legs wiggling in the air — while Suiter drilled her furiously. She seemed to be enjoying it, which was doubtful, since Maya and Justine lived together and were a couple — recently married in their home state of Massachusetts.

Justine, in fact, was just now providing 'the money shot.' She stood over Suiter, knees slightly bent, gripping a hold bar on the ceiling and letting nature take its course down the client's shoulders and back.

Suiter panted out in time with his own thrusts, his voice rising toward climax. 'That's right . . . That's right . . . That'sa girl, that'sa fucking girl.'

Nicholson rolled his eyes in disgust and muted the mating sounds. He didn't need to hear this idiot's twaddle right now. Later in the week, he'd pick out a nice thirty-second clip to send to Mr. Suiter at his home office. Something with full frontal and choice words always seemed to do the job best.

Because as much as these men were willing to

pay for getting spanked on a Saturday night, or even just to fuck a woman who wouldn't ask what they were thinking about afterward, Tony Nicholson knew that they were always — *always* — willing to pay even more for the privilege of keeping those dirty little secrets to themselves.

All of them — except Zeus.

30

'What have you got?'

'License DLY 224, a dark blue Mercedes McLaren. Leased to a Temple Suiter.'

'The lawyer?'

'Presumably. Who else would it be? Guy's got more money than God.'

Carl Villanovich put the camera down and rubbed his eyes vigorously. It had been three straight nights of surveillance in the woods of Blacksmith Farms, and he was stone-cold sick of the duty.

He unfolded a tripod from his pack and mounted the camera to give himself a break. The image played on a laptop next to him as he zoomed out for a long shot of the house exterior.

The place was huge, limestone from the look of it, with three-story columns in front. It had probably been a plantation house at one point. There was a converted barn in the back and several other outbuildings, all of them dark tonight.

'Here comes another one.'

His partner, Tommy Skuba, fired off several shots with a high-speed digital SLR as a wine red Jaguar coupe came rushing out of the woods. Villanovich went in tight on the Jag's license number when it swung around the oval loop in front of the house.

'Got that?' he asked.

'Got it,' came the voice on his headset. Command center was seventy-five miles away in Washington, watching everything in real time.

There was no valet out front. The new arrival parked himself and rang the bell. Almost instantly, a tall, gorgeous black woman in a shimmery dress answered the door, smiling, and let him right in.

'Skuba, stay on the windows.'

'I know, I know. Doin' my best to make Steven Spielberg proud. Jaguar must be a regular.'

Villanovich rubbed both hands up and down his face, trying to stay sharp. 'Any chance of calling this early tonight? We've already got more than we need here, don't we?'

'Negative,' command came back right away. 'We want you there for departures.'

Another round of shots from Skuba's camera pulled Villanovich's attention back to the house. The Jag's driver had just passed a window on the stairs, walking with a girl on his arm. Tall and black, but not the woman from the front door.

'Jesus Christ.' Skuba lowered the camera and muted his headset. 'Did you see the rack on her? I don't mind saying, I'm a little jealous out here. And, uh, horny.'

'Don't be. Quantico's on the case now,' Villanovich told him, still watching the empty window. 'When this place goes down, they're all going down with it.'

31

Before Nana was allowed to come home, I had to meet with Dr. Englefield one more time. In the confines of her office on the first floor at St. Anthony's, the doctor was considerably more relaxed and easygoing and human.

'We've unloaded the fluid in your grandmother's chest and gotten her blood pressure back to a baseline level, but that's only a start. She, and you, are going to have to be vigilant. Regina won't admit it, but she's over ninety years old. This is a serious problem.'

'I understand,' I said. 'And so does my grandmother — believe it or not.'

Nana was already on a whole new regimen of medications — ACE inhibitors, diuretics, and a hydralazine-nitrate combination that had been shown especially effective with African American patients for some reason. There was also a new no-salt diet to think about, and daily weight monitoring to make sure she wasn't retaining excess fluid.

'It's a lot to get used to all at once,' Dr. Englefield said, offering a rare half smile. 'Lack of compliance is a major contributor to cardiac arrest for someone in her position, and family support is crucial. It's critical.'

'Believe me, we'll do whatever it takes,' I told her. Even Jannie had been researching congestive heart failure online.

'I'd also recommend bringing in a home care provider any time you and your wife are out of the house.' Englefield had met Bree only once in passing; I didn't bother to correct her. 'Of course, that might be a tough sell with your grandmother. I suspect it will be.'

I grinned for the first time. 'I see you've been getting to know each other. And yes, we've already started looking into it.'

The doctor smiled too — for about a tenth of a second. 'Regina was lucky to have someone on hand when she collapsed the other day. You'd be wise to make sure she's just as lucky if — or when — it happens again.'

It wasn't hard to see why Nana had dubbed this one 'Dr. Sunshine.' But if she was trying to scare me, it was definitely working.

32

The doctor and I went upstairs to see Nana together. There was safety in numbers after all. Wasn't that right?

'Mrs. Cross,' Dr. Englefield said, 'you're doing quite well, all things considered. I'd recommend one more night's stay and then we can send you off.'

'I like that word, *recommend*,' Nana said. 'Thank you for your recommendation, Doctor. I appreciate it. Now, if you'll excuse us, my grandson is going to take me home. I have things to do today, cakes to bake, thank-you notes to write, and so on and so forth.'

With a quick shrug from Englefield, I let it go. So did she. Forty-five minutes later, Nana and I were on our way home.

In the car, Nana reminded me of an old chocolate Lab we'd had when I was a kid in North Carolina, just before my parents died. The window was down and she was letting the air blow over her while the world flew by outside. I half expected her to start quoting Dr. King. *Free at last, free at last . . .*

Or maybe some choice line of Morgan Freeman's from *The Bucket List*.

She turned to me and patted the upholstery with both hands. 'How do they get these seats so comfortable? I could sleep much better here than in that hospital bed, I'll tell you that.'

'So you won't mind that we turned your room into a den,' I deadpanned.

She cackled and started to recline the seat. 'Just watch me.' But when she got too low, her laugh turned into a coughing jag. Her lungs were still tentative; it doubled her over with a hacking sound that went right to my gut.

I pulled over and got a hand behind her until I could raise the seat again.

She waved me off, still coughing but better. My own heart was working overtime. This recovery was going to be an interesting dance, I could tell.

The coughing episode seemed like a good segue, so once we were moving again, I said, 'Listen. Bree and I have been thinking about getting someone at the house — '

Nana gave a wordless grunt.

'Just for when we're at work. Maybe half a day.'

'I don't need some oversolicitous stranger hovering over me and fluffing my pillows. It's embarrassing. And costly. We need a new roof, Alex, not nursemaids.'

'I hear you,' I said. I'd been expecting that answer. 'But I'm not going to feel comfortable leaving the house otherwise. We have enough money.'

'Oh, I see.' She folded her hands in her lap. 'This is all about what *you* want. I understand perfectly now.'

'Come on, let's not argue. You're going home,' I said, but then I caught a little eye roll from her. She was just busting my chops because she could

106

— for the sheer fun of it.

Which was *not* to say she'd agreed to anything about any 'nursemaid.'

'Well, at least the patient's in a good mood,' I said.

'Yes, she is,' Nana answered. We were coming onto Fifth Street, and she sat up a little higher in her seat. 'And no one, not even the great Alex Cross, is going to get under her skin on a day as nice as this one.'

A few seconds later, she added, '*No nursemaids!*'

33

A hastily made banner hung over the front door: it said *Welcome Home, Nana!* in a half dozen colors.

The kids came streaking out as soon as they saw us. I ran interference and scooped Ali off the ground before he could tackle Nana on the walkway.

'Gently!' I called to Jannie, who had already put the brakes on some.

'We missed you so much!' she shrieked. 'Oh, Nana, welcome home! Welcome, welcome!'

'Give me a real hug, Janelle. I'm not going to break.' Nana turned on like a lightbulb and grinned.

Ali insisted on carrying Nana's suitcase, which he thunk-thunk-thunked up the steps behind us, while Nana took my arm on one side, Jannie's on the other.

When we came into the kitchen, Bree was on the phone. She flashed a big smile Nana's way and held up a just-one-second finger.

'Yes, sir. Yes. I will. Thank you so much!' said Bree into the receiver.

'Who was that?' I asked, but Bree was already rushing over to give Nana a hug of her own.

'Gently!' Ali said, which cracked Nana up.

'I'm not a basket of eggs,' she said. 'I'm a tough old bird.'

We settled in at the kitchen table after Nana

made it clear she'd go to bed when 'real people' did, thank you very much.

Once we were sitting, Bree cleared her throat like she had an announcement to make. She looked at each of us, then started in. 'I've been thinking that maybe this whole idea of hiring someone to be here with Nana might not go over so well. Is that correct?'

'Mm-hm.' Nana gave me a look that said, *See? I'm not so hard to figure out.*

'So . . . I'm going to cut back at work and stay home with you for a while, Nana. That is, if you'll have me.'

Nana beamed. 'That's so thoughtful, Bree. And you put it so well. Now *that* is a health care plan I can live with.'

I was a little stunned. 'Cut back?' I asked.

'That's right. I'll stay available for whatever you need on Caroline's case, but everything else, I'm farming out. Oh — and Nana, *here*.' She got up and took a sheaf of papers off the counter. 'I printed these recipes out from the net. See if any of them look good to you. Or not. Whatever. You want some tea?'

While Nana was reading, I followed Bree over to the stove. One look in her eyes and I realized that it would be wrong for me to ask if this was what she really wanted. Bree had always done what she wanted, and I mean that in a good way.

'Thank you,' I said quietly. 'You are the best.' She smiled to let me know that thanks weren't necessary here, and also that she definitely was the best. 'I love her too,' she whispered.

'*Eggplant?*' Nana held up one of the pages

109

she'd been reading. 'You can't make decent eggplant without salt. It's just not possible.'

'Well, keep looking,' Bree said, going over to sit down next to Nana. 'There's a ton more recipes. What about the crab cakes?'

'Crab cakes could work,' Nana said.

I just hung back and watched the two of them for a while. It felt like a real circle-of-life moment. I noticed the way Bree leaned into Nana when they laughed, and the way Nana always seemed to keep a hand on Bree, as if they'd been buddies forever. God willing, I thought, they would be for a long time to come.

'Angel's food cake with chocolate icing?' Nana said, and beamed mischief. 'Is that on your good-to-eat list, Bree? Should be.'

34

When I got a call from my FBI friend Ned Mahoney the next day, I never would have guessed it had to do with Caroline's murder case. All he told me over the phone was to meet him at the food court at Tysons Corner Center in McLean. Coming from anyone else, it would have seemed a strange request. Since it came from Ned, whom I trusted implicitly, I knew something was up.

Ned was a pretty big deal who had once headed the Hostage Rescue Team at the FBI training facility out in Quantico. Now he had an even bigger job, supervising field agents up and down the East Coast. We'd worked together when I was an agent at the Bureau, and again more recently, at a bizarre showdown with dirty cops from SWAT and some drug dealers in DC.

I sat down across from Ned at an orange plastic table with white plastic chairs, where he was gulping coffee.

'I'm pretty busy these days. The hell do you want?' I said, and grinned.

'Let's walk,' he said, and we got right back up. 'I'm busy too. Monnie Donnelley says hello, by the way.'

'Hello back at Monnie. So, Ned, what's on your mind? Why the John le Carré cloak-and-dagger stuff?' I asked as we left the food court at a brisk pace.

'I know some interesting things about Caroline,' he told me, point-blank. 'Honestly, Alex, I wouldn't be talking to you if she wasn't your niece. This whole thing is getting hinkier and more dangerous every day.'

I stopped walking across from a store with David Sedaris books stacked up high in the window. 'What *whole* thing? Ned, start me at the beginning.' Mahoney is one of the smartest cops I've ever known, but information moves through his brain too fast sometimes.

He began walking again, eyes scanning the mall. He was starting to make me nervous. 'We've had a surveillance team on a certain location in Virginia. Private club. Very heavy hitters. Alex, I'm talking about people who can go over both our heads — in more ways than one.'

'Go on,' I said. 'I'm listening to every word.'

He looked at the ground. 'You know that your niece was, um . . . '

'Yeah. I know the forensics, all the other details. I saw her at the medical examiner's.'

He threw the rest of his coffee into a garbage can. 'It's possible, even probable, that Caroline was murdered by someone at that club.'

'Hold on.' We stopped again. I waited for a blond mother with three small towheads and an armful of Baby Gap bags to go by. 'Why is the Bureau involved?'

'Technically, Alex? Because a body was transported across state lines.'

I thought of the mobster who'd been found and then lost: Johnny Tucci. 'You're talking about the punk from Philly?'

'We have no interest in him. Chances are he's dead anyway. Alex, this club is frequented by some of the more important people in Washington. It's gotten heavy at the Bureau in the last couple of days. *Top* heavy.'

'I assume you mean Burns is involved.' Ron Burns was the Bureau's director, and a decent guy. Mahoney shook his head; he wouldn't answer that one directly, but I could figure it out for myself.

'Ned, whatever happens, I'm only going to help.'

'I figured as much. But listen, Alex. You should assume you're being watched on this one. It's going to get nasty like you wouldn't believe.'

'The nastier the better. Just means somebody cares. I'll take my chances with that.'

'You already have.' Ned clapped me on the shoulder and offered a grim smile. 'You just didn't know it until now.'

35

The meeting with Ned was useful, but it had also given me a headache, so I was playing a little Brahms in the car on the way back to Judiciary Square. I picked up a voice mail from Ramon Davies's secretary as I sped along the streets of DC. The superintendent wanted to see me as soon as possible. That didn't sit too well on top of Ned's warning at the mall. The last time Davies called, it was to tell me that Caroline had been killed.

When I got to the Daly Building, I bypassed the elevator and jogged up the stairs to the third floor. Davies's office door was open, and I rapped two knuckles on the frame.

He was hunched over paperwork at his desk. The wall behind him was hung with some of his large collection of commendations, including MPD's Detective of the Year for 2002. I had the award for '04, but no big office to put a plaque up in. Actually, the certificate was in a drawer someplace at home; at least I thought it was.

Davies nodded when he saw me. We weren't exactly friends, but we worked well together and there was respect on both sides. 'Come in, and close the door.'

As I sat down, I couldn't help noticing my own handwriting on some of the photocopied pages he was studying.

'Is that Caroline's file?' I asked.

Davies didn't answer at first. He sat back and eyeballed me for a few seconds. Then he said, 'I had a call this morning from Internal Affairs.'

There it was — just about the last thing I wanted to deal with right now. Internal Affairs used to be called the Office of Professional Responsibility. Before that, it was — Internal Affairs. MPD is nothing if not fluid that way.

'What did they want?' I asked.

'I think you know. Did you threaten that anchor asshole Ryan Willoughby at Channel Nine? He says you did. So does his assistant.'

I sat back and took a breath before I answered. 'It's bullshit. Things got a little heated, that's all.'

'Okay. I had another call yesterday, from a Congressman Mintzer. Want to guess what he was calling about?'

I couldn't believe it — though it was typical enough Washington power-playing and outright bullying. 'Both of their phone numbers were found in Caroline's apartment.'

'I don't need you to give me the 101. Not yet anyway.' He held up the file to illustrate his point. 'I just need to know that you've got a cool head on this.'

'I do. But this isn't just another homicide investigation, and I don't mean because my niece was killed and cut up into pieces.'

'Damn straight it's not, Alex. That's the whole point. These complaints could become a problem. For you and for the entire investigation.'

I was talking to Davies, but I was also trying to think this thing through. Citizen complaints

115

— when they're investigated — can end up at one of four conclusions. They can be sustained, determined unfounded, deemed unprovable for lack of evidence, or the officer can be exonerated because no regulation was broken. I felt confident that at worst, I was in the last category.

Davies wasn't done with me, though. 'I give you more leeway than just about any detective in this division,' he said.

'Thank you. I'm handling it okay, right? Despite appearances.'

That got a microscopic grin. He studied me for another few seconds and then sat back. When he started putting away his notes, I knew we were over the hump. At least for right now.

'I want you on this investigation, Alex. But believe me when I say that the minute — and I mean the minute — anyone tries to take this over my head, I'm pulling you off.'

He stood up then, my sign to get out of there while I still could. 'Keep me in the loop. I don't want to have to call you again. You call me.'

'Of course,' I assured him, and then I left. If I stuck around longer, I'd have to tell him about my meeting with Ned Mahoney, and that was something I couldn't afford to do right now. Not if Davies was already considering reining me in.

I'd tell him everything later. Just as soon as I had some answers myself.

36

Tony Nicholson recalled a particular short story that had been popular when he was a schoolboy. He thought it was called 'The Most Dangerous Game.' Well, he was playing such a game now, only in real life, and it was much more dangerous than some story in an anthology.

Nicholson stared at the monitors on his desk — watching and waiting, forcing himself to go slowly on the scotch. Zeus was due any minute, at least he was scheduled to appear, and Nicholson had a decision to make.

For months now, it had been the same game with this madman. Nicholson kept the carriage barn apartment vacant at all times, booked escorts whenever Zeus demanded it, and then tortured himself wondering if it would be suicide to record one of these little parties of his.

Nicholson had seen plenty in the few sessions he'd watched, but he had no idea exactly what Zeus was capable of, or even who he was. The man definitely played rough, though. In fact, some of the escorts he'd had sessions with had completely disappeared; at least they'd never come back to work after seeing Zeus.

Just after 12:30, a black Mercedes with tinted windows pulled up to the front gate. No one buzzed; Nicholson admitted the car remotely, then sat back, waiting for it to show up at the top of the drive.

His fingers played compulsively back and forth over the keyboard's touchpad. *Record, don't record, record, don't record.*

Soon enough, the Mercedes passed in front of the house, then continued around toward the carriage barn in back — its destination. As always, the car's plates were covered.

Before Zeus, the apartment had been a private VIP suite for any preapproved client who could afford it. The fees started at twenty thousand a night, and that was just for room and board. The suite was outfitted with the finest liquors and wines, a fully stocked gourmet kitchen, a marble steam room and Swiss shower, two fireplaces, and a full complement of electronics, including separately wired phone lines with routing software and multifrequency voice scramblers to make outgoing calls untraceable.

Nicholson pulled up the living room view — where two girls were waiting, as ordered. All they knew was that it would be a 'party of one' and they'd been promised time and a half for the evening, a minimum of four thousand each.

When the door from the parking bay below opened, both of them stood up at once and started to primp.

Nicholson's body tensed as he watched Zeus stride into the room, looking like any other client with his crisp blue suit, briefcase in hand, and a tan overcoat on his arm.

Except for one thing — Zeus wore a mask. Always. Black. Like an executioner.

'Hello, ladies. Very pretty. Very nice. Are you ready for me?' he asked.

118

That was what he always said too.

And in the voice he always used — too deep to be his real speaking voice.

Another element of disguise.

So who was this creepy, powerful, rich bastard?

37

Through the narrow peepholes in his mask, Zeus studied the two girls and thought they were gorgeous, just spectacular to look at. One was tall, with long dark hair and alabaster skin. The other was a short dark beauty who was probably Hispanic.

They had obviously been instructed not to ask about the mask, or who he might be, or anything of a personal nature. This was good — his mood couldn't have been any better.

'I think we're going to have a good time tonight,' he said. That was all they needed to know for now, and actually, he had no idea how tonight might go, only that it was completely in his control. He was, after all, Zeus.

They took his words as a cue to speak and introduced themselves as Katherine and Renata. 'Can I take your coat?' Katherine asked, and somehow managed to make it sound seductive. 'Get you something to drink? What would you like? We have it all.'

'No, thank you. I'm fine for now.' He was polite, but definitely reserved, even strange. For one thing, he never touched anything outside the bedroom. His people knew as much and would work accordingly.

'Let's go on in,' he said. 'You're the most beautiful girls I've seen here, by the way. I don't know which of you is prettier.'

Everything in the bedroom was laid out as it should be. The windows were curtained; there was a bottle of Grey Goose vodka, a new box of latex gloves on the dresser, and nothing else — no knickknacks, no carpets, no bedding except for a fitted rubber sheet covering the mattress.

'This is interesting.' Katherine sat down and ran her hand over it. 'Decor by Rubbermaid.'

Zeus made no comment.

He had the two girls undress first, then took off his own clothes, except the mask, folding everything onto the dresser so he could leave the club just as neat and pressed as when he'd arrived.

Finally, he opened his briefcase.

'I'm going to tie you girls up,' he said. 'Nothing too scary. They told you about this, correct? Good. Have either of you been handcuffed before?'

The shy one, Renata, shook her head no. The other, Katherine, put a come-fuck-me look into her eyes and nodded. 'Once or twice,' she said. 'And you know what? I still haven't learned to be a good girl.'

'Don't do that, Katherine,' he told her. She looked at him as if she didn't know what he was talking about. 'Don't ever play-act for me. Please. Just be yourself. I can tell the difference.'

Before there could be any more nonsense, he tossed a pair of cuffs onto the bed. 'Put those on, please. What I'd like — I want you to share them. One cuff for each of you.'

While the girls clipped the cuffs on, he slipped

121

his hands into a pair of gloves and took out the rest of his gear: two more pairs of cuffs, a new skein of hardware store rope, two red rubber ball gags with black leather straps.

'Just lie back now,' he said, and went over to Renata first. He could see something interesting now, mounting concern in her eyes, the beginning of fear.

'Give me your free hand,' he said. Then he cuffed her wrist to the bedpost. 'Thank you, Renata. You're very sweet. I like compliant women. It's my vice.'

As he walked around to the other side, Katherine arched her back a little and widened her eyes, more vacant than scared.

'Please don't hurt us. We'll do anything you want; I promise,' Katherine said.

She was getting him pissed — already. Like some cockteasing little wife. Doing her coital duty. He slapped on the last cuff and secured it to the other bedpost and started fitting the gag into her mouth before she could say any more and ruin tonight.

'I can tell you're still acting, and you're not good at it,' he told her. 'Now you're making me a little angry. I'm sorry. I don't like myself when I get like this. You won't either.'

He tightened the strap at the back of her head. He used all of his strength, and he was a powerful man. The girl tried to say something, but it came out as a muted grunt. He'd caused her pain. Good. She deserved it.

When he stepped back, the look on Katherine's face had changed completely. She was afraid of him now. That wasn't something you could fake.

'Much better,' he said. 'Now, let's see if I can think of anything else to improve that performance of yours. Oh, how about these?'

He reached into his black briefcase and pulled out a Taser gun. And pliers.

'Katherine, that's wonderful. Your improvement is just outstanding. It's all in the eyes.'

38

Nicholson felt as if he'd been drinking coffee all night instead of expensive scotch. He squinted at the headlights on Lee Highway, wishing for nothing more than a nightcap, an Ambien, and a few hours away from his own tortured thoughts.

It was done, anyway. He'd wiped the hard drive and taken the disk away with him. He'd recorded Zeus's session with the two girls. He'd witnessed the horror show. The question now was what to do with it.

It was tempting to drive around all night, put the thing in his safe-deposit box, and hopefully never go back to it again. On the other hand, he thought, if the need did arise, he'd be smart to keep it closer at hand. Just in case.

Nicholson had never indulged in the idea that this scheme of his could go on forever. The discreet club and the dirty blackmail had been a delicate balance. With Zeus in the mix, it was untenable, and the madman showed no sign of slowing down.

If Nicholson wanted out, he was going to have to disappear, and sooner rather than later.

One contingency plan after another ran through his head as he drove.

The offshore account in the Seychelles had just over two million in it. There was a hundred and fifty thousand coming from Temple Suiter, and then the Al-Hamad party next week, which promised to be good for at least as much. It was no lifetime reserve, but it was certainly enough to get him out of the country and keep him more than comfortable for a while. Definitely a couple of years, maybe longer.

He could fly through Zurich and lie low for a few weeks, until he could get a second passport. Lots of countries offered acquisition programs; Ireland might draw the least notice. Then he could use it to fly back out again, perhaps heading east. He'd always heard the trade in flesh was outrageous in Bangkok. Maybe it was time to find out.

Meanwhile, there was Charlotte.

God, what had he been thinking when he married her? That he would turn that lump of clay into something worth keeping? She'd been a little nothing of a London schoolteacher when they met; now she was a little nothing of an American housewife. It was like some kind of cruel joke — on him.

One thing was certain. Mrs. Nicholson would definitely not be making the trip east, or wherever he ended up. The only question was whether he should find someone to finish her off — just one more body at this point, and well worth the twenty or thirty thousand it would cost. Anything to keep that gob of hers from flapping after he was gone.

It was just after four a.m. when Nicholson finally got home. His mind was still racing as he came down the short, curved slope of his driveway, and he nearly rear-ended the black Jeep four-door parked right in front of the garage.

'What the hell?'

His first cogent thoughts were of the disk in his glove box, and of Zeus. *Jesus, was it possible somebody already knew about the recording? Could it be true?*

Not wanting to find out, Nicholson jammed the car into reverse, but even that was too little, too late.

A fat man was already at his side window, pointing a handgun and shaking his head *no*.

39

What was this — *The Sopranos?* It certainly looked like it to Nicholson.

There were two of them. A second hoodlum-looking gent stepped into the glow of the headlights, pointing another gun at his face.

The fat one opened Nicholson's door for him and then stepped back. The guy's mouth hung open a little, and his cheap golf shirt was tucked in, leaving an impressive curve of belly suspended in midair. It seemed inconceivable that someone as sloppy as this should be working for Zeus — which left the obvious question.

'Who the hell are you?' Nicholson asked. 'What do you want with me?'

'We work for Mr. Martino.' The accent was New York, or Boston, or *something*. East Coast American.

Nicholson slowly got out of the car, keeping both hands in sight. 'Okay then, who the hell is Mr. Martino?' he asked.

'No more stupid questions.' The corpulent thug gestured Nicholson toward the house. 'Let's go inside. We're right behind you, bub.'

It occurred to Nicholson that he'd already be dead if this were a straightforward hit. So that meant they wanted something else. *What?*

They were barely inside the front door when Charlotte Nicholson's thin, very irritating voice came seeping down from the upstairs hall.

'Babe? Who's that with you? Isn't it late for guests?'

'It's nothing. Not your concern. Go back to bed, Charlotte.'

Even now, he felt like throttling her, just for being where she shouldn't be.

Her bare splayed feet and legs came into the light from the foyer as she took a step down. 'What's going on?' she called out again.

'Did you not hear me? *Go. Now.*' She seemed to pick up on his tone, anyway, and floated back into the darkness. 'Stay up there,' he told her. 'I'll come get you later. Go to sleep.'

He took his two unexpected guests through to the great room at the back, for more privacy. Also, the bar was there, and Nicholson headed straight for it.

'I don't know about you fellas, but I could use a drink — ' he said, then felt a sharp crack at the back of his skull. He stumbled down onto his knees.

'What the fuck do you think this is, a social call?' shouted the fat guy.

Nicholson felt angry enough to fight, but he was in no position to do it. Not even close. So he pulled himself up, then onto the sofa. Thankfully, his vision was slowly coming back into focus.

'So what the hell do you want at four in the morning?'

The fat one hovered over him. 'We're looking for one of our guys. He came down here about a week and a half ago, and we haven't heard from him since.'

Christ, he wanted to lay out this fat bastard, but that wasn't going to happen, at least not right now. But someday — somewhere.

'I'm going to need more information than that. *What* guy? Give me a hint.'

'The name's Johnny Tucci,' said Fatboy.

'Who? Never heard of him. Tucci? Did he come to my club? Who is he?'

'Don't bullshit us, man.' The smaller punk pushed in close now, with a rush of cigarette and body stink. 'We know all about your little place in the country, okay?'

Nicholson sat up straight on the couch. This might have more to do with Zeus than he'd thought. Or maybe with his business on the side?

'That's right,' the punk went on. 'You think Mr. Martino sends his people down here for a vacation?'

'Listen, I still have no idea what you're talking about,' he told them. That much was partly the truth.

Fatboy hunkered down on the burled-wood coffee table and lowered his gun for the first time. It might have been an opening, if the other punk weren't so close by.

'I'm going to lay it out for you, then,' he said, in an almost conciliatory tone. 'One of our guys is missing. Whoever's been contracting with our boss isn't easy to track down. So far, all we've got is you. And that means our problem just became your problem. You understand?'

Nicholson was afraid that he did. 'What do you expect me to do . . . about *our* problem?'

The guy shrugged, then scratched his stubbly

chin with the barrel of his gun. 'Bottom line, we've got to deliver somebody back to Mr. Martino. So you do some asking around, find out what you can, or you'll be the one we bring back.'

'Or the little lady up on the stairs,' the other one said.

'You can have the little lady,' Nicholson said. 'We'll call it even.'

The heavy man smiled finally, and then he stood up. Tonight's business was clearly done.

'I'll take that drink to go,' he said to Nicholson. 'You just stay put.'

He waddled over to the bar, where his buddy was already helping himself to as many bottles as he could carry in both arms.

Once the two punks were gone and Nicholson had his drink and some ice for his head, he noticed they'd cleaned him out of Johnnie Walker only to leave a Dalmore 62 sitting right there on the bar. It was a four-hundred-dollar bottle, and seemed as ominous a sign as anything else.

If these two losers were onto him, then everything was unraveling faster than he'd thought possible.

Now, who the hell was Johnny Tucci?

40

For Suarez and Overton, every exchange with Zeus was a dead drop — no face-to-face meetings, ever, by mutual agreement with whoever was actually paying their fees. They went into the suite at Blacksmith Farms after him, sanitized the space, and took away whatever needed taking away, including the bodies.

Just before dawn, their no-profile G6 bumped along the familiar dirt track in the backwoods of Virginia. Its rear end was riding a little low because of the weight in the trunk.

'Let me ask you this,' Suarez said to his partner. 'He's obviously filthy rich. Why does he risk it? What is he — completely crazy?'

'On some level, sure.'

'On some level? How about 24/7/365 he's crazier than a shithouse rat on speed? How does he get away with it — *how?*'

'Well, for one thing — do *you* know who he is, Suarez?'

'You're right, I don't. But somebody has to know. Somebody has to stop him eventually.'

'What can I tell you — welcome to the wackadoo world of the rich and famous. Can you say wood chipper?'

41

Remy Williams didn't trust these two guys at all. Never had, not from the start of the contract. When they pulled up to the cabin and didn't even get out of the car, he knew something was up. Something more than the usual dirtbag routine.

'How's it going, fellas?' He shuffled on over like the piece of white trash he was supposed to be. 'What've you got for me this time?'

'Two female.' The driver looked up, though not quite into his eyes. What was this: *Did the Latino have a conscience?* 'One of them has a bullet in the chest. You'll see.'

'Oh, yeah? What'd you shoot her for?'

'I don't know, maybe because we're still chasing down the last one who ran off.'

The guy was baiting him, Remy could tell, but he wasn't sure why or, really, what these murders were all about. He was just a cog, didn't have all the pieces, figured probably no one did. Like JFK. Like RFK. Hell, like O.J.

'Seems to me you shot the last one too,' he said, playing along. 'Maybe she didn't run off a'tall. Might just be lying out in those woods somewhere, turning into mulch. As we speak. Coulda just been found by hikers.'

'Yeah, maybe.' The ex-agent took a deep breath, starting to get a little showy with his aggravation. 'Listen, if you could just clean out the trunk, we'll be on our merry way.'

Remy scratched at his crotch — a little overkill, maybe — and then shuffled around to the back of the car. The driver popped the trunk for him. *Jesus! Look at this.*

The two bodies were double wrapped in black poly sheeting and sealed with packing tape. These guys were pros at what they did; he had to give them that much. *But who the hell was hurting these girls in the first place? What was the big picture here? Who was the killer?*

He dragged both 'packages' out of the trunk and onto the canvas tarp he'd already spread. His tools were laid out on a big hickory stump, and there was an extra gallon of gas next to the chipper.

'Which one'd you say was shot?' he called over to the spooks.

'Tall one. Left chest. What a waste. Girl was a real looker.'

He rolled her over and slit the plastic down the middle, pushing just hard enough with the tip of his bowie knife to leave a thin red trail in its wake. When he pulled back the wrapper, he found a small crater just above the very well-formed left breast. The body was still warm — in the nineties or high eighties. Dead only a few hours at most.

'Okay, got it. You want me to pull the slug or do you care?'

'Pull it. Get rid of it.'

'All righty. *Done.* Anything else?'

'Yeah. Close the trunk.'

A few seconds later, the two smartass bastards were gone.

Distrust aside, Remy didn't mind their arrogance, mostly because he knew it worked in his favor. It probably never even occurred to those two how expendable *they* were.

Or how vulnerable.

In fact, they'd already done a good bit of the work for him when they erased their own identities. Now they were just a couple of spooks, and Remy knew as well as anyone that when the time came, there was nothing easier to make disappear than a ghost.

He could do that — hell, he'd done it before. Made a career of it, actually.

He unwrapped the second girl — another real looker. Seemed like maybe she'd been strangled. And bitten? He massaged the girl's lukewarm breasts, played around a little bit more, then took the two of them up the hill to the chipper.

What a waste was right. Who the hell would do such a thing? Somebody even crazier than he was?

42

I had another clandestine meeting with Ned Mahoney Saturday afternoon — this time at a busy parking garage on M Street in Georgetown.

As I pulled in, I couldn't help thinking about those Deep Throat scenes in *All the President's Men*, the book and the movie. There was a definite cloak-and-dagger thing happening here. Why was that? What in hell was going on?

Ned was already waiting when I got out of the car. He handed me a manila folder with the Bureau's seal on it. Inside, I found some notes and a collection of photos, copied two to a page. 'What's this?'

'Renata Cruz and Katherine Tennancour,' he said. 'Both missing, presumed dead.'

Each picture showed one of the girls, in several locations around town, with a variety of mostly white, much older men.

'Is that *David Wilke?*' I asked, pointing at someone who looked very much like the current chair of the Senate Armed Services Committee.

Ned nodded. 'That's David Wilke, all right. Both women have powerful men as regular clients, which is why we've been tracking them to begin with. And Katherine Tennancour, at least, worked at the club out in Virginia.'

I didn't say a word, just stared at Mahoney.

'I know exactly what you're thinking,' he said.

'Might as well break out the legislative directory while we're at it.'

This whole thing was getting more insidious by the minute. There was no way to track this killer — or this network, if that's what we were looking at — without exposing all kinds of very dirty laundry in the process. A lot of innocent family members' lives would be ruined — and that was just the start of it.

House and Senate majorities, not to mention presidential elections and governorships, had been lost over a lot less than this. No one would be going down without a fight either; I already had a bad taste of that from Internal Affairs. Anyone who thinks that cops look forward to these sensational 'career-making' cases has never been in the middle of one.

'Jesus, Ned. It's like waiting for a hurricane to happen right here in DC.'

'More like running after one — looking for trouble,' he said. 'A real category-five shitstorm. Don't you just love Washington?'

'Actually, I do. Just not right at this minute.'

'So listen, Alex.' His voice went serious again. 'The Bureau's all over this. It's about to go *pop*. I'd totally understand if you want to back off, and if you do, now would be a good time. Just hand the envelope full of goodies back.'

I was a little surprised by the offer. I thought Ned knew me a lot better than that. Which meant, of course, that his offer carried a serious warning.

'Does that mean you're ready to hit the club out in Virginia?' I asked him.

'I'm waiting on the ex parte right now.'

'And?'

Ned grinned, and if I'm not mistaken, he looked just a little relieved. 'And you should probably leave your phone on when you go home tonight. I'll be calling.'

43

The good news was I got to have a nice dinner with the family. I even got to spend some time hanging out with the kids afterward, just before all hell would probably break loose, probably like nothing I'd ever experienced before. It all depended on *who* was at that private club tonight.

Jannie had been teaching Ali to play Sorry, one of the most boring games in the universe, but I liked playing just about anything with the two of them. I goofed around between my turns, stealing pieces off the board and telling old jokes to Ali. Things like 'Why is six afraid of seven?'

'Because seven ate nine!' Jannie cackled. She loved to be the spoiler, and Ali was a perfect audience. The boy just loves to laugh. He's the least serious of my three kids by far.

Nana sat off to the side, watching us over the top of *A Thousand Splendid Suns*, one of the books she'd been tearing through these days. She and Bree had settled into a tentative partnership, with Bree slowly asserting herself around the house and Nana learning she could afford to let go of a few things she'd always controlled — like how to load the dishwasher.

It was all good — until the phone rang.

Usually, I expect the kids to put up an immediate stink when that happens. '*Don't answer it, Daddy*' had become a common refrain

138

around our house. So when both of them just looked away, waiting for the inevitable, I felt even worse.

I checked the ID. It was Mahoney. As promised.

'I'm sorry; I really do have to take this,' I said to Ali and Jannie.

Their silence was loud and clear as I went out to the hall to answer.

'Ned?'

'We're a go, Alex. There's a Holiday Inn off Exit 72 in Arlington. I can meet you in the parking lot if you come now. Right now.'

44

It was called Operation Coitus Interruptus, which only goes to prove that there are some people in the FBI with a sense of humor.

Ned's full team had convened at a small farm in Culpeper County, about an hour and a half west of DC and not far from Shenandoah National Park. It was a strange, foreboding mix: Mahoney and his co-case agent, Renee Victor; six HRT agents; three crisis negotiators from the Tactical Support Branch; and a ten-man FBI SWAT team.

I'd been expecting an all-HRT team, but I wasn't concerned in the least. FBI SWAT has some of the best tactical units in the world. This was going to be quite a show.

There was also a rep from Virginia State Police, who had two collection wagons on standby, and me. I'm not sure what strings Ned had to pull to have me there, but I appreciated it, and also knew that he figured I would add value. We all gathered around the tailgate of someone's pickup for a quick briefing from the big guy.

'There will be some heavy hitters inside, but for us, it's going to be SOP all around,' Ned told the group. 'I want SWAT in first, then agents, and I want all exits secure at all times. You should be prepared for any scenario, including sexual situations and even violent resistance. I'm not expecting the latter, but it's possible;

140

anything is. The idea is to work fast and safe, and to clear this place out as cleanly as we can.'

Surveillance showed that the main house had entrances on the north, south, and east sides. Mahoney divided us into three units accordingly. I'd be going in the front door with him. There were also several outbuildings, which were supposed to be empty, at least tonight. I couldn't help wondering about the kind of parties held in them.

Before we left, Ned gave me an FBI jacket and a new Aramid vest from the back of his car. The vest was lighter than anything I'd used before, which was okay, since we were hiking in from a couple of miles away.

It took forty-five minutes to get there through pretty thick woods and brush. After the first mile or so, we switched to night vision only, those with goggles leading those without.

All conversation dropped off at that point, except for the occasional radio exchange between Mahoney and the SWAT commander.

The main house came up quickly over a steep rise, all three stories of it. We hung just out of sight, about seventy-five yards off the front. Ned sent SWAT out to do a quick three sixty, and I borrowed a pair of binoculars for a better look while we waited for the action to start.

It was a really large limestone *mansion*; there's no other word for it. And the driveway was a virtual car show tonight — Mercedes, Rolls, Bentley, even a vintage Lamborghini and a red Ferrari.

Tall mullioned windows ran along the first

floor, which was well lit inside, but there were no people that I could see. Presumably, the action was taking place upstairs, where all the windows were dark or at least shaded.

Was this where Caroline had been killed? The thought came over me like a shroud. Was it also where her body had been so horribly desecrated? For that matter, were we about to crack open somebody's butcher shop or just a rich man's playground? It was a strange feeling to have no idea what to expect.

Word finally came back to Mahoney. I couldn't hear anything from his headset, but it looked like the main event was about to happen. He radioed a standby to the other units, which had spread out around the property, and then gave me that gallows humor grin of his.

'You ready for Coitus Interruptus?'

'As I'll ever be,' I said.

'Here we go, then. Should be a gas.' He went back to his headset and counted off. 'All units, on the ready. Don't hurt anybody; don't get hurt.'

A few seconds later, SWAT was out of the woods with the rest of us just behind, sprinting toward the impressive house of ill repute.

45

An expensive-looking walnut front door splintered and then gave way. SWAT was inside with no difficulty. I had my Glock out, hoping I wouldn't have to use it. The last time Ned and I had worked together, we'd both been shot.

Not this time, I hoped. This was white-collar crime, wasn't it? As soon as we got the 'all clear' from SWAT, Ned left two men at the door, then led everyone else inside.

My first impression was just, well, *money*.

The foyer was three stories high, with a checkerboard marble floor and huge chandeliers dangling like outrageous jewels overhead. The furniture was gleaming antiques, and there was something odd about the light. It looked like gold in here.

The second impression I got was of stunningly beautiful women — a lot of them — some in evening gowns, others in various stages of undress. Three were naked and not being very shy about it, hands on their hips like we'd just busted into an apartment they all shared.

The escorts, expensive ones. From clean-cut all-American to exotic Far Eastern.

I moved through the foyer and turned right, past another agent shuttling two dark-skinned men speaking Arabic and a tall black woman toward the front. All three were naked, and they were cursing out the agents as if they were household help.

I passed open, empty parlors on either side, then came to a glass-walled smoking room at the end of the house. It stank of cigars and sex, but nobody was inside at the moment.

When I doubled back, I could hear shouting from near the entrance. Somebody was objecting to our presence — and loudly.

'Get your hands off me! Don't touch me, you wanker!' A tall blond man with an English accent was attempting to come down the big main staircase while two FBI agents held him back.

'This is an illegal search, *goddamnit!*' The Englishman had some spine; I could see that much. They finally had to put him down on the marble landing just to get a zip tie around his wrists.

I took the stairs two at a time, to where Mahoney was trying to question the guy. 'Are you in charge here? You're Nicholson, right?'

'Piss off! I've already called my attorney. You're trespassing, every one of you.' He was well over six feet and didn't seem to be losing steam. 'You're breaking the law just being here. This is private property. Goddamnit, let me up! This is an outrage. This is a *private* party in a *private* house.'

'Keep him separated from the others,' Mahoney told the agents. 'I don't want Mr. Nicholson talking to anyone else.'

We quickly established a couple of holding areas on the first floor and started working through the house, culling the paying customers from the staff, taking names as best we could.

'Yes, my name is Nicholson — very soon you won't be able to forget it!' I heard from one of the rooms. '*Nicholson*, like the moving-picture star.'

46

It was as bizarre a raid as I'd seen since I'd been on the force. Pretty funny, actually, if you have a sense of humor like mine.

We pulled one joker out of a concrete-block room, where he was still manacled to the wall in his thong underwear, presumably ditched there by his dominatrix. In fact, most of the people I saw were in one state of undress or another — completely naked, satin underwear, skimpy see-through robes — and one soaking-wet couple in towels, including turbans, the male smoking a cigar.

The men were a mix of Saudi and American. From what I gleaned, one was a billionaire by the name of Al-Hamad. He was having a birthday party that night. *And a very happy fiftieth to you. One you won't forget.*

We kept the English manager — if that was what he was — in a small study downstairs. By the time I got back to him, he'd settled into a stubborn silence. When I asked about the bruise on his cheek, Mahoney told me he'd taken to spitting at the arresting officer. Never a good idea.

I stood in the doorway, watching him sulk on an antique settee, surrounded by high shelves of books I couldn't imagine anyone had ever read. He was obviously a nasty son of a bitch and presumably a pimp. But was he also a killer? And why was he acting so arrogant about the raid?

His lawyer got there less than an hour later, wearing suspenders and a bow tie in the middle of the night. If I'd seen him on the street, I'd never have expected he was tied into something like this. He was Dilbert, minus the pocket protector.

Unfortunately, his paperwork was very good.

'What's this?' Mahoney asked, as the lawyer handed it over to him.

'Motion to quash. As of this moment, your ex parte's void, and this raid is illegal. My client will generously allow you five minutes to clear out. After that, we're looking at contempt of court and criminal trespassing.'

Mahoney did a slow double take between the lawyer's little bug eyes and the motion to quash. Whatever he saw seemed to have the intended effect. He dropped the pages to the floor and walked away as they fluttered. Then I heard him shouting orders and shutting everyone down, the entire raid.

I picked up the motion and started scanning. 'Who the hell's your judge at one in the morning?' I asked the lawyer.

He actually reached up and flipped the page for me, pointed. 'The Honorable Laurence Gibson.'

Of course, I thought. Senators, congressmen, billionaires for clients — why not a judge?

Part Three

WITH OR WITHOUT YOU

47

I got home early Sunday morning, somewhere between the newspaper delivery trucks and the overzealous joggers heading to the park.

Whoa! What was this?

I found Nana in the sunporch, fast asleep in one of the wicker chairs. Other than her ancient pink terry slippers, she was already dressed for church in a gray flannel skirt and white sweater set. This would be Nana's first service since the hospital visit, and the whole family was going.

I put a hand on her shoulder, and she woke with a shrug. All it took was one quick look at my face. 'Bad night?' she asked.

I flopped down on the love seat across from her. 'Am I that obvious all the time?'

'Only to the initiated. All right, tell me what happened. Talk to me.'

If this were any other case, I would have pleaded exhaustion, but Nana deserved to know about it. Still, I kept the details down to a PG rating; there was no need to over-emphasize the dark side of Caroline's life. Nana knew, I was sure. She always seemed to, somehow.

By the time I got to the part about the geeky lawyer with the 'motion to quash,' I started getting worked up all over again. I'd just wasted a whole night, and I'd run out on Ali and Jannie to do it.

'I think Jannie has that pouting, cold-shoulder

thing down pat, though,' I said. 'How were they after I left?'

'Oh, you know. They'll survive,' she said, but then added, 'Assuming that's all you need them to do.'

It was like a pat on the head and a smack on the cheek at the same time. Pure Nana Mama.

'So that was your twin sister waving me out the door last night? Telling me it was all good. See, I could have sworn it was you.'

'Now, don't get defensive on me, Alex.' She sat up a little straighter and cricked her neck, massaging it on one side. 'I'm just saying, the children don't always care *why* you're gone, Alex. They just know that you are. Especially little Damon.'

'You mean Ali.'

'That's what I said, isn't it? The boy's only six, after all.'

I leaned in for a better look at her. 'How much sleep did you get last night?'

She made her *pssh* sound. 'Old people don't need sleep. It's one of the secret advantages. Reason I can still whip you in a debate. Now, help me up and I'll start some coffee. You look like you could use it.'

I had a hand on her elbow and she was halfway up, when she stopped suddenly and sagged a little.

'What is it?' I asked.

'Nothing. I just, um . . . '

At first she looked confused. Then all at once, her face creased with pain and she doubled over in my arms. Before I could even get her back down again, she'd passed out.

Oh God, no.

Her small body was like nothing to hold in my arms. I laid her gently on the love seat and felt for a pulse at her neck. *There was none.*

'Nana? Can you hear me? Nana?'

My heart was flying now. The doctors at St. Anthony's had told me the signs to look for — no movement, no breath, and she just lay there, horribly still.

Nana was in cardiac arrest.

48

It was another nightmare — the EMTs in the house, the blur of the ambulance ride, questions at the emergency room. Then the terrible waiting.

I stayed with Nana all day and all night at St. Anthony's. She'd survived the heart attack, which was about as much as anyone would say for now.

They had her on a ventilator to help her breathe, with a tube taped over her mouth. There was a clip on her finger to measure her oxygen level, and an IV to keep the medications coming. More wires ran from Nana's chest to a heart monitor by the bed, its pulsing lines like some kind of electronic vigil. I hated that screen and relied on it at the same time.

Friends and relatives came and went all day and into the evening. Aunt Tia was there with some of my cousins, and then Sampson and Billie. Bree brought the kids, but they weren't allowed in, which was just as well. They'd seen more than enough at home when the ambulance had come and taken Nana away again.

And then there were the 'necessary' conversations. Different staff members wanted to talk to me about the DNR order in her file, about options regarding hospice, about religious affiliation, all *just in case*. Just in case what — Nana never woke up?

No one tried to chase me out after visiting hours, as if they could, but I appreciated the consideration. I sat with my forearms on the edge

154

of the bed, sometimes to rest my head, other times to pray for Nana.

Then, sometime in the middle of the night, she finally stirred. Her hand moved under the blanket, and it was like all those prayers of ours were answered in that one small motion.

And then another tiny motion — and her eyes slowly opened.

The nurses had said that I should stay calm and speak quietly if that happened. For the record, it was no easy feat.

I reached up and put a hand on her cheek until she seemed to know I was there.

'Nana, don't try to say anything right now. Don't try to argue either. There's a tube in your throat to help you breathe.'

Her eyes started moving around, taking it all in, staring at my face.

'You collapsed at home. Remember?'

She nodded, but just barely. I think she smiled too, which felt huge.

'I'm going to ring for the nurse and see how soon we can get you off this machine,' I said. 'Okay?' I reached for the call button, but when I looked back, her eyes had closed again. I had to check the monitor just to reassure myself she was only sleeping.

All the yellow, blue, and green lines were doing their thing, just fine.

'Okay, tomorrow morning, then,' I said, not because she could hear me but because I needed to say something.

I only hoped there would be a tomorrow morning.

49

Nana was wide awake and off the ventilator by noon the following day. Her heart was enlarged and she was too weak to leave intensive care, but there was good reason to believe she'd be coming home again. I celebrated by sneaking the kids into the room for the quickest, quietest Cross family party ever.

The other hopeful news was on the work front. An FBI lawyer named Lynda Cole had established probable cause and gotten the Bureau back onto the property out in Virginia. By the time I reached Ned Mahoney on his cell, the FBI had a full Evidence Response Team on site.

Bree spelled me at the hospital — Aunt Tia would spell Bree later — and I drove out to Virginia in the afternoon to have another look around Blacksmith Farms.

Ned met me out front so he could walk me through with his creds. The primary area of interest was a small apartment out back. The access was an interior staircase from a three-bay parking garage underneath.

Inside, the place looked like a suite at the Hay-Adams. The furniture was all soft linens and upholstery, mostly in lighter tones. There was a decorative dropped ceiling over the dining area, and a highly polished walnut-manteled fireplace.

If you subtracted the techs in their tan cargos

156

and blue ERT polo shirts, the place was pristine.

'It's the bedroom that's the puzzle,' Ned said. I followed him in through a set of curtained French doors. 'No carpet, no knickknacks, no bedding, nothing,' he said, stating the obvious. Other than a bare bed, dresser, and two night-stands, it looked like someone had recently moved out.

'Prints and fibers came up with nothing. So we went to luminol.'

That explained the portable UV lamps set up in the room. Mahoney turned off the ceiling light and closed the door. 'Go ahead, guys.'

Once they powered up, the whole room seemed to go radioactive. The walls, the floor, the furniture, all fluoresced bright blue. It was one of those occasions when my life actually did feel like an episode of *CSI*.

'Someone cleaned in here professionally,' Mahoney said. 'And I don't mean Merry Maids of Washington.'

One of the limitations with luminol is that although it can bring out traces of blood, it also responds to some of the things people use to get rid of blood, like household bleach. That's what we were looking at. It was as if the room had been painted with Clorox.

This looked like a crime scene for sure. And maybe a murder scene.

50

The next thing that happened, nobody saw coming. It was maybe half an hour later, and I was still on the case at Blacksmith Farms.

A rumble of conversation came from the apartment's living room, and Ned and I went out to see what was going on. Several techies were gathered around a bearded guy on a short ladder near the door. He had the plastic cover of a smoke detector in one hand, with the exposed unit on the ceiling above him. That's what everybody was staring at.

The tech reached up with a pencil and pointed at an innocuous plastic nub tucked into the circuitry. 'I'm pretty sure it's a camera. Fairly sophisticated.'

Talk about grinding the gears.

Immediately, Ned ordered a second sweep of both buildings. Everyone turned off their cell phones, and all the televisions and computers we could find were disconnected. That would keep them from interfering with the radio-frequency detectors.

Once the search got going, it was fast work. Ninety minutes later, most of the on-site personnel were gathered in the main house foyer for a briefing. I saw a few familiar faces, including the assistant director in charge, Luke Hamel, and also Elaine Kwan from the Behavior Analysis Unit, my old office.

I was surprised the case hadn't been graded major

yet, just based on the firepower in the room.

The special agent in charge of ERT was Shoanna Spears. She was tall and big boned, with a heavy Boston accent and a tiny ivy tattoo that just peeked over the top of her white oxford collar. She stood on the grand staircase to address the group.

'Basically, there's nowhere in the house that isn't covered. We found cameras in every room, including the bathrooms and the apartments out back.'

'How do we find out what all those cameras have been *filming?*' Hamel asked the question percolating in everyone's brains.

'Hard to say. These are wireless units; they can transmit to any base station within a thousand feet, maybe more than that. We did find a hard drive on the third floor with the right software, but no archived files. That means either that all the surveillance was done live or, more likely, that somebody took the files off site.'

'In which case we'd be looking for what?' Mahoney spoke up from the back of the room. 'Disks? A laptop? E-mails?'

Agent Spears nodded. 'Keep going,' she said. 'There's nothing terribly sophisticated about those files. They can pretty much be stored anywhere.'

You could feel the energy in the room dip. We were all ready for some good news. And then we got it.

'For what it's worth,' Spears went on, 'there seems to be only one set of prints on the hardware upstairs. We're running them through IAFIS now.'

159

51

'I don't understand any of this, Tony. Why can't you at least tell me *where we're going?* Is that too much to ask?'

The truth — and Nicholson had only come to realize it that afternoon — was that he didn't have the stomach for cold-blooded murder. Not by his own hand, anyway. He'd always believed that if he had to, he could easily put a pillow over Charlotte's face or slip something lethal into her morning coffee, but that wasn't going to happen, was it? And now it was too late to have her hit by someone else, which would have been a snap.

He threw a few last things into his duffel, while Charlotte harped at him from the far side of the bed. The Louis Vuitton bag he'd set out for her was still empty, and his patience was running out. He badly wanted to punch her in the face. But what good would that do?

'Darling.' The word nearly caught in his throat. 'Just trust me here. We have a plane to catch. I'll explain everything once we're away. Now, pick out a few things and let's go. Let's *go*, sweetheart.' *Before I get really angry and murder you with my bare hands.*

'It's about those men from the other night, isn't it? I knew something wasn't right with them. Do you owe somebody money — is that it?'

'Goddamnit, Charlotte, are you listening at

160

all? It's not safe here, dimmy. For either of us. The best we could hope for would be jail at this point. That's the *best*, do you understand? It only gets worse from there.'

Depending on who gets to us first was the rest of his thought.

'*We?* What do you mean, *we?* I haven't done anything to anyone.'

Nicholson rushed around the bed and threw an armful of clothes from her closet into the bag, hangers and all.

Then the red leather jewelry box he'd bought her in Florence, forever ago — a lifetime ago, when he'd been young, in love, and most definitely dumb as a bag of bricks with a hard-on.

'We're leaving. *Now.*'

She trailed after him, more afraid of being alone than anything else, which he was counting on. That got them as far as the front hall before Charlotte melted down completely. He heard something between a moan and a scream, and turned to see her half-crouched on the polished slate floor. Black lines of makeup ran down her cheeks with the tears; she always wore too much of the stuff, like some kind of tart, and he should know.

'I'm so scared, Tony. I'm shaking all over. Can't you see that? Can't you see anything besides your own needs? Why are you being like this?'

Nicholson opened his mouth to say something bland and conciliatory, but what came out instead was 'You really are too stupid for words, do you know that?'

He dropped her bag and took her up roughly

by the arm, didn't care if he yanked it from its socket. Charlotte pulled back, kicking and screaming, literally, as he started to drag her across the floor. All he had to do was get her to the car, and then she could pop an aneurism for all he fucking cared about the dumb, stubborn cow his wife had become.

But then the first slam came at the front door.

Something — not someone — had just smashed into it from the outside, hard enough to leave a long, forked crack down the middle. Nicholson looked out a window just quickly enough to realize what it was — a battering ram. And he knew then that it was probably too late to save even himself.

The second vicious and powerful swing came right away. It popped the lock set and dead bolt like children's toys, and the door exploded open.

52

'*Run.*'

That was the only advice that Tony Nicholson had for his wife before he dropped her arm and sprinted toward the back door himself. All priorities were now relative. Survival was not, and it definitely could go to the fittest.

He got as far as the kitchen, where he came face-to-face with a short, solid-looking Hispanic man coming the other way. *Now, who the hell was this?*

There was a blur of motion, then an excruciating crack at the side of his knee. Nicholson vaguely registered the pipe wrench in the man's hand as he went down hard and stayed down.

At first there was only pain, a big red ball of it exploding up and down his leg.

Then came the handcuffs. They bit into his wrists before he knew they were there.

Handcuffs?

Next, the Hispanic intruder dragged him by the collar all the way back into the living room, where he dropped him midpoint on the rug.

Charlotte was sitting in one of the Barcelona chairs with a strip of silver tape plastered over her mouth.

A second man — were there really only two of them? — stood over her, watching Nicholson with faint interest, almost boredom, like he did this kind of thing every day.

They weren't FBI or police; that much seemed clear. And they were nothing like the two goons from last week. Their clothes were dark, and they wore black balaclavas pulled up off their faces and latex gloves on their hands.

Not exactly cops, but close. Former cops? Special Forces?

The one who had attacked him was smash nosed, with dark eyes that seemed to be looking down at an unworthy specimen more than anything.

'The disk?' was all that he said.

'Disk?' Nicholson gutted out the word between clenched teeth. 'What the hell are you talking about? Who are you two?'

'*Two* — I like that number.'

The man looked at his stainless-steel watch. 'You have about two minutes.'

'Two minutes or what?' Nicholson asked, but then he saw the answer to his question.

The taller one took out a clear plastic bag and pulled it down over Charlotte's head. She struggled, but he had no trouble wrapping bands of the silver tape around her neck, sealing her head inside the plastic.

Nicholson could see Charlotte's expression change as she realized exactly what was happening. He even felt a pinch of pity, maybe even lost love, something emotional and, well, human. For the first time in years, he felt a connection to Charlotte.

'You're insane! You can't do this!' he yelled at the man holding down his wife.

'You're the one doing this, Mr. Nicholson. You're in complete control of the situation, not us. This is all on you. For God's sake, make us stop.'

'But I don't even understand what you want. Tell me what it is!'

He lunged for Charlotte, but the injured knee took him right back down, wedged embarrassingly between the couch and the coffee table.

'Please, tell me what you want! I don't understand!' Nicholson begged at the top of his lungs as convincingly as possible. It was the performance of a lifetime, and it had to be.

By the time he got himself onto the couch, Charlotte had gone still.

Her familiar blue eyes were wide open. Her head lolled against her shoulder like some marionette waiting to be picked up. It was grotesque, with the plastic bag still on, and easy to respond to.

'You bastards! You fucking bastards, you killed her! Now do you believe me? Is that what it takes?'

The two men were as cool as ever. They exchanged a glance. A couple of shrugs.

'We should go,' the white guy said. The other nodded, and for a second Nicholson thought he'd pulled it off, that maybe 'we' meant only the two of them. It didn't. One of them picked up Charlotte and the other dragged Nicholson.

As he was forced to hobble on his good leg toward the door — and God knew where after that — Nicholson had the strangest thought he'd had all day. He wished he had been nicer to Charlotte.

53

Ned Mahoney and I were in my car, headed east on I-66 toward Alexandria, when the call came in that we were too late. Virginia State Police were reporting that they'd found Nicholson's house empty. There were signs of a break-in and a struggle, two packed suitcases left behind, both of the Nicholsons' cars still in the garage.

An APB was in effect, but without a specific vehicle to look for, it didn't carry much hope of an apprehension.

The plan was still to convene at the Nicholson house. ADIC Hamel was calling in another Evidence Response Team right away. And Mahoney phoned someone at the Hoover Building to do some fast digging on Nicholson.

He also had one of the Bureau-issue Toughbooks in the car, which let him double up on research. He started feeding me information rapid-fire, the way Ned always does when he's keyed up.

'Well, our boy's never been arrested, naturalized, federally employed, in the military — no big surprises. He doesn't have any known aliases either. And he doesn't cross-reference in any Bureau file, under Tony or Anthony Nicholson.'

'I don't think he's our killer,' I said.

Mahoney stopped what he was doing and gave me his attention. 'Because?'

'There're too many loose ends here,' I explained. 'Nicholson's obviously one of them,

166

but that's all he is, Ned. It's like that old story about the five blind men and all the elephant parts.'

'Which makes Nicholson what — *the asshole?*'

I had to laugh. Mahoney is never without a quick response, and he's at his best when the pressure's on.

'I think someone came after the same thing we're looking for, only they got to him first. Which just means they have more puzzle pieces to work with than we do.'

'Or' — Mahoney held up a finger — 'he staged his own disappearance. It wouldn't be hard — drop a few suitcases, bust up some furniture, and he's halfway over the Atlantic with his little snuff film collection while we're still dusting the house for prints.'

We batted possibilities around some more, until another call came in. Whatever it was got Mahoney excited — again. He punched an address into his laptop.

A few seconds later, we were following the GPS onto the Beltway toward Alexandria — but not to Nicholson's house.

'Avalon Apartments,' Mahoney said. 'Nicholson came up on a tenant database. Guess he missed a payment or something.'

'A rental?' I said. 'In the same town where he already lives?'

Mahoney nodded. 'Lives with his *wife*,' he said, 'who I'm betting is at least fifteen years older than whoever we find behind door number two. What do you say — twenty bucks?'

'*No bet.*'

167

54

Tony Nicholson leaned forward from the backseat, as far as the cuffs would allow. He could see that the lights on the second floor were on.

'We don't need to be here,' he said. 'She doesn't know anything. I promise you.'

The one who had ruined Nicholson's leg opened the passenger door. 'Who knows?' he said. 'Maybe you talk in your sleep.'

He got out and went to the front door. Then he used one of Nicholson's keys to let himself in.

Nicholson was thinking that he still might be able to save himself, and maybe Mara. He had a surreal image of her beautiful face trapped inside a plastic bag.

The driver was tall and blond — like him — with pale eyes and a square forehead. He looked more intelligent than the spic. Maybe he was more reasonable too.

'Listen,' Nicholson said in a whisper. 'I do know what you're looking for. I can help you get it, but not without some kind of exit strategy for me.'

The man sat straight and still, staring out the windshield as if Nicholson hadn't spoken.

'I'm willing to make a deal, is what I'm saying.'

Still nothing from the front seat.

'For the disk. Of *Zeus*. Do you hear me? I'll

tell you where it is.'

'Yeah,' the blond guy finally said. 'You will.'

'So . . . why won't you make a deal? Now? Here? Why the hell not?'

The driver's fingers drummed lightly on the wheel. 'Because we're going to kill you anyway. You and the girlfriend.'

Nicholson felt a hollow beating in his chest, and he was finally feeling as if nothing mattered anymore. He laughed, a little desperately.

'Jesus, friend, I don't mean to tell you your job, but then why the hell would I — '

All at once, the driver turned, reached down, and squeezed the soft parts of Nicholson's mangled knee.

The pain was instant and stunning. His jaw dropped open even as his throat closed up. Nicholson couldn't breathe, much less scream, and in the strange silence, his tormentor's low voice was easy to hear.

'Because at some point, friend, you're going to stop wanting to live and start wanting to die. Understand? And if you haven't told us what we want to know by then — believe me, you will.'

55

The car door opened and Mara slid in, thin hips first, with the other man's hand cupping her blond head of hair. Nicholson saw him tuck a .45 into his waistband before he slammed shut the car door behind her.

His girlfriend looked understandably freaked out. Hell, she was only twenty-three years old. Her arms came together in front, with a sweater draped over them to hide the cuffs. He'd given her that sweater as a present. Cashmere. From the Polo store in Alexandria. Happier days.

'You okay?'

'Jesus, Tony, what's going on? He told me he was the police. Showed me a badge. Is he?'

'Just don't say anything,' Nicholson told her quietly. His injured leg felt as though it were going to explode. It was nearly impossible to focus, and Mara's being here only made matters worse. A whole lot worse, actually. Nicholson loved her.

She was the complete opposite of Charlotte. For one thing, she knew too much. For another, she was New York Irish Italian. Keeping their mouths shut wasn't exactly a strong suit for most New Yorkers.

'What do they want?' she pressed. 'Where are they taking us? Tony, *tell me.*'

'That's a bloody good question.' Nicholson said, and kicked the back of the seat with his good foot. He shouted at them. 'Where the fuck do you think you're taking us?'

That got him a backhand across the cheekbone with the .45. He felt the pain, but it was getting hard to care. In fact, pain could be considered a good thing — it meant he was still alive, didn't it?

'Whatever this is, I don't work for him anymore,' Mara was already telling the two men in front. 'You have to believe me. I'll tell you anything you want to know. I was the bookkeeper.'

'Shut up, Mara,' Nicholson said. 'Won't do any good anyway.'

'He's been shaking people down. Important people. For money. Taping them and — '

He leaned into her, which was about all he could do. 'Mara, I'm warning you.'

'Or what, Tony? It's a little late for warnings, isn't it? I shouldn't even be here.'

Her dark brown eyes flashed fear and anger, the same things he was feeling, so it was hard to completely blame her. 'I'm talking about big names,' she rattled on. 'Rich guys. Politicians, Wall Street, lawyers, that kind of thing — '

'Yeah, yeah.' The driver cut her off. 'Tell us something we don't already know. Otherwise, like the man said — shut up, Mara.'

56

Mahoney called in our new position as we followed the GPS off the Beltway and onto Eisenhower Avenue. It was getting dark, but the roads were still crowded with commuters. I wondered vaguely when nine-to-five had become an anachronism.

A mile and a half up Eisenhower, we came to a row of identical four-story townhouses fronting the street.

A break in the road marked the entrance with a sign welcoming visitors to Avalon at Cameron Court.

The GPS led us through the mini-maze of the compound inside. It was one of those upscale developments, 'communities,' with their own everything. Rents here were as high as thirty-five hundred a month, according to Mahoney and his laptop.

'You know, my aunt lives in a place like this, down in Vero Beach, Florida. They have a two-pet maximum, but she's got four identical little dogs. Just walks them two at a time.'

I sort of listened, until we came onto Nicholson's block. 'Hey, Ned. See that?' A dark blue sedan was just pulling out of a driveway about fifty yards ahead. 'Is that Nicholson's building?'

Mahoney sat up and closed the laptop. 'Could be. Let's find out.'

The other car started up the block, heading right toward us. It had DC plates. Two men in front, two passengers in back who were harder to see.

As we passed, I looked in, and for just a second I locked eyes with Tony Nicholson.

57

As soon as my siren came on, the dark blue sedan took off up the block and then spun around the corner. I had no idea who these guys were — mob, guns for hire, or what — but the way they tore out of there told me Nicholson and his girlfriend were in some serious trouble.

Ned was already on the phone. 'This is Mahoney. I have command of the target, Nicholson. We're in pursuit of a blue, Pontiac G6, DC plates.'

We came around another corner, and I saw them stopped at the compound's exit.

'One for the good guys!' Ned said, and pumped a fist. There was a solid stream of traffic on Eisenhower blocking them in, and for maybe a second, I thought we might get through this cleanly.

Then the Pontiac's doors opened on both sides and two men came out — firing!

A bullet pierced my windshield with a dull popping sound before Ned or I could get out. I threw open my door and rolled onto the street. Mahoney also got out the driver's side and stayed low.

From where I was, in a gully, I could only see the sedan's driver. He looked military to me, tall, with a blond buzz cut — and still firing. I didn't shoot back, didn't dare.

The problem was the traffic stopped behind

him. There wasn't a safe shot I could take. He seemed to figure that out, and broke for the nearest building.

As he passed the large Avalon sign fronting the complex, I fired off a fast, controlled double tap. Two shells kicked over my shoulder. The blond man went down with the second one.

But we weren't out of this yet, not by a long shot. Mahoney was up and firing. I could see the other man now, down in the street. He had a wet hole in the leg of his pants, but he got up again.

'Drop your weapon!' Mahoney shouted, as the man began to hobble away.

I came around to cover from a second angle, just as the guy raised a .45 at Mahoney.

Both our shots got off before his. He spasmed twice when they hit, and still managed to pull the trigger one more time. His shot nearly clipped Ned, who dropped and fired back. The last bullet caught the guy in the shoulder.

The shooter was alive when we got to him, wide-eyed and tremoring, his finger still on the trigger. Ned stepped on his wrist and pulled the .45 out of his hand.

'Hang in there,' I told him. 'Ambulance is on its way.'

He was in bad shape, though. A wound in his stomach was pumping blood, too much and too fast. While Mahoney ran to Nicholson and the woman, I pulled off my jacket and pressed it to the wound.

'Who do you work for?' I asked.

I wasn't sure if he could hear me. He didn't look scared, but his eyes were like saucers. When

175

he tried to swallow, foamy blood came through his lips. My jacket was already soaked.

'*Tell me!*' I finally shouted at him. 'Who sent you here?'

The gunman's breath hitched, and his grip went tight on my arm — just before everything went lax. He died without saying a word that might help us understand, well, anything about what was happening.

58

Our two dead soon became three, when Charlotte Nicholson, her face blue, the body still warm, turned up in the Pontiac's trunk.

Tony Nicholson and his presumed girlfriend, Mara Kelly, were both mute except to say that they hadn't done anything wrong and they had no idea who the dead men were. That's as much as we got before the FBI took them into custody.

By now, the response team had swelled to three Bureau cars, Alexandria police, EMTs, and the local sheriff's department. As soon as I could, I called Bree to check in.

That's when I realized that my phone had been off for hours — ever since the sweep at the private club out in Culpeper. When I turned it on, there were three voice mails waiting — all from Bree.

Right away I got nervous.

I listened to the first message. 'Hey, it's me. Listen, the doctors are concerned about Nana's kidney function. They say her fluid levels aren't what they should be. There's no prognosis yet, but you should give me a call. Love you.'

I turned toward my car now and started walking, not at all sure I wanted to hear the second message.

'Alex, it's Bree. I tried the Bureau, but nobody seems to know where you are. I don't have Ned's cell. I'm not sure what else to do. Nana isn't good. I hope you get this soon.'

I was running, but the third message nearly stopped me cold on the spot.

'Alex, where are you? I hate to leave this on your phone, but . . . Nana's gone into a coma. I'm going back in now, so you won't be able to reach me anymore. Get here as soon as you can.'

59

The function being held at One Observatory Circle tonight was relatively informal, a Maryland crab boil for several midlevel staffers and their families. That meant jackets with no ties — until the vice president went to shirtsleeves just before dinner and his male guests followed suit.

Agent Cormorant, however, kept his jacket on. It was specially tailored to conceal a .357 SIG Sauer pistol holstered under his right arm, and though the event was distinctly low-threat, it was not in Cormorant's professional DNA to take anything for granted, especially not these days.

Secret Service had been covering the sprawling Victorian residence since 1972. The Rockefellers had never moved in, but the Mondales, Bushes, Quayles, Gores, and Cheneys had all lived here before the Tillmans. Every corner of the place was well documented, literally. Cormorant knew the house better than his own two-bedroom condo on M.

So when he needed a private word with the vice president, it was second nature to access the library through a back sitting room, to avoid being seen coming or going by any of the guests.

Tillman poured himself a scotch rocks and waited by the mantel while Cormorant closed and latched doors at both ends of the room.

'What is it that can't wait, Dan?' Tillman asked.

'I should tell you right now, sir, that I'm about to step way out of line here,' Cormorant said.

Tillman sipped his drink. 'That's something new. The warning, I mean.'

The two men were friends, as much as men in their positions could be. Someday they'd share fishing trips and holidays, but for now, it was Mr. Vice President and Agent Cormorant — protectee and protector.

'Sir, I think it's time you brought the president in on Zeus. Specifically the fact that someone connected to the White House or the Cabinet might be a killer.'

Tillman's expression hardened instantly and he set his drink down. 'The president knows that much. I took care of it. We still need facts. We need a name.' Tillman had already been briefed about the FBI raid in Virginia, but not on the latest developments. Cormorant quickly brought him up to speed, including the cameras found at the sex club.

'No one's talking specifically about Zeus yet, but if any recordings happen to be found, it won't matter what he calls himself.'

'When did this come out?' Tillman asked. He seemed visibly shaken now.

'Today. This afternoon.'

'And how do you know about it already?'

Cormorant maintained eye contact with the VP, and also what he hoped was a discernibly respectful silence.

'Right,' Tillman said. 'Never mind. Go on, please. Sorry I interrupted you.'

'It's actually the attorney general who might

be able to do something about this. If there were any manageable pretense for sidelining the investigation or even slowing it down — '

Suddenly Tillman seemed angry, but it was always hard to tell with him.

'Hang on right there. You want the president to lean on the AG? Do you even know what you're suggesting? A Cabinet member could be involved.'

'It's not about what I want, sir. This has always been about protecting President Vance and this administration.'

A burst of laughter came from just beyond the foyer-side door. Cormorant didn't waver, except to lower his voice a notch.

'I'm not suggesting we try to bury this scandal. I just need a little space to see if we can find out who Zeus is. If I can do that, then the White House will be in a better position to control the information when it comes out — and it *is* going to come out, sir, one way or another, sooner or later.'

'What does Reese have to say about this?' Tillman asked. 'You ask him? Does he know about the cameras?'

'I briefed the chief of staff this afternoon, but nothing was said about bringing everything to the president. I wanted to speak with you first.'

'Don't play me against him, Dan. And don't play me against President Vance. The president has my complete loyalty.'

'I'm not trying to, sir — '

'No. All right. Here's what you're going to do.' Tillman had a way of shifting from inquiry to

181

decision without warning, and it had just happened. 'Talk to Gabe about this, and speak your mind with him. If he wants to bring it back to me, we'll go from there. Otherwise, you and I never had this conversation.'

The vice president was already halfway to the door when Cormorant's voice rose for the first time.

'Walter!' It was the kind of protocol breach that could send an agent down the ranks fast, under most circumstances, anyway. 'I can find him. Zeus. Just give me the time to do it.'

Tillman stopped, but he didn't turn around. 'Talk to Gabe' was all he would say, and when he continued out of the room, Agent Cormorant had no choice but to follow.

The conversation was over, and the crab was getting cold in the other room.

60

I ran my siren all the way across the Potomac and into the city until I was parked in the lot outside St. Anthony's Hospital. My mind hadn't stopped racing since I'd heard Bree's voice mails. How could this have happened? Just this morning, Nana had been sitting up; she'd been talking to us; she'd been *getting better*.

When I got off the elevator on six, the first familiar face I saw was Jannie's. She was parked on the edge of one of the molded plastic chairs just outside the ICU. When she saw me, she ran into my arms and held me tight.

'Nana's in a coma, Daddy. They don't know if she's going to wake up or not.'

'Shhh. I know, I know. I'm here now.' I felt her go from stiff to limp as the tears started. Jannie was so strong and so fragile at the same time. *Just like Nana*, I couldn't help thinking as I held her. 'Have you seen her?' I asked.

She nodded against my chest. 'Only for a minute or so. The nurse told me I had to wait out here.'

'Come on,' I said, taking her hand. 'I think I need you for this.'

We found Bree sitting next to Nana's bed, in the same chair I'd slept in the night before. She got up and put her arms around both of us.

'I'm so glad you're here,' she whispered.

'What happened?' I whispered back. In case Nana could hear, I suppose.

'Her kidney function just spiraled, Alex. They have her on dialysis now, and she's back on the hydralazine, the beta blockers . . . '

I could barely hear Bree's words, or sort out their meaning. My legs were weak, my head spinning in fast little circles.

Nothing could have prepared me for how much worse Nana looked.

She was on the ventilator again, this time with a tracheotomy right into her throat. There was a feeding tube in her nose now, and the dialysis too. But the worst by far was Nana's face — all pinched and drawn down, like she was in pain. I had thought she would just look asleep, but it was much worse than that.

I squeezed in to sit by her. 'It's Alex. I'm here now. It's Alex, old woman.'

I felt as if I were on the opposite side of a thick piece of glass from Nana. I could talk to her and touch her and see her, but I couldn't actually reach her, and it was the most helpless sensation I'd ever known. I had this terrible sick feeling that I knew what was coming next.

I'm usually good in a crisis — it's what I do for a living — but I was barely holding it together. When Jannie came over to stand beside me, I didn't bother to try and hide the tears coming down my cheeks.

This wasn't just happening to Nana. It was happening to all of us.

184

And as we sat there watching Nana, a tear ran down her cheek.

'Nana,' we all said at once. But she didn't speak back to us or even try to open her eyes.

There was just that single tear.

61

When I wasn't sleeping that night, or getting out of the nurses' way every few hours while they checked their patient, I was talking to Nana. At first, I stuck to the soft stuff — how much we loved her, how much we were pulling for her, and even just what was going on in the room.

But eventually it sank in for me that all Nana ever wanted was the truth, whatever that happened to be. So I started to tell her about my day. Just like we had always talked, never thinking about the reality that our talks would have to end eventually.

'I had to kill someone today,' I said.

It seemed like there should have been more to say about that, once I'd said it out loud, but I just sat there quietly. I guess this was where Nana was supposed to come in.

And then she kind of did — a memory, anyway, from an earlier time when we had a similar conversation.

Did he have a family, Alex?

Nana had asked me that before anything else. I was twenty-eight at the time. It was an armed robbery, at a little grocery store in Southeast. I wasn't even on duty when it happened, just on my way home. The man's name, I'll never forget, was Eddie Clemmons. It was the first time anyone had ever shot at me, and the first time I'd ever fired in self-defense.

And yes, I told Nana, *he had a wife, though he didn't live with her. And two children.*

I remember standing there in the front hall on Fifth Street with my coat still on. Nana had been carrying a basket of wash when I came in, and we ended up sitting down on the stairs, folding clothes and talking about the shooting. I thought it was strange at first, how she kept handing me things to fold. Then, after a while, I realized that at some point, my life would start to feel normal again.

You're going to be fine, she had said to me. *Maybe not quite the same, but still, just fine. You're a police officer.*

She was right, of course. Maybe that was why I needed so badly to have the same conversation again now. It was strange, but all I really wanted was for her to tell me it was going to be okay.

I picked up her hand and kissed it and pressed it against my cheek — anything to connect with her, I guess.

'Everything's going to be all right, Nana,' I said.

But I couldn't tell if that was the truth or not, or exactly whom I might be lying to.

62

I woke up with a hand pressing on my shoulder and someone whispering close to my ear. 'Time to go to work, sweetheart. Tia's here.'

My aunt Tia set her big canvas knitting bag down at my feet. I'd been awake and then asleep again half a dozen times through the night; it was strange being here, with no windows and no real sense of time, and Nana so sick.

She looked about the same to me this a.m. I wasn't sure if that was good or bad. A little of both, maybe. 'I'm going to wait for morning rounds,' I told Tia.

'No, sweetheart, you're going to go.' She nudged my arm to get me out of the chair. 'There's not enough room in here, and Tia's calves are killing her. So go on. Go to work. Then you can come back and tell Nana all about it, just like you always do.'

The knitting came out automatically, with the big colorful wooden needles she always used, and I saw a thermos and a *USA Today* in the bag too. The way she settled right in made me remember she'd been through this before, with my uncle, then with her younger sister, Anna. My aunt was almost a professional at caring for the very sick and dying.

'I was going to bring you some of that David Whyte you like,' Tia said. At first I thought she was talking to me. 'But then I thought no, let's keep you riled up, so I brought the *newspaper* instead. You know they're outsourcing the statue for Dr. King's memorial to China? *China?* Do you believe that, Regina?'

Tia's not a sentimental woman, but in her own way, she's a saint. I also knew there was no chance she'd let Nana catch her crying, coma or no coma. I leaned down and kissed the top of Tia's head. Then I kissed Nana too.

'Bye, Tia, Nana. I'll see you both later.'

My aunt kept right on chattering, but I heard Nana answer me. Another echo or memory or whatever these were.

Be good, she told me. *And Alex, be careful.*

Actually, I wouldn't be in any physical danger right away. Technically, I was on administrative leave after the previous day's shooting. Superintendent Davies kept it down to two days, which I appreciated, but even that was time I couldn't afford. I needed to talk with Tony Nicholson and Mara Kelly. Now. So I asked Sampson to set up some interviews under his name. Then I would just go along for the ride, be another set of ears and eyes.

63

The detention center down in Alexandria is a big old redbrick building at the dead end of Mill Road.

It was where they held Zacarias Moussaoui until he was sentenced to the supermax facility in Florence, Colorado — which, by coincidence, was the last known residence of Kyle Craig, a serial killer and major piece of unfinished business for me to get to one of these days. It's amazing how small and incestuous the world of major crime can start to feel once you've spent enough time immersed in it, as I had. Just thinking about Kyle Craig got me riled up inside.

Nicholson and Ms. Kelly were being held on the first and second floors, respectively. We had put them in separate interview rooms and then had to shuttle between the two by elevator.

At first, neither of them was willing to say anything except that they'd been the victims of kidnap and assault. I let that go on for a while, several hours, and even subtly let Mara Kelly know that her boyfriend was holding firm. I wanted to build up her trust in Nicholson before I tried to tear it down to nothing.

Next time into the room, I laid a photocopied page on the table in front of her.

'What's this?' she asked.

'See for yourself.'

She leaned in, tucking in a loose strand of hair

with a white-tipped fingernail. Even here in an interrogation room, Kelly had the kind of gentility that struck me as more practiced than real. She spoke of herself as an accountant, but she'd only finished a year of junior college.

'Plane tickets?' she said. 'I don't understand. What are these for?'

Sampson hunkered low over the table. He's six nine and more than a little intimidating when he wants to be, which is most of the time when he's on the job.

'Montreal to Zurich, leaving last night. You read the ticket? You see the names?'

He tapped a finger on the page. 'Anthony and Charlotte Nicholson. Your boyfriend was getting ready to run on you, Mara. He and *his wife*.'

She pushed the page away. 'Yeah, I've got a computer and a color printer too.'

I took out my cell phone and offered it. 'There's a number for Swiss Air right there. You want to call and confirm the reservation, Mrs. Nicholson?'

When she didn't answer, I decided to give her a few minutes alone to stew. Actually, she was right — we had faked the tickets. By the time we came back, she was ready. I could see she'd been crying, and also that she'd tried to wipe away any sign of tears.

'What do you want to know?' she asked. Then her eyes narrowed. 'What do I get for it?'

Sampson made eye contact with her and held it. 'We'll do everything we can to help you.'

I nodded. 'This is how it works, Mara. Whoever helps us first, we help them.'

I turned on the tape recorder and set it down. 'Who were the men in the car? Let's start there.'

'I have no idea,' she said. 'I never saw them before in my life.' I believed her.

'What did they want? What did they say?'

Here she paused. I had the sense she might be ready to bury Nicholson, but it wasn't a corner she would turn all at once. 'You know, I warned him something like this could happen.'

'Something like what, Mara?' Sampson asked. 'Be a little more specific.'

'He's been blackmailing clients of the club. It was supposed to be our 'new-life money.' That's what Tony always called it. Some new life, right?' She gestured around the room. '*This* is it?'

'What about names? Dead names, made-up ones, whatever you heard. What do you know about the people he was blackmailing?'

Mara Kelly was warming to this, and as she did, her tone got more bitter and sarcastic. 'I know that he always covered his bases. Both sides of the aisle. That way, if anyone talks, everyone loses. And if anything happened to Tony, I was supposed to blow the whole thing wide open.' She sat back and crossed her slender arms. 'That was the idea, anyway. That was the threat he made to the dumbasses he was blackmailing for getting a little nookie.'

'And everyone paid up?' Sampson asked her.

Her eyes traveled around the room again like she couldn't believe she was here, that it had all come to this.

'Well, if that was true, we wouldn't be having this conversation now, would we?'

64

It didn't take long for Tony Nicholson to start talking a blue streak about the club and the blackmail scheme after that. I'd seen it so many times before, the way suspects will start competing with each other once they sense the ground is shifting. To hear him tell it, Mara Kelly had set up the entire back end: Asian underground banking, public key cryptography — everything they needed to stay out of reach for as long as they had.

'Why do you think they came after her too?' he kept asking us. 'Don't be fooled by the pretty face. That bitch isn't nearly as stupid as she appears.'

I guess you could say those two were no longer an item. Now things might get interesting.

Nicholson had been sitting on the same rickety folding chair for hours, with his injured leg stuck out to the side in an immobilizer. From the twisted look on his face, he was coming due for a pain pill.

'Okay,' I said. 'That's a start, Tony. Now let's talk about the real reason we're here.'

I took out a file and started laying photos on the table. 'Timothy O'Neill, Katherine Tennancour, Renata Cruz, Caroline Cross.'

There was a moment of genuine surprise on his face — but just a moment. Nicholson was cool under fire. 'What about them?'

'They all worked for you.'

'It's possible,' he said. 'A lot of people work for me.'

'It wasn't a question.' I pointed at Caroline's picture. 'She was found mutilated beyond recognition. Did you catch that on camera too, Nicholson?'

'I seriously don't know what you're talking about. I have no idea what you're getting at. Try making sense when you bother to open your mouth.'

'How did she die?'

Something seemed to click suddenly, like a spark in Nicholson's eyes. He looked down at the picture and then back up at me.

'You said Caroline Cross? That's your name, isn't it?' When I didn't answer, his mouth spread into a grin. 'Excuse me, Detective, but I think maybe you're in over your head.'

I got up very fast. If the table hadn't been bolted to the floor, I might have pinned Nicholson to the far wall with it.

But Sampson got to him first. He shot around the table and pulled the chair right out from under him. Nicholson flopped onto the floor like a caught fish.

He started to scream. 'My leg! My goddamn leg! You bastards! I'll sue you both!'

Sampson didn't seem to hear. 'You know Virginia's a death penalty state, right?'

'What is this, Abu fucking Ghraib? Get the hell away from me!' Nicholson gritted his teeth and pounded the floor. 'I didn't kill anyone!'

'But you know who did,' I shouted back.

'If I had anything to trade, don't you think I'd use it? Help me up, you stupid assholes! Help me up, here. Hey! *Hey!*'

We walked out instead. And while we were at it, we took the chairs with us.

65

Four hours later, in the name of 'coming clean' and telling us what he knew, and most of all, getting the best deal he possibly could, Nicholson offered up access to a safe-deposit box in DC. He said it contained evidence that could help us. I had doubts, but decided to take my progress with him incrementally.

It took some scrambling, but by the next morning Sampson and I were outside the Exeter Bank on Connecticut with fully executed paperwork, a key from Nicholson's desk, and two empty briefcases in case there really was evidence to retrieve.

This place was no ordinary savings and loan, starting with the fact that we had to be buzzed in from the street. The lobby had a do-not-touch kind of feel to it — not a pamphlet or a deposit slip in sight.

From the reception desk, we were directed up to a row of glass-walled offices on the mezzanine. A woman inside one of them put down her phone and turned to look at us as we started up the stairs.

Sampson smiled and waved at her. 'Feels like a damn James Bond movie,' he said through his teeth. 'Come in, Dr. Cross. We've been expecting you.'

The branch manager, Christine Currie, was indeed expecting us. Her brief smile and handshake were about as warm as yesterday's oatmeal.

'This is all a bit irregular for us,' she said. Her accent was stuffy and British, and more upper-crust than Nicholson's. 'I do hope it can be done quietly? Can it be, Detectives?'

'Of course,' I told her. I think we both wanted the same thing — for Sampson and me to be back on the street as soon as possible.

Once Ms. Currie had satisfied herself with our paperwork and compared Nicholson's signature in half a dozen places, she led us out to an elevator at the back of the mezzanine. We got on and started down, a very rapid descent.

'You guys do free checking?' Sampson asked. I just stared straight ahead, didn't say a word. Stuffy environments sometimes set John off. Stuffy people too. But most of all, bad people, criminals, and anybody who aids and abets.

We came out into a small anteroom. There was an armed guard by the only other door, and a suit-and-tie employee at an oversize desk. Ms. Currie logged us in herself, then took us straight through to the safe-deposit room.

Nicholson's box, number 1665, was one of the larger ones at the back.

After we'd both keyed the flap door, Ms. Currie pulled out a long rectangular drawer, then carried it to one of the viewing rooms off an adjacent hallway.

'I'll just be outside, whenever you're ready,' she said in a way that sounded a lot like *Don't take too long with this*.

We didn't. Inside the box, we found three

197

dozen disks, each one in its own plastic sleeve and dated by hand in black marker. There were also two leather binders filled with handwritten pages of notes, lists, addresses, and ledgers.

A few minutes later, we left with all of it in our briefcases.

'God bless Tony Nicholson,' I said to the unflappable Ms. Currie.

66

For the rest of the afternoon, Sampson and I holed up in my office with a pair of laptops. We stayed busy watching and cataloging the extra-curricular sex lives of the rich and mostly famous. It was surprisingly repetitive stuff, especially given everything that Tony Nicholson was set up to provide at the club.

The roster of power players, on the other hand, was one big holy shit after another. At least half the faces were recognizable, the kind of people you'd see at a presidential inauguration. In the front row.

The clients weren't just men either. Women were outnumbered about twenty to one, but they were there, including a former US ambassador to the United Nations.

I had to keep reminding myself that every one of these people was — at least technically — a murder suspect.

We set up a log, using the date stamps embedded on each recording. For every clip, we wrote down the name of the clients we recognized and flagged the ones we didn't. I also made a note of where each 'scene' took place at the club.

My primary interest was the apartment over the carriage barn, which I'd come to think of as a kind of ground zero for this whole nasty murder puzzle.

And that's where we started to pick up some legitimate momentum. Right around the time I thought my eyes were going to burn out of my head, I started to notice an interesting pattern in the tapes.

'John, let me see what you've got so far. I want to check something.'

All of our notes were handwritten at this point, so I laid the pages out side by side and started scanning.

'Here . . . here . . . here . . . '

Every time I saw someone had used the apartment, I circled the date in red pen, ticking off entries as I went. Then I went back over everything I'd circled.

'See this? They were using the studio in the back pretty regularly for a while, and then, about six months ago, it just stops cold. No more parties back there.'

'So what happened six months ago?' Sampson asked. The question was more rhetorical than anything, since we both knew the answer.

That's when the killing started.

In which case — where were the rest of Nicholson's disks?

67

After work, I picked up some Thai food on Seventh and brought it to Bree at the hospital. It wasn't the kind of dinner date she deserved, but anything besides Swiss steak and Jell-O from the cafeteria had to be a big improvement.

It looked like she had a whole mobile-office thing going on, with her laptop and a little printer and files spread out on the counter in the back. The laptop was open to Web MD, and she was busily taking notes when I came in.

'Who ordered the panang curry and pad thai?' I called from the doorway.

'That would be me,' Bree said.

She picked her way past all the equipment and gave me a kiss hello.

'How's our girl been doing?' I asked.

'Still fighting. She's amazing; she really is.'

Nana looked a little more peaceful, maybe, but otherwise seemed about the same. Dr. Englefield had already warned us not to get too invested in the minutiae. You could drive yourself crazy scrutinizing every little tic and twitch, when the important thing was to keep showing up and never lose hope.

While I unpacked the food, Bree caught me up on the day. Englefield wanted to keep Nana on beta blockers for the time being. Her heart was still weak, but it was steady, for what that was worth. And they were going to take the dialysis down to three times a day.

'There's a new resident, Dr. Abingdon, you should talk to about that,' Bree said. 'I've got her number right here.'

I traded a plate of food and a bottle of water for it. 'You're doing too much,' I told Bree.

'This is the closest thing I've ever had to a real family,' she said. 'You know that, don't you?'

I did. Bree's mother died when she was five, and her father never expressed much interest in his children after that. She'd been raised by a series of cousins more than anything, and when she left home at seventeen, she never looked back.

'All the same,' I told her, 'you can't take off from work indefinitely.'

'Sweetie, listen to me. I hate that this is happening. There's nothing good about it. But as long as this is the deal, then I am right where I want to be. End of story, okay? I'm fine with it.'

She twirled up a forkful of rice noodles and popped them into her mouth, with a grin I hadn't seen in a while. 'Besides, what are they going to do at work, replace me? I'm too good for that.'

I couldn't argue there.

Honestly, I'm not sure I could have done everything Bree was doing. Maybe I'm not that generous. But I do know that she made me feel lucky, and incredibly grateful. There was never going to be enough I could do to thank her for this, but Bree didn't seem to want any payback.

We spent the rest of the evening with Nana, reading out loud from *Another Country*, an old favorite of hers. Then, around ten o'clock, we kissed her good night, and for the first time since this had happened, I went home to sleep in my own bed. Right next to Bree, where I belonged.

68

When Ned Mahoney called me the next day and said I should meet him at the Hirshhorn sculpture garden, I didn't question it for a single moment. I left the office right away and marched over there.

The beat goes on. In double time. Now what does Ned want? What has he found out?

He was waiting on one of the low cement walls when I came down the ramp from the Mall side. Before I even reached him, he was up and walking — and when I did come alongside, he started briefing me without so much as a hello. I knew Ned well enough to understand when I should just shut up and listen.

Apparently, the Bureau had already secured an administrative subpoena to get a look at Tony Nicholson's overseas bank records. They'd gotten a whole list of deposits, originating accounts, and names attached to those accounts, through something called the Swift program.

Swift stood for the Society of Worldwide Interbank Financial Telecommunications. It's a global cooperative based in Belgium that tracks something on the order of six trillion transactions every day. The database doesn't include routine banking — they don't necessarily know when I go to the ATM — but just about everything else is in there. The program was under all kinds of legal scrutiny, since it had

204

come out that the US government was using it to track terror cells, post 9/11. Whatever the obstacles, though, someone at the Bureau had gotten around them.

'If this were my case, which it isn't, I'd follow the numbers,' Mahoney said, still peppering me with information. 'I would start with the biggest depositors into Nicholson's account and work my way down from there. I don't know how much time you'll have, though, Alex. This thing is unbelievably hot. Something is not right here, in a big way.'

'Isn't the Bureau already on it? They have to be, right?'

It was the first question I'd asked in five minutes of nonstop talk. Ned was as manic as I'd ever seen him, which is saying a lot, since he's usually a buzz saw on Red Bull.

'Honestly, I don't know,' he said with a shrug. He shoved his hands into his pockets, and we started another lap around the sunken garden.

'Something's sure up, Alex. Here's an example. I don't understand it, but the whole case has been moved out to the Charlottesville Resident Agency, which is a satellite. They'll work with Richmond, I guess.'

'Moved? That doesn't make any sense. Why would they do that?'

I knew from past experience that the Bureau didn't swap cases around midstream on a whim. It almost never happened. They might cobble a task force between offices to cover a wider area, but nothing like this.

'Word came down from the deputy director's

office yesterday — and they transferred the files *overnight*. I don't know who the new SAC is, or if there even is one. Nobody'll talk to me about this case. As far as they're all concerned, I'm just a guy running a lot of field agents. I shouldn't even be on this anymore. I definitely shouldn't be *here*.'

'Maybe they're trying to tell you something,' I said, but he ignored the joke. It was pretty lame, anyway. I just wanted to calm Ned down a little if I could. I wanted him to speak slowly enough that I could follow.

He stopped by the big Rodin in the garden, took my hand, and shook it in an oddly formal way. 'I've got to go,' he said.

'Mahoney, you're freaking me out a little here — '

'See what you can get done. I'll find out what I can, but don't depend on the Bureau in the meantime. *For anything*. Do you understand?'

'No, Ned, I don't. What about this bank list you were just talking about?'

He was already walking away, up the stone stairs toward Jefferson Drive.

'Don't know what you mean,' he said over his shoulder, but he was patting his coat pocket when he said it.

I waited for him to leave, then checked my pocket. There, along with my keys, was a black-and-silver thumb drive.

69

Ned could lose more than his job for handing over the kind of sensitive information he'd just given me. He could go to jail too. I owed it to him to do as much with the list as I could. So I took his advice and started right at the top — with Tony Nicholson's biggest single 'benefactor.'

If someone had told me a month ago that Senator Marshall Yarrow of Virginia had a connection to a scandal like this, I would have been highly skeptical. The man had too much to lose, and I don't mean just money — though he had plenty of that too.

Yarrow was a billionaire before he was fifty, riding the dot-com wave in the nineties and then getting out. He'd turned part of his fortune into a Bill Gates-style foundation, run by his wife, focused on children's health initiatives in the United States, Africa, and East Asia. Then he leveraged all that good will, and another big pile of money, into a Senate campaign that no one took too seriously — until he won. Now Yarrow was in his second term, and it was an open secret in Washington that he'd already formed an off-the-books exploratory committee, with his eye on the next presidential election.

So yes, plenty to lose — but he wouldn't be the first Washington politician to blow it all on hubris, would he?

With a little calling around, I found out that Yarrow had a working lunch in his office that day, followed by a one thirty TVA caucus meeting, both in the Russell Senate Office Building. That would put him in the southwest lobby just before one thirty.

And that's when and where I went after him.

At one twenty-five, he came off the elevator with a retinue of power-suited aides, all of them talking at once. Yarrow himself was on the phone.

I stepped into his line of sight with my badge out. 'Excuse me, Senator. I was hoping for a minute of your time.'

The one woman in the group of aides, strikingly blond, attractive, late twenties, stepped between us. 'Can I help you, Officer?'

'It's Detective,' I told her, but kept my eyes on Yarrow, who had at least put a hand over his cell. 'Just a few questions for Senator Yarrow. I'm investigating a large credit card fraud case in Virginia. Someone may have been using one of the senator's cards — at a social club out in Culpeper?'

Yarrow was very good. He didn't even flinch when I referred to the club at Blacksmith Farms.

'Well, as long as it's quick,' he said, just reluctantly enough. 'Grace, tell Senator Morehouse not to start without me. You all can go ahead. I'm fine with the detective. I'll be right along. It's okay, Grace.'

A few seconds later, the senator and I were alone, as much as you could be in a place like this. For all I knew, the three-story coffered dome over our heads carried sound everywhere and anywhere.

'So, which credit card are we talking about?' he asked, with a perfectly straight face.

I kept my voice low. 'Senator, I'd like to ask you about the half-million-dollar transfers you've made to a certain overseas account in the past six months. Would you rather talk about this somewhere else?'

'You know what?' he said, as brightly as if he were being interviewed by Matt Lauer on the *Today* show. 'I just remembered a file I need for this meeting, and I already sent my aides on. Would you mind walking with me?'

70

The first thing I noticed about Marshall Yarrow's private office was how many pictures of himself he had mounted on the walls. There seemed to be a visual clique of 'important' people he wanted to be seen with. There was one with the president and one with the vice president. Tiger Woods. Bono. Arnold and Maria. Bob Woodward. Robert Barnett. He was obviously a well-connected man, and he wanted everyone who walked into this office to know it right away.

Yarrow perched on the edge of a huge cherry inlaid desk and made a point of not asking me to sit down.

I'd known I was going to have to be aggressive at first, but now I wanted to back off and see what I could accomplish with a little tact. If Yarrow chose to put up a firewall, it would be hard to get around without subpoenas.

'Senator, let me start by taking any association you may have with that social club off the table. It's not why I'm here,' I told him. That wasn't entirely true, but it was good enough for the time being.

'I never said I was associated with any club,' he said. It was a balls-of-steel moment on his part, especially considering the sex acts I'd seen him performing on more than one of Nicholson's tapes.

I didn't push it. 'Fair enough, but you should

210

know that my focus here is extortion, not solicitation.'

'Please don't push your way in here doling out some puzzle pieces and holding onto others, Detective,' Yarrow said, suddenly more aggressive. 'I'm too smart and too busy a man for that. What *exactly* are you hoping to walk away with here?'

'Good question, and I have an answer. I want you to tell me that those bank transfers are exactly what I think they are.'

There was a long standoff; I guess he was waiting for me to blink.

Then he finally said, 'Yeah, okay, let's get this out on the table. I've been to Blacksmith Farms, but for entertainment purposes only. And I *don't* mean myself. We're talking about out-of-town guests, contributors, visitors from the Middle East, that sort of thing. It's a part of the job, unfortunately.

'I get them in, have a drink or two, and then leave them to it. That's it. Believe me' — he held up his left hand and waggled a gold-banded finger — 'I can no sooner afford to piss Barbara off than I can my whole constituency. There's been no solicitation here. Nothing to be blackmailed for. Am I clear on that?'

I was starting to get real sick of people pretending that none of this was happening.

'I'm sorry, Senator, but I have evidence to the contrary. Digital video evidence. You sure this is the way you want to go?'

Senator Yarrow never missed a beat, and he even remembered to pick up the file he'd supposedly forgotten in the office.

'You know, Detective, my caucus meeting started five minutes ago, and if I don't get this important water bill moving today, it's not going anywhere. Assuming there aren't any charges here, you're going to have to excuse me.'

'How long is your meeting?' I asked.

He flipped a card from his pocket and held it out between two fingers for me. 'Give Grace a call. We'll get you on the schedule,' he said.

I could feel the firewall starting to rise, higher and higher, faster and faster.

71

I brought some music to Nana's room that night, a mixed artist CD, the *Best of U Street*, with a lot of the big names from when she went to the clubs there with my grandfather and friends — Basie, Sarah Vaughan, Lena Horne, and Sir Duke himself, the great Mr. Ellington.

I let it play quietly on Bree's laptop while we visited.

The jazz singers' weren't the only familiar voices in the room. I'd also brought along Jannie and Ali. This was the first night the nurses had allowed Ali into the room. He was so quiet and respectful, sitting right next to Nana's bed. Such a good little boy.

'What's this for, Daddah?' he asked in the younger-sounding voice he used when he was a little nervous and unsure of himself.

'That's the heart monitor. You see those lines? They show Nana's heartbeat. You can see that it's steady right now.'

'What about that tube there?'

'That's how Nana gets food while she's in the coma.'

Then, suddenly, he said, 'I wish Nana was coming home soon. I wish it more than anything. I say prayers for Nana all day long.'

'You can tell her yourself, Ali. Nana's right here. Go ahead, if you want to say something.'

'She can hear me?'

213

'She probably can. I think so.' I put his hand on Nana's and my hand on top of his. 'Go ahead.'

'Hi, Nana!' he said as if Nana were hard of hearing, and it was difficult not to laugh.

'Inside-the-house voice, buddy,' Bree said. 'But good enthusiasm there. I'll bet Nana heard you.'

72

Jannie was more reserved with her grandma. She moved kind of awkwardly around the room, like she just wasn't sure how to be herself. Mostly, she hung back by the door until I motioned her over.

'Come here, Janelle. I want to show you and Ali something interesting.'

Ali hung on my arm, and Jannie came to look over my shoulder. It was tight in the little space next to the bed, but I liked us pressed in that way, a unit, hopefully ready for whatever came our way.

I took a picture out of my wallet. It was the one I'd found in Caroline's apartment, and I'd been carrying it with me.

'Now, this is Nana Mama, your uncle Blake, and me. Way back in 1976, if you can believe it.'

'Daddy! You look ridiculous,' Jannie said, pointing at the red, white, and blue hat jammed onto my seventies Afro. 'What are you wearing?'

'It's called a boater. It was the Bicentennial, America's two hundredth birthday, and about a million people were wearing them that day. Very few looked so jaunty, though.'

'Oh, that's really too bad.' Jannie sounded somewhere between embarrassed and filled with pity for her poor, clueless father.

'Anyway,' I went on, 'about five minutes after this picture was taken, a big Washington

215

Redskins float came by in the parade. They were throwing out mini footballs, and Blake and I just about lost our minds trying to catch one. We ran after the float for blocks without even a second thought for poor Nana Mama. So you know what happened next, right?'

This was mostly for the kids, but also for Nana — like we were sitting around the kitchen table and she was over at the stove, eavesdropping. I could just imagine her standing there, stirring something good and pretending not to listen in, getting a wisecrack ready for me.

'It took her hours to find us, and let me tell you, when she did, you have never seen Nana that mad in all your life. Not even close.'

Ali stared at Nana, trying to imagine it. 'How mad was she? Tell me.'

'Well, do you remember when she quit us and moved out for a while?'

'Yeah.'

'Madder than that, even. And remember when a certain someone' — I poked Ali in the ribs — 'drove' the vacuum cleaner down the stairs and put scratches all over the wood?'

He played along and dropped his jaw wide open. 'Madder than that?'

'Ten times madder, little man.'

'What happened, Daddy?' Jannie chimed in.

The truth was, Nana had slapped both of us across the face — before she hugged us silly and then bought us a couple of red, white, and blue cotton candies, as big as our haircuts, on the way home. She'd always been a little old-school that way, at least back then. Not that I ever held the occasional whupping against her. That's just the way it was in those days. Tough love, but it seemed to work on me.

I picked up her hand and looked at her, so frail and still in the bed, like some kind of place marker for the woman I'd known for so long and loved so dearly, possibly since before I could remember.

'You made sure we never ran off like that again, didn't you, Regina?'

Two seconds ago, I'd been making jokes. Now I was feeling overwhelmed, and if I had to guess, I'd say I was feeling a lot of the same emotions Nana had that day on the Mall before she found Blake and me, safe and sound.

I was scared and I was desperate, most likely because I was exhausted from fighting back all the worst-case scenarios in my head. More than anything, I wanted our family to be back together, the way it was supposed to be, the way it had always been.

But I doubted it was going to happen, and I couldn't really face that yet, or maybe ever.

Stay with us, Nana.

73

The next morning started early, too early for most of the other detectives on the case. I had a list of names from the diaries in Nicholson's safe-deposit box, and Sampson had confirmed current addresses for twenty-two escorts who'd worked the club in Virginia at one time or another.

Starting at eight, I sent out five teams of two uniformed officers each, to pull in as many from the list of escorts as we could find.

Presumably these were night birds we were going after. First thing in the morning seemed like a good bet. I wanted to talk to as many of them as possible, before any cross talk could start mucking things up and making this investigation even trickier than it was already.

Sampson also called in a favor from our friend Mary Ann Pontano in the Prostitution Enforcement Unit. She arranged for us to use the office they shared with Narcotics on Third Street, and Mary Ann would also be sitting in for at least some of the interviews. I wanted a white female face on our side of the table, to go against the mostly white female prostitutes.

By ten o'clock, we had an impressive fifteen of the twenty-two names accounted for.

I spread them out into every conference room, interview space, cubicle, and hallway available, and I don't think I made any new friends in

Narcotics that morning. Too bad. I didn't much care that I might be inconveniencing somebody.

The place was a total zoo, including the four extra officers I kept around to make sure nobody walked out on us. The rest of the team I sent back out to look for the escorts who hadn't turned up. The possibility that some of them might never be found was something I'd have to worry about later.

The interviews started slowly. None of these very pretty women trusted us, and I couldn't blame them much for that. We didn't hold back on details of Caroline's murder, or the possibility of others. I wanted the young women to realize the kind of danger they'd been in, working for Nicholson, working for anyone in the escort business. Anything to get them to talk to us.

A few of the women quickly admitted to recognizing Caroline's picture. She'd gone by the name Nicole when she was at the club, which wasn't often from the sound of it. She was 'nice.' She was 'quiet.' In other words, they told me nothing I could use to find her murderer.

Instead of lunch, I took a walk around the block to clear my head, but it didn't help much. Was I wasting my time here? Were we asking the wrong questions? Or should we just let the escorts go and try to salvage the afternoon for something else?

This was the classic problem for me: I never knew when to stop, because stopping always felt like quitting. And I wasn't ready for that yet. For one thing, I still vividly remembered Caroline's 'remains.' I feared there were several others who'd died the same horrible way.

I was on my way back up Third Street, feeling no better than before, when my phone rang. Mary Ann Pontano's name was on the ID.

'I'm outside,' I answered. 'Trying to clear my head — if that's possible. Taking a walk.'

'Only place I didn't look,' she said. 'You should get back in here and talk to this girl Lauren again.'

I started walking faster. 'Red hair, shearling coat?'

'That's the one, Alex. Seems like her memory's warming up. She's got a few interesting things to say about one of the missing girls, Katherine Tennancour.'

74

Just like every other escort we'd pulled in today, Lauren Inslee was slender, well-endowed, and absolutely gorgeous. She was a former model in New York and Miami, a graduate of Florida State University, an escort for men with a taste for perky cheerleader types. Nicholson obviously had a variety of tastes to satisfy, but his general aesthetic was 'expensive.'

'Katherine's dead, isn't she?' That was the first thing Lauren asked when I sat down with her. 'Nobody will tell me anything. You want *us* to talk, but you people won't say a word about what happened.'

'That's because we don't know, Lauren. That's why we're talking to you.'

'Okay, but what do you *think?* I don't mean to be morbid. I just want to know. She was a friend of mine, another Florida girl. She was going to be a lawyer. She'd been accepted at Stetson, which is a really good school.'

Lauren played with a paper napkin the whole time she spoke, tearing it into tiny pieces. A slice of the pizza we'd brought in sat untouched on a plate next to the torn shreds of napkin. I believed that all she wanted to hear was the truth. So I decided to give it to her.

'The police report says there's no indication that she packed a bag at her apartment. Given the amount of time it's been — yes, there's a

221

good chance she's not coming back.'

'Oh, God.' The girl turned away, fighting tears, hugging herself tightly.

It was getting more depressing in here by the second. We were in one of the larger interview rooms, with graffiti burning right through the latest paint job on the walls and scorch marks on the floor from years of cigarette butts.

'Detective Pontano says that you mentioned something about a specific client at Blacksmith? And maybe Katherine. Lauren, tell me about the client.'

'I don't know,' she said. 'Maybe. I mean — I know what Katherine told me. But that place was all rumors all the time.'

I kept my voice even and as calming as possible. 'What did she tell you, Lauren? We're not going to arrest you for anything you say in here. You can believe me on that. This is a big homicide case. I don't give a damn about vice.'

'She said she had a private scheduled with someone, a big hitter she called Zeus. That was the last time I ever talked to Katherine.'

I wrote it down. *Zeus?*

'Is that some kind of alias? Or was it Katherine's code for the client?'

She dabbed at her eyes. 'An alias. Almost everyone uses booking names. You know — Mr. Shakespeare, Pigskin, Dirty Harry, whatever strikes their fancy. It's not like you don't end up face-to-face. But it does mean nobody's real name gets written down anywhere. Believe me, it's safer for everybody that way.'

'Sure it is.' I nodded. 'So Lauren, do you know

who Zeus is? Any idea?'

'I don't know. Honestly. This is what I'm saying, trying to say. *Supposedly*, he had something to do with the government, but Katherine could be gullible that way. I didn't even think twice about it when she told me.'

My mind was racing ahead a little now. 'Gullible how? Can you expand on that for me? What do you mean?'

Lauren sat back and pushed both hands through her hair, away from her face. I think finally talking about Katherine was a relief for her — if not for me.

'This is the thing you need to understand,' she said, and leaned in closer. 'Clients lie about what they do all the time. Like, if you think they're more important than they really are, you'll work harder, or let them go bareback or whatever crazy shit it is they're fantasizing about. So I never believe half of what I hear. In fact, I just assume that the ones who talk about their lives are lying. The men with the real power? Those are the ones who keep it all to themselves.'

'And Zeus?'

'Honestly, I don't even know if he exists. It's just a name. The name of a Greek god, right? *Greek?* Maybe that's a clue? His sexual preference?'

75

I never got to make up my own mind about what I thought of Lauren's story — because the next morning, it was made up for me.

I was gassing up my rental at a 7-Eleven on L Street near home, mostly thinking about how I missed my own car. It was in the shop for new glass after the shootout in Alexandria, and I wanted it back — *yesterday*. There's just no substitute for familiarity, the old faithful comfort zone, even the cup holder in just that spot where you automatically reach.

When the cell phone rang, it was a blocked number, but I'd been answering everything since Nana went into the hospital. I didn't even think about it.

'Dr. Cross?' It was a woman's voice, a little formal, no one I knew. 'Please hold for the White House chief of staff.'

Before I could respond, I was put on hold. I was stunned — not just by the call itself but by the timing. *What the hell was going on here? What now? The White House was calling? Could this be for real?*

It didn't take long for Gabriel Reese to come on the line. I recognized his distinctive voice right away, probably from seeing him on the news and the occasional Sunday morning show like *Meet the Press*.

'Hello, Detective Cross, how are you today?'

he began in a chipper enough tone.

'I guess that depends, Mr. Reese. May I ask, how did you get my number?'

He didn't answer, of course. 'I'd like to meet with you as soon as possible. Here in my office would be best. It's all been cleared up the line. How soon could you be available?'

I thought about Ned Mahoney and how agitated he had been the other day. How paranoid he had seemed about the records from the investigation getting out. Well — I guess they were out.

'Excuse me, Mr. Reese, but what is this about? Can I at least ask that?'

There was a pause on the line, carefully chosen, maybe; I wasn't sure. Then Reese said, 'I think you already know.'

Well, I did now.

'I can be there in about fifteen minutes,' I said.

Then Reese surprised me again.

'No. Tell me where you are. We'll pick you up.'

76

A livery car with a military driver got to my location within a few minutes. The driver followed me to a nearby parking garage, waited, and then took me to the White House.

We came in at the Northwest Appointment Gate, off Pennsylvania. I had to show my ID twice, to the sentry at the gate and then to the armed guard who greeted me at the West Wing turnaround. From there, a Secret Service agent walked me straight in through the entrance closest to the Rose Garden.

I'd been to the White House enough times to know that I was on a fast track, leading straight to the chief of staff's office.

I also understood that they didn't want my visit to attract attention, the reason for the escort.

Gabriel Reese had a reputation as a wonk more than a bulldog, but also for the kind of covert power he wielded here. He and President Vance went back years. More than a few pundits had labeled him the de facto vice president of the administration. What that meant to me was Reese had either initiated this meeting on his own or at the president's request. I didn't think I liked either possibility.

My Secret Service escort delivered me to a woman whose voice matched the one from before, on the phone. She offered coffee, which I declined, and then walked me right in to meet Gabriel Reese.

'Detective Cross, thank you for coming.' He shook my hand across his desk and motioned for me to sit in one of the tall wing chairs. 'I'm so sorry about your niece. It must have been a horrible shock. I can't even imagine.'

'It was, thank you,' I said. 'But I have to tell you, I'm a little uneasy with the amount of information you have about this case.'

He looked surprised. 'It would be much stranger if I didn't. Anything to do with the White House is the Secret Service's job to know.'

I tried to cover my surprise. *What did my murder investigation have to do with the White House? What was going on?*

'In that case, I would have thought I'd be meeting with them,' I said. 'The Secret Service.'

'One thing at a time,' he said. Fine — that was about all my nervous system could handle anyway.

There was nothing aggressive about Reese's manner; he just seemed very sure of himself. Actually, he seemed younger in person, even a little preppy looking, with a button-down collar and conservative tie. You'd never know to see him that his thumbprint was on American policy all over the world.

'For now,' he went on, 'I'd like to hear about how the investigation is coming along. Bring me up to speed about the way you see things, what you've found out so far.'

This interview was getting stranger by the minute.

'It's coming along fine, thanks.'

'I meant — '

'I think I know what you meant. With all due respect, though, Mr. Reese, I don't report to the White House.' *Not yet anyway.*

'I see. Of course you're right. You're absolutely right. My apologies for overreacting.'

I'd already gone further than I meant to, but so had Reese. I decided to stay on the offensive with him.

'Have you ever heard the name Zeus in connection with any of this?' I asked.

He considered the question for a second. 'Not that I can recall. And I think I would, a name like Zeus.'

I was pretty sure he was lying, and it reminded me of something Lauren Inslee had said about her clients: Why would someone like Reese even answer my question, *except* to lie?

When the phone on his desk buzzed, he picked it up right away. He watched me while he listened, then stood as soon as he hung up. 'Would you excuse me for a minute? I'm sorry about this. I know how busy you are.'

As he walked out of the room, a Secret Service agent stepped into the open door with his back to me. I couldn't help wondering what would happen if I tried to leave. Instead, I just sat there and attempted to get my bearings. Why was the White House chief of staff involved with my case? How?

Soon enough, there were voices outside, just a low murmur that I couldn't understand from where I was sitting.

The agent in the door stepped out and another one took his place. He came in and glanced quickly around the office. His eyes played right over me, the way they did the rest of the furniture.

Then he moved aside to make way for the president, who walked into the room smiling.

'Alex Cross. I've heard so much about you. All of it good,' she said.

77

The president's vibe was completely different from Reese's. She was almost collegial the way she shook my hand and settled onto the tufted leather couch instead of behind the desk. Not that it did anything to put me at ease.

'I've read your book,' she told me. 'Years ago, but I remember it well. Very interesting stuff. And so very scary because it's all true.'

'Thank you, Madam President.'

I admired Margaret Vance. She'd done a lot to get both sides of the aisle talking to each other. She and her husband, Theodore Vance, were both powerful figures not only in Washington but around the world. All things being equal, I would have liked to work with the president. But things were definitely not equal right now.

'I'd like to ask you a favor, Dr. Cross.' She nodded at her agent to leave us alone, and I waited for him to close the door.

'Regarding my investigation?'

'That's right. I think you'll agree it's important this case not proceed in a way that could threaten innocent people, or especially national security, or even the everyday workings of our government. Allegations can be just as harmful as indictments if they're brought to light in the wrong way. You know that, of course.'

'Yes,' I agreed. 'I have a bit of experience with that.'

'So you can appreciate the delicacy here.' She was talking more at me than to me, and seemed to think this was all already settled. 'I'd like you to meet with one of our lead agents, Dan Cormorant, get him up to speed, and transition the case into his care.'

'I'm not sure that I'm in a position to do that,' I told her. 'For several reasons.'

'It won't be a problem. The Service's uniformed division has all the statutory authority of the Metropolitan Police.'

I nodded. 'Within the city limits, that's true.'

It was like I wasn't even speaking anymore, the way she went on. 'And of course, all the field resources any investigation could possibly need. We've got the best in the world working for us here.' She stopped and looked at me over the top of her glasses. 'Present company excluded, of course.'

My, my, my. It's a truly original feeling to have your ass kissed by the leader of the free world. Too bad I couldn't enjoy it for more than a few seconds. I've got a pretty good internal compass, but for all I knew, it was sending me right over an edge I'd never come back from.

'President Vance,' I said. My heart might have been thudding, but my mind was still clear. 'I'd like to take all of this under advisement and respond sometime in the next twenty-four hours, either in writing or in person, whichever you prefer.'

She didn't try to hide how she felt about that. Two lines showed up around her mouth like parentheses.

'I'm not here to negotiate, Dr. Cross. This meeting is a courtesy, and an extraordinary one at that. I assumed someone like you preferred not to be walked over. That was obviously my mistake.' She stood up and I followed suit. 'Frankly, I'm surprised. I've been told you were a bright man and a patriot.'

'A patriot in a very difficult position right now, Madam President.'

Vance didn't address me after that. The last thing I heard her say was to the agent on the other side of the door as she left.

'Show Dr. Cross out. We're done here.'

Part Four

BURNING DOWN THE HOUSE

78

The murder mystery was turning out to be more like a plague, spreading and infecting anyone who touched it, killing them.

Adam Petoskey sat up suddenly on the couch, all five foot four of him. His heart was kicking at the inside of his chest. Something besides a terrifying nightmare had just woken him, though there had been plenty of those lately too.

What was it?

What now?

His apartment was dark except for the TV. He'd been watching *The Daily Show* when he dropped off, finding solace in the droll humor of Jon Stewart.

Now there was an infomercial on, people laughing and screaming about some weight-loss thing. Maybe that's what woke him.

Paranoia was his roommate these days, and one hairy bitch to be cooped up with too. He hadn't left the apartment in a week. Literally a week. The phones were unplugged, the shades were drawn at all times, and garbage was piling up by the back door — ever since he'd nailed it shut on that first night when he couldn't sleep a wink.

There were things Adam Petoskey knew — things he wished to hell he didn't know.

Working for Tony Nicholson and his girlfriend, Mara, cooking the books and looking the other

way, had been shitty enough. *Not* working for
him, not hearing a word from him, as it turned
out, was even worse.

Like tonight, just to use a handy example. He
stood up off the couch, still a little shaky.

Halfway to the kitchen, he stopped. For the
hundredth time that week, he felt almost sure
someone was behind him.

And then, before he could even turn around
— *someone was.*

A strong arm looped across his throat and
pulled hard, until his feet nearly left the floor.
Duct tape was pressed over his mouth. He heard
it rip in the back and felt it stick and tighten.

'Don't fight, Mr. Petoskey. You fight — you
lose — you die.'

A hard finger pressed into the spot between
his shoulder blades and moved him toward the
bedroom door. 'Let's go. This way, my friend.'

Petoskey's brain squirmed. He was a numbers
man, after all. He could run equations and
probabilities like a machine, and right now,
everything he knew told him to do as this guy
said. It was even a strange kind of relief,
following someone's orders after seven days of
solitude in this hellhole.

In the bedroom, the man turned on a light. He
was no one Petoskey recognized — tall and
white, with gray-flecked dark hair. His gun had
one of those extensions on it, a silencer, if the
ones on TV were any indication.

'Pack a bag,' he said. 'Don't leave anything
out. Clothes, wallet, passport, whatever you need
for a long trip.'

Petoskey didn't hesitate, but a whole new raft of questions floated into his crowded mind as he started to pack. Where was he going? What kind of long trip? And how could he possibly convince anyone of the truth, that he'd never had any intention of telling a soul what he knew?

One thing at a time, Petoskey. Clothes, wallet, passport . . .

'Now get in the bathroom,' the man told him. 'Pack everything you'll need in there.'

Right, he thought, clinging to the task at hand. *Don't leave anything out. Toothbrush, toothpaste, shaver . . . condoms? Sure. Why not be positive?*

The master bath was tiny, with barely enough room to stand between the pedestal sink, toilet, and shower.

Petoskey opened the medicine cabinet, but then he felt another poke between his shoulder blades.

'Get in the tub and lie down, little man.'

It made no sense, but nothing did right now. Was he going to be tied up in the tub? Robbed? Left behind after all?

'No,' the man said. 'The other way, with your head down by the drain.'

And suddenly it all became horribly clear. For the first time, Petoskey screamed — and he heard just how tiny his voice was from behind the tape. This was it. This was really it. Tonight, he disappeared forever.

He knew too much — the famous names, all their dirty secrets.

237

79

I had fewer and fewer people I could talk to about this murder case anymore. Lucky for me, Nana was still one of them.

For a few days, I'd been holding back on her. Somehow it seemed wrong to bring the extra stress into her room at the hospital. But as the days had passed, and these visits of mine turned into their own kind of normal, I started to realize something. If Nana were awake through all of this, she would have been asking about Caroline's case every day. No doubt about it in my mind.

So I didn't hold back anymore.

'It's not going well, old woman. Caroline's murder case,' I told her that night. 'I'm overwhelmed, to be honest. I've never been in a position like this before. Not that I can remember, anyway.

'Ramon Davies is ready to take me off. The Bureau was going at it full clip, and now I don't even know where they are on it. I've got the White House breathing down my neck, if you can believe that. *Believe* it.

'And these are supposed to be the good guys, Nana. I don't know. It's getting harder and harder to tell the difference anymore. It's like somebody said: You can love this country and hate our government.'

It was quiet in the room, as usual. I kept the heart monitor volume down when I was there, so the only sounds besides my own voice were the hiss of the ventilator and an occasional snatch of conversation from the nurse's station down the hall.

Nana's condition hadn't changed, but she just seemed sicker to me. Smaller, grayer, more distant. It felt as though everything in my life was sliding in the same direction these days.

'I don't know where to go with any of this. One way or another, it's going to come out, and it's going to be huge when it does. I mean like Watergate huge, old woman. There'll be hearings and spin, and probably no one's ever going to know the real story — but I feel like I'm the only one who even wants to open that particular door. I want to know. I need to know.'

There was one other thing about the quiet. It meant that I could hear Nana talking back.

Poor Alex. An army of one, huh? What else have you got?

It wasn't a rhetorical question. She'd really want to know. So I gave it some thought . . . I had Sampson on my side. I had Bree, of course. I had Ned Mahoney — somewhere out there.

And I had one other rainy-day idea I'd been sitting on. It wasn't the kind of thing that could be undone once it was started, but hey, how much rainier did I expect it to get?

I reached through the bed rail and put my hands on Nana's. Things like touch had become more important than ever to me — any way I could connect with her, for as long as I could.

The room's ventilator hissed. Someone laughed down the hall.

'Thank you, old woman,' I said. 'Wherever you are.'

You're welcome, she communicated somehow, and we left it at that. As always, Nana had the last word.

80

And people continued to die. Anyone who knew anything was at risk.

It was two thousand miles from Virginia back to the island of Trinidad and the bright blue house where Esther Walcott had grown up, just outside the capital city of Port of Spain. That's where she'd run to after the raid on Mr. Nicholson's club.

Mum and Bap had welcomed her home with open arms and, more important, asked no questions about the life she'd left behind so abruptly in America.

Two years of hostessing and recruiting for the club in Virginia had left her with a nice bank account, if nothing else, and she planned on putting it toward a hair and nail boutique of her own, maybe even something at Westmall, like she'd always imagined as a girl. It seemed like the perfect way to start her life over.

But when she woke up on that third night home with a man's hand pressed tightly over her mouth, and heard the American accent in her ear, Esther knew that she hadn't run far enough.

'One peep and I'll kill everyone in the house. *Everyone*. Do you understand what I'm saying, Esther? Just nod.'

It was almost impossible not to scream. Her breath was coming in fast, high-pitched gasps, but she managed to nod yes.

'Good girl, smart girl. Just like at the club in America. Where's your suitcase?' She pointed to the closet. 'Okay. Very slowly, now, I want you to sit up.'

He got her propped up in bed and pasted a length of tape over her mouth before he let go. It was seventy-five degrees out, but she was shaking as if it were thirty. The touch of his rough hands on her stomach and breasts made her feel practically naked. And vulnerable. And sad.

When a light showed under her door, Esther's heart flip-flopped — a rush of hope at first, but then dread. *Someone was coming!*

The intruder turned to her in the semidark and held a finger to his lips, reminding her of what was at stake. Her family.

A moment later, there was a soft knock. 'Esther?' It was her mother's voice, and all at once, more than she could take. Her right hand flew up and clawed the tape off her mouth.

'Run, Mummy! Man has a gun! Run!'

Instead, the door to the bedroom flew open. For a moment, Esther saw the wide shape of her mother shadowed against the light from the hall.

There was a soft popping sound, nothing like a regular gunshot, but Miranda Walcott clutched her chest and collapsed to the floor without another word.

Now Esther was screaming — and couldn't have stopped if she'd wanted to. Next she heard her father's voice, coming closer. He was running!

'*Esther? Miranda?*' he called out.

The intruder left her side, heading for the

door, and she threw herself after him, if only to catch his ankles, make him fall somehow.

Instead, she hit the floor hard and again heard the awful popping sound.

Something shattered in the hall, and her poor Bap crashed against the wall.

Sparks of white light played at the edges of Esther's vision, and the room swam even as she scrambled up onto the bed again. With both fists, she pushed and clawed through the screen mesh in the window.

It wasn't far to a patch of black sage bushes below, and she was more outside than in when strong hands latched onto her ankles and started to pull. Her body scraped hard over the wooden sill as she reversed direction.

One more time, Esther screamed, knowing that the neighbors would hear, but also that it was too late to matter.

They were going to kill everyone who knew anything.

And anyone else in the way.

81

Damon had come home for the weekend, which was a great thing for everybody. I'd bought him a ticket and asked him to make the trip, partly because of Nana, partly because all of this upset was making us miss him more than ever.

Anyway, I wanted the kids together in one place, even if it was only for a couple days.

We started with a welcome home dinner for Day, including a lot of his favorites: Caesar salad for everyone, with anchovies for me; Nana's sloppy joes in sourdough bowls that the younger two had hollowed out; and Jannie's monkey bread for dessert. It was the first time she'd ever made the bread by herself, without Nana's help. Everything about Day's visit was happy and sad at the same time.

It was interesting to see the changes around the house through Damon's eyes. Jannie, Ali, and I had gotten used to Bree coordinating schedules, helping with homework, and putting meals on the table. For Damon, though, it was all new. Mostly, he didn't comment other than a lot of 'thank yous,' which were much appreciated by Bree.

I waited until we'd heard about life at Cushing Academy and had enjoyed our meal together before I steered the conversation around to Nana Mama.

'Let's talk about it,' I finally said.

Jannie gave a sigh. She was the one who kept the most informed, but emotionally, I think this was harder for her than anyone. She and Nana were incredibly close; they did everything together, and had since Jannie was a baby.

'What do you mean, Dad?' Damon asked. 'We all know what's going on. Don't we?'

'Just what I said — we should talk. Nana could get better soon. That's what we're hoping for. Or she could be in a coma for a while. It's also possible . . . that she won't wake up again.'

'She could *die*,' Jannie said, a little rudely. 'We get it, Dad. Even Ali does.'

I looked over at Ali, but he seemed all right so far. In his way, he was older than his age. Both Nana and I had talked to him like an adult, respected his intelligence, since he was around four years old. One of my theories, and Nana's, about raising kids is that you cannot give them too much love, but that the environment inside your house has to bear a relationship to what they will face on the outside. So no excess coddling or making excuses for unacceptable behavior.

I nodded Janelle's way. 'We all get it. We're all sad and we're angry. C'mere, everybody. Maybe I'm the only one who needs a little help right now.'

We gathered close for a group hug, and it was better that way, thinking about Nana without speaking.

Bree was the first to break down, and then everybody was in tears. No shame in that, nothing but love on display. That may not work for all families, but it sure does for us.

245

82

By Monday, I was ready to make my next move on the case. Her name was Wylie Rechler, although her readers knew her as simply 'Jenna.' She'd been helpful to the FBI and Metro before; in particular, she had aided Vice.

Wylie Rechler was DC's answer to Cindy Adams and Perez Hilton, with a hugely popular gossip blog called Jenna Knows. She'd used it to break a couple of smaller Washington stories over the years — Angelina Jolie's nomination to the Council on Foreign Relations, Barack Obama's closet cigarette habit — but most of her space was dedicated to the social and sex lives of the 'people who matter most,' as her home page called them.

Sampson and I caught up with the popular gossipist that afternoon at the Neiman Marcus store in Friendship Heights. Wylie was launching a new designer scent, whatever that means, also called Jenna Knows. With the smell of cheap perfume as thick in the air as it was, I kept thinking of it as 'Jenna Nose' instead.

She was set up in the middle of the store, near the escalators. Pretty ladies in black smocks were spritzing passers-by, while Jenna herself autographed bottles from a big pyramid of red-and-black boxes on a C-shaped counter.

When she saw our detective badges, she put a perfectly manicured hand up to her chest. 'Oh,

246

God! I've finally gone too far, haven't I?' It got a good laugh from the crowd behind us.

'I was wondering if I could persuade you to take five,' I asked her. 'It's important.'

'*Mais oui.*' Wylie stood up with a little flourish. 'Excuse me, ladies, but gossip awaits. The Metro Police know all. But — will they tell all?'

Some of the theatricality dropped off as soon as we were away from the crowd. 'I'm not actually in any trouble here, am I?' she asked.

'Nothing like that,' Sampson said, and held the door for her out to Wisconsin Avenue. 'We just need some help.'

We waited until we were in my car to go on. Then I just asked her point-blank. 'I'm wondering if you've heard anything about a sex club for heavy hitters? Out in Virginia? Place called Blacksmith Farms. We're looking, first of all, for some verification.'

She'd been rustling inside a little red clutch purse, but now she stopped cold. 'You mean it's true?'

'I'm just wondering what you've heard. Names, stories, anything at all.'

'Nothing in a while,' she said, pulling out a lipstick. 'Not enough to make a story I could go with. I figured it was — what? — a ridiculous *suburban* myth?'

'Aren't you in the business of publishing rumors?' Sampson asked her.

'Honey, I'm in the business of being as accurate as I can be and not getting my ass sued. I learned that the hard way blogging on Condi Rice's love life. And just for the record, there's no such thing as an old rumor in Washington.'

'How do you mean that?' I asked.

'I mean you can't swing a stick around here without hitting some investigative reporter looking to make a name for themselves. Rumors either turn into headlines real quick or they're dead on arrival. When I didn't hear any more about that one, I figured it was a dead end.'

She smiled happily and started reddening her lips in the rearview mirror. 'Until now, anyway.'

'That's another thing,' I said, catching her eye. 'I need you to sit on this for a while.'

'*Excuse me?* You do know what I do for a living, don't you?'

'And I assume you know what I do,' I said. 'This is a murder investigation, Jenna, not a game. Do you understand what I'm saying here?'

'Okay, now you're scaring me,' she said, returning the lipstick to her purse. Then she finally opened up and gave me a few names she'd heard connected to the sex club. *New* names, which was helpful.

'Listen.' I handed her two of my business cards. 'Call me if you hear anything else, and please give me your number too. As soon as this thing is ready to go, I'll bring you whatever I have. Do we have a deal?'

'That depends.' She fanned herself with the cards. 'How do I know you're the type to return favors?'

I chose my words carefully. 'I'm here talking to you because I need you and I know you've been helpful to Metro before. That also means I can't afford to piss you off. Is that honest enough for you?'

She took out a little gold pen, scribbled some digits, then kissed the card. She handed it back to me with a lipstick imprint next to the number.

'Delicious,' she said.

I took the card. 'No, you had it right a minute ago — scary.'

83

I was surprised to hear from one of Tony Nicholson's attorneys the next afternoon. It wasn't the bow-tie-and-suspenders nerd from the night of the raid, but someone else entirely. This one sounded even more expensive, with a 202 phone number on the ID. The heart of the heart of the capital.

'Detective Cross, my name is Noah Miller. I'm with Kendall and Burke. I believe you're familiar with my client Anthony Nicholson?'

'I've been trying to meet with your client since last week,' I told him. 'I've left half a dozen messages for *Anthony*.'

'At Nyth-Klein?' he asked.

'That's right.'

'Yes, they represent the LLC and its holdings in Virginia. We've taken over individual representation for Mr. Nicholson — which brings me back to the subject at hand. I want to be very clear that I'm making this call at his request, and that he's choosing to ignore counsel on the matter.'

That got my attention. 'How soon can I see him?' I asked.

'You can't. That's not why I'm calling. Please listen carefully. What I have for you is a safe-deposit key, if you'd like to come pick it up. Mr. Nicholson says it's important to your investigation. He also believes that the Metro Police are his best chance of staying alive. He doesn't want to deal with the FBI.'

I was Googling Kendall and Burke while we spoke. 'I've already been to Nicholson's safe-deposit box,' I told him, as the firm came up on my screen. Big, reputable one on K Street.

'Yes, I know. This is in the same bank but a different box,' he said, and my hands stopped over the keyboard. What would Nicholson have in a second box? More important, how could we protect him? And from whom?

'Can I assume you'll come pick this up today?' Miller continued.

'Definitely, but let me ask you something,' I said. 'Why Metro? Why me? Why wouldn't Nicholson give this up to the Federal Bureau?'

'Honestly, my client doesn't trust the people who are holding him — or, frankly, the integrity of their investigation. One more thing — he wants to make sure his cooperation doesn't go unnoticed.'

I couldn't help a little smile. How weird, to suddenly be on the same side of the fence as Tony Nicholson, ah, Anthony. It sounded like he was getting as paranoid as I was — and maybe for good reason.

'Twenty-twenty K Street, fourth floor?' I asked, printing it off the screen.

'Very good, *Detective* Cross. Make it between one thirty and two o'clock. I'll be gone after that.'

'I'll see you at one thirty,' I said, and hung up on Lawyer Miller before he could hang up on me.

84

It didn't take long to snag the key from Nicholson's attorney at Kendall and Burke, and not much longer than that to get in and out of the Exeter Bank. It was as if the lawyer, Noah Miller, and the bank manager, Ms. Currie, were competing to see who could get me out of their lives faster. Fine with me.

It turned out that the only thing in the new deposit box was a single, unmarked disk, which was about what I'd expected. I drove straight back to the Daly Building with it and called Sampson on my way. He was already there, so it was no problem to meet as soon as I arrived with the disk.

In fact, the big man was sitting with his feet up, fooling around on a laptop, when I came into my office.

'Did you know Zeus was also called the Cloud Gatherer?' he said. 'His symbols are the thunderbolt, eagle, bull, and oak. Oh, and he was a pederast too. Rumored to be.'

'Fascinating,' I said. 'Get your shoes off my desk and slide this in.'

I handed him the disk and closed the door behind me.

'What is it?' Sampson asked.

'Tony Nicholson thinks it's his life insurance.'

Seconds later, the video started playing.

Right away, I recognized the bedroom from

the carriage barn apartment at Nicholson's club. It looked the same except for some clean sheets on the bed and maybe a few more knickknacks.

A time signature at the bottom of the screen put it at 1:30 a.m. on July 20 of the previous summer.

'Can those signature numbers be faked?' I asked Sampson.

'No doubt. Why? Do you think Nicholson is screwing with you?'

'Maybe. Probably. I don't know yet.'

After about thirty seconds, the image hiccupped, and the time jumped ahead to 2:17 a.m.

Now there was a girl on the bed, wearing nothing but black lace panties. She was blond and petite, with black cuffs on her wrists that were strapped to the posts over her head. Her legs were spread open as wide as humanly possible.

There was no sound, but the way she was moving looked more alluring than scared or defensive to me. Still, I had a fierce knot in my stomach. Whatever this was, I didn't think I wanted to see it proceed.

A man walked into the frame — a real creep wearing full S&M garb, with either rubber or latex pants and a long-sleeved shirt. Also heavy boots and a fitted hood that zipped all the way up the back of his head. Other than the fact that he was tall and well muscled, I couldn't tell much more about him.

'He knows the camera's there,' Sampson said. 'Maybe he wanted this filmed.'

'Let's just watch, John.'

I couldn't talk much right now. I was already thinking about what had happened to Caroline, possibly in this room, and maybe at the hands of the same creep we were watching.

Zeus, or whoever it was, bent over the girl and placed a black kidney-shaped blindfold over her eyes. 'There's a ring,' I said. 'On his right hand.'

It looked like a class ring, but the image quality wasn't good enough to make it out.

He took his time, pulled a few more things out of the dresser, a spreader bar that he cuffed to both of her ankles; a small brown bottle of something, possibly amyl nitrate.

When he waved it under her nose, the blond girl's face went very red. Then her head lolled from side to side.

Sampson and I watched silently as they had sex. Most of the time, the creep kept one hand on the mattress for balance and the other over her throat. It looked like he was performing asphyxophilia to me, controlling the girl's oxygen, giving it and then taking it away.

The girl played along and didn't seem distressed, which was distressing to watch. Then suddenly he arched up off of her, climaxing, I think, and raised his free hand like he'd just won some kind of contest.

All his weight appeared to be on her throat, and suddenly her movements became jerky and desperate. Her legs jutted straight out under him. It was a horrible thing to watch, like it was happening right now, and there was nothing we could do to stop it.

The more the blond girl struggled, the more

excited he got, until finally her body went limp and she stopped moving altogether. Only then did he kiss her.

'Oh, Christ,' Sampson said under his breath. 'What's the matter with the world?'

The killer climbed off the bed after that. There was no lingering, no fetishizing with the body. In less than a minute, he was gone from the private suite.

Twenty seconds later, the video cut out altogether.

'Come on, John. We're going to Alexandria. We need to find out if that was Zeus.'

85

At the detention center in Alexandria, Sampson and I walked in through the visitors' area. We went down a familiar path — past Records and Door 15, where inmates are released, until we got to the Command Center.

At that point, our police IDs were enough to get us buzzed through another pair of steel doors, to the booking desk.

All that was the easy part.

As usual, three guards were stationed on the desk. Two of them were middle-aged and hung in the background. One younger guy had the grunt job of processing walk-ins like us. A gold tooth caught the light when he spoke.

'State your business.'

'Detectives Cross and Sampson, MPD. We need a temporary custody order on two prisoners, Anthony Nicholson and Mara Kelly.'

'You got a letter on file?' He was already picking up the phone.

'We've interviewed them before,' I said. 'Just a few follow-up questions and we're out of here.'

It was worth a shot, anyway. Maybe there was a crack we could fall through.

The deputy wasn't on the phone for long, and he shook his head at me as he hung up.

'Well *A*, you don't have a letter for today, and *B*, it don't matter anyway. Your people are gone, Nicholson and Kelly both.'

'Gone?' I couldn't believe what I'd heard. 'Please tell me you mean they were transferred.'

'I mean *gone*, man.' He flipped open a black binder on the desk. 'Yep, right here. Eleven hundred hours today. Someone named Miller posted — *Jesus* — full cash bonds on both of them. A quarter mil each.'

That got the attention of the other two guards, and they came to look over his shoulder. One of them whistled low. 'Must be nice,' the other one said.

'Yeah, right?' the kid agreed.

This wasn't their doing and it wasn't their fault, but they were the ones standing in front of me.

'What is going on around here?' I said. 'Nicholson is a major flight risk. Did anybody bother to check on that? He had plane tickets booked the day he was arrested!'

The young guard was staring at me now. The other two had hands on their batons. 'I hear you, man, but you've got to step back, *right now.*'

I felt Sampson pulling on my shoulder. 'Don't waste your breath here, Alex. Let's go. Nicholson and the girl are gone.'

'This is a disaster, John.'

'I know, and it's done. Come on.'

I let him pull me away, but I would have paid good money to take a swing at someone. Tony Nicholson, for one. Or that smug lawyer Miller.

Even as we were leaving, I could hear the guards talking about their former prisoners. 'Fuckin' Richie Riches, man. They get their own breaks and everyone else's too.'

257

'Yeah, right? It's like they say, the rich just get richer, and the poor — '

'Work here.'

The last thing I heard was the guards laughing among themselves.

86

What an incredible circus! Whether or not it was Nicholson's own money that got him out, he still would have needed a federal judge to sign the Form 41, and someone else even higher in the food chain to broker the deal.

The cover-up was getting broader and deeper and dirtier every day, wasn't it? I think I was more awed than shocked by the whole thing, and worse, I suspected it wasn't close to being over.

John and I went through the motions of running out to Nicholson's house and then Mara Kelly's apartment, but we found exactly what we expected.

There was yellow police tape on the doors, but no indication that anyone had been there for at least a couple of days. Even if they had been, they were long gone now. I doubted that we would ever see Nicholson or Kelly again.

Before we got back on the highway, I asked Sampson to pull over at an Exxon station near Mara Kelly's apartment. I bought a little Nokia prepaid phone for thirty-nine dollars and used it to dial the number I'd gotten the other day.

Wylie Rechler answered on the first ring. 'This is Jenna. Talk to me.'

'It's Detective Alex Cross, Jenna. We met the other day out in Friendship Heights,' I said. 'Are you ready to jump into this thing?'

I heard a melodramatic little gasp on the other

end. 'Honey, I was ready the last time we chatted. What have you got for me now?'

'Ever heard the name Tony Nicholson?'

'I don't think so. No, definitely not. Should I have?'

'He's the one with the little black book you'd love to get your hands on, not that any of us ever will. Until eleven o'clock this morning, he was in federal custody. Now he's out on bail, and if I had to guess, he's on his way out of the country. With the little black book.'

'What does this mean for me?'

'It could mean a lot, Jenna. *If* you help me out. I want you to put a bug in Sam Pinkerton's ear at the *Post*,' I said. 'Could you do that?'

'I suppose I could.' She paused, and then her voice dropped. 'Sam covers the White House. You know that, correct?'

'That's right.'

'Oh Jesus, I'm wet — excuse my French. Okay, so what's Mr. Pinkerton going to have for me when I call? *If* I call.'

I told Jenna the truth. 'Maybe nothing right away. But you two might make a pretty good team on this one. You'll have all the right angles covered.'

'I think I'm in love with you, Detective.'

'That's another thing,' I said. 'Sam pretty much hates my guts. You'll probably get a lot further with him if you don't happen to mention my name.'

As I hung up, Sampson was giving me a once-over from the driver's seat. 'I thought Sam Pinkerton was a friend of yours.'

'He is.' I pocketed the new phone next to my old one. 'I'm just trying to keep it that way.'

87

I had one more place to be that afternoon, and I asked Sampson to drop me off.

One of Washington's favorite sons, and one of my favorite people too, Hilton Felton, had died a while back, too young at the age of sixty. I'd spent countless nights listening to Hilton play at Kinkead's in Foggy Bottom, where he'd been the house pianist since 1993. That's where they were having a memorial concert for him.

Something like a hundred and fifty people squeezed in to celebrate Hilton's life, and, of course, hear some great music from his friends. It was all very beautiful and relaxed and wonderful in its own way. The music could only have been better if Hilton had been there to play it himself.

When Andrew White got up and played one of Hilton's original compositions, it made me feel incredibly lucky to have known the man behind that music, but also deeply sorry to know that I'd never hear him play it again in the way that only Hilton could.

I missed him terribly, and all the while I was there, I couldn't stop thinking about Nana Mama too. She was the one who first took me to hear Hilton.

88

After the emotional stop at Kinkead's I caught a cab over to Fifth Street, then went upstairs to work. As if things weren't already interesting enough, we had a couple of unwanted visitors at the house that night. It was around eleven when Bree came up to my office in the attic to tell me the news.

'Alex, we've got company outside. Two guys in a Ford Explorer, parked across the street for the last hour. Cups on the dash, no coming and going. Just sitting there, watching the house. Maybe watching you up here.'

Bree has the best instincts I know, so I didn't doubt that we had a new problem. I holstered my Glock and slid on a windbreaker over it.

Then I stopped in Damon's room on my way downstairs for his old Louisville Slugger. A good piece of ash, not aluminum.

'Please don't come out,' I asked Bree at the front door. 'Call dispatch if there's a problem.'

'If there's a problem, I'm calling dispatch *and* I'm coming out,' she said. I took off out the front door and down the stoop. The Explorer was parked just past the house on the opposite side. The driver was getting out when I took my first swing and obliterated his left taillight.

'What the fuck are you doing?' he screamed at me. 'Are you nuts, man?'

In the streetlight, I could see he was hefty but

not fat, with a shaved head and a nose that had been broken a few times. I'd been thinking government, but now that I'd seen him, he looked more like a *Yellow Pages* PI.

'Why are you here watching my house?' I shouted at him. 'Who are you?'

His partner got out on the other side, but they both kept their distance.

'Alex?' I heard Bree coming up behind me. 'Are you all right?'

'I'm fine,' I shouted back. 'Washington plates, DCY 182.'

'Got it,' she said.

The bald-headed guy flashed his palms for me. 'Seriously, just take it down a notch, man. We know you're a cop.'

'I'll take it down when you tell me what you're doing here where I live.'

'We're not in for anything heavy, all right? I'm not even wearing a piece.' He opened his overshirt to show me. 'Somebody hired us to keep an eye on you for a little while. That's all this is.'

'On *me*?' I cocked the Slugger a little higher. 'Or me and my family?'

'On you. *On you*.' I didn't know if he was telling me the truth or just what I wanted to hear.

'Who are you working for?' I asked.

'We don't know. Seriously. It's a cash job. All I know is what you look like and where you've been today.'

That didn't do much to calm me down. I stepped over and took out another taillight.

'*And where have I been?*'

'You're working a murder case for Metro. Something to do with a detainee in Alexandria, and for fuck's sake, lay off the car already!'

Something had just flipped about this case. It hit me hard, in a way I couldn't deny. *The people I'd been pursuing were starting to pursue me now.*

'You know, you should be more careful,' the second PI told me.

I took a step in his direction. 'Why is that?'

'We're not the ones you need to worry about. Whoever this is, and whatever they don't want you doing — they've got some suction. That's all I'm saying. You can take it for what it's worth.'

'Thanks for the warning.' I pointed up the street. 'You're done here. If I catch either of you in this neighborhood again, I'm going to arrest you and have this car towed, you got it?'

'Arrest us?' Now that he was over the hump, the first guy decided to show a little chin. 'What are you going to arrest us for?'

'I'm a cop, remember? I'll think of something.'

'What about my car, man? That's like five hundred bucks damage!'

'Charge it to your clients,' I told him. 'Believe me; they can afford it.'

89

I got called into Ramon Davies's office again the next morning. He even had a desk jockey waiting outside the door to my office when I got there.

'What does he want?' I asked the officer. There were no good possibilities running in my mind, only very bad ones. Like more bodies.

'I don't know, sir. Just to meet with you. That's all I was told.'

I've heard that Woody Allen leaves his actors alone when they're doing well and only directs them if there's a problem. Davies is kind of the same way. I hated these walks to his office.

When I got in there, he had someone waiting with him. I recognized the face from the White House but didn't know the name until Davies introduced us.

'Alex Cross, this is Special Agent Dan Cormorant. He's from Secret Service. He'd like to talk to you.'

Cormorant was the one who had accompanied President Vance into the chief of staff's office the other day when I visited. I assumed he was here at his boss's behest.

'We've met, sort of,' I said, and shook his hand. 'I don't suppose you have anything to do with the two PIs outside my house last night?'

'Don't know what you're talking about,' he said.

'Imagine that.'

'Alex.' Ramon cut me off with a raised voice

265

and hand signal. 'Be quiet and let's get to this.'

Cormorant and I sat down across the desk from him.

'I'm not going to dwell on how we got here right now,' Davies said, and the implication was clear. We'd talk about it later, in private. 'But I will tell you what's going to happen next. Alex, you're going to make yourself available to Agent Cormorant and provide him with any case-related materials he needs. When that's finished, you're going to report back to me that you're ready for a new assignment. I've got a quad homicide in Cleveland Park with your name written all over it. Big case, serious crime.'

I heard the words, but my mind was elsewhere. If I had to guess, I'd say that Ramon was embarrassed at having the Secret Service foisted on him, probably by the chief himself. He'd never spoken to me like this before, but I decided to bite my tongue until I had a chance to see what Cormorant was all about.

The meeting ended pretty soon after that, and I walked out with Cormorant, back toward my office.

'How long have you been with the presidential detail?' I asked him. 'That's some rarified air.'

'I've been with the Service for eight years,' he said, not quite answering my question. 'Philadelphia PD before that, and for what it's worth, I know how much you don't want me here.'

Rather than getting into it, I asked, 'So where are you guys on Tony Nicholson at this point? Where is he now? If I can ask that kind of question.'

He smiled. 'How much do you already know?'

'That he was in Alexandria until eleven o'clock Friday morning, and now he's nowhere to be found. At least not by Metro.'

'Then we've got the same information,' Cormorant said. 'That's part of why I'm here. This is a *big* mystery, Detective Cross. And a dangerous one.'

He struck me as a little looser than a lot of the guys I knew at the Service, although that's all relative. And the question remained — was he here to legitimately pursue this case or to bury it?

In my office, I took out the latest disk from Nicholson and handed it to him. 'Most of the physical evidence is with the Bureau, but this is new.'

He turned it over in his hands. 'What is it?'

'Is the name Zeus already familiar to you? I'm guessing it is.'

He looked at me but wouldn't answer.

'Cormorant, do you want my help or not? I would actually like to help.'

'Yes, I've heard the name Zeus,' he said.

'Supposedly, this is him. On the disk.'

'Supposedly?'

'It's a homicide. White male assailant with a distinctive ring on his right hand. I'm not going to make any assumptions, and you shouldn't either.'

It's comments like that last one I should really work a little harder at keeping to myself. I saw Cormorant stiffen right up.

'What else do you have?' he asked. 'I need to

267

hear everything, Detective.'

'I need a little time to pull my notes together. But I can get you whatever I have by tomorrow,' I told him.

'What about copies?' He held up the disk I'd given him. 'How many of these are floating around?'

'That's the only one I know of,' I said. 'It came out of Nicholson's safe-deposit box. He was using it to bargain. Of course, if we could find him — '

'Okay, then.' He shook my hand again. 'We'll talk soon.'

After he was gone, I ran over the conversation in my head and wrote down everything I could remember. How many lies had Cormorant told me already? And by the same token, other than the one I'd just told him about copies of Nicholson's disk, how many more would I have to tell before this was over?

90

Here's how crazy/paranoid things were getting. I had stopped using my own phone, and stuck to prepaid ones, changing the number every forty-eight hours or so.

After my meeting with Cormorant, I ran out to get a new one and used it to call Sam Pinkerton at the *Washington Post*.

Sam and I originally met at the gym where we both work out. He's more into Shotokan, whereas I'm straight boxing, but we'd spar anyway, and have a drink once in a while too. So it wasn't completely out of left field for me to call and ask if he felt like grabbing a quick one at Union Pub after work.

I spent the rest of the afternoon chasing Tony Nicholson's shadow and pretty much getting nowhere that I hadn't been before.

Then, just after five, I walked up Louisiana and along Columbus Circle to meet with Sam.

Over a beer, we shot the breeze and played catch-up, about how our kids were doing, what we thought of the DC school budget fiasco, even the weather. It felt good to sit and have a seminormal conversation for a little while. My days had been too crowded for regular life lately.

On the second round, things heated up and got a whole lot more pointed.

'So what do you have brewing at work these days?' I asked.

He leaned back in the booth and tilted his head at me. 'Did this meeting just start?'

'Yeah. I've got a case going, and I'm trying to take the temperature on a few things out there.'

'As in, *over there?*' He pointed in the general direction of the White House, which was his beat, and only a few blocks from the bar. 'Are we talking about legislation or something else? I think I already know the answer.'

'Something else,' I said.

'I assume you don't mean the president's sixtieth-birthday thing?'

'Sam.'

''Cause I can get you in if you want. The grub's going to be pretty good. You like Norah Jones? She'll be performing. And Mary J. Blige.'

He knew he was doing me a favor, and he wasn't going to let it go by without busting on me a little.

'Okay, here's something,' he said. 'You know the blog Jenna Knows? I get a call the other day from Jenna herself. Now, you've got to consider the source on something like this, but suffice to say she had some pretty wild shit. I can't go into any detail right now. You might want to buy me another drink in about two days.' He drained his glass. 'Unless you want to tell me what the hell you're working on.'

'No comment. Not just yet,' I told him. And I also thought, *Mission accomplished.* Whatever else happened, this thing was at least set in motion, with or without me.

'There is one other thing, though,' I said. 'It's a little unconventional.'

270

'My favorite convention,' he said, and spun his finger in the air at the waitress for another round.

'Off the record. If anything happens to me in the next few days or weeks, I want you to look into it.'

Sam went still and stared at me. 'Jesus Christ, Alex.'

'I know it's a strange thing to say. More than a little, I guess.'

'Don't you have — I don't know — an entire police department looking after you?'

'It depends on how you mean that,' I said, as the next round came to the table. 'Let's just say I'm calling for backup.'

91

Two weeks ago, hell, *last* week, Tony Nicholson had been popping five-hundred-dollar bottles of champagne when he was thirsty. Now here he was, huddled in the rain at a filthy I-95 truck stop like some third world alien on the run.

Mara waited inside, watching through the plate glass window of the Landmark Diner. When he looked back, she tapped her wrist and shrugged, like maybe he'd forgotten they had somewhere else to be.

He knew, he knew.

The alternative to this had been no alternative at all — rotting in a cell at the Alexandria Detention Center. At least now there was the promise of passports, plane tickets, and enough cash to get them off this plasticized continent for good.

But his contact was late, and Nicholson felt a little more paranoid with every passing minute. On top of it all, his bad knee was only getting worse in the rain and cold, and it throbbed like a sonofabitch from standing too long.

Finally, another five minutes later, there was movement in his line of vision.

A panel truck of some kind flashed its lights from across the front parking lot. Nicholson looked over, and the driver motioned him to come that way.

He motioned again — more urgently.

Nicholson's heart jumped into his throat. *Something was off.* It was supposed to have been a car, not a truck, and the meeting point was supposed to be right here, where people could see. Where nothing funny could happen.

Too late. When he looked back at the diner again, Mara was gone. A little boy stood where she'd been, hands cupped around his face behind the glass, looking out at him like this was a remake of *Village of the Damned.*

Pulse racing, Nicholson motioned to the driver that he'd be right back, and gimped toward the door at what he hoped was a natural enough pace.

Inside, the restaurant and newsstand were mostly empty, with Mara nowhere in sight.

A quick check of the deserted ladies' room told him what he already knew: This had just officially become an individual sport. He continued out the back door by the loos and kept moving.

The rear lot was quiet and looked empty. He'd parked the rental maybe fifty yards away, which right now seemed like fifty too many. When he checked over his shoulder, someone was coming out the same door he'd just used — maybe the truck driver, maybe not; it was hard to tell in the blowing mist and rain.

He broke into an excruciating, lopsided run, but now he could hear faster steps than his own slapping the wet pavement behind him.

Out of the corner of his eye, he saw the panel truck again, skirting the lot. *Pete's Meats*, it said on the side, and even now some part of his brain registered the irony.

Mother of God, I'm dead. So's Mara. Maybe she is already.

He got as far as one hand on the rental-car door. A calloused palm slapped over his mouth, absorbing any scream he had to offer. The man's arms were massive, and Nicholson felt himself twisted around as though he were a small child.

For a split second, he felt sure his neck was about to be broken. Instead, something stabbed up under his chin, creating a stomach-churning flash of pain and disorientation.

His vision fluttered. Parking lot, sky, and car all swam together in a blur, until the curtain came down for Tony Nicholson and everything went far, far away.

92

Nicholson woke up in the dark, on cold ground, but at least he was alive. He was completely naked, he realized, and his wrists and ankles were bound.

A horrible ache blazed up in his neck when he tried to look around. But he was still in the game, which was all that really counted now, wasn't it?

There was a building of some kind behind him, dimly lit from the inside. Everything else was just shadows and trees. A stack of firewood, maybe. Machinery of some kind near the building. What? A snowblower? Lawn mower?

'He's waking up,' a voice said, not far away from him.

Nicholson heard footfalls and the sound of sloshing water. As the steps came closer, a flashlight beam lit the ground in front of him. He saw a pair of feet in dark cordovans.

'Welcome back, Tony. Thought we lost you back there. Here you go!'

When the splash of water hit, it jolted him like an electric shock. His whole body seized with the cold, and his breath came in crazy accordion gasps he couldn't control.

'Get him up,' someone else said.

They hoisted him under the arms until his bare ass landed on a wooden chair. The flashlight caught just glints of things — a face, a stump, a

275

flash of silver in someone's hand. Gun? Phone?

'Where's Mara?' he slurred, as she suddenly came to mind.

'Don't worry about her right now. Least of your problems. Trust me on that.'

'We had an arrangement!' He sounded pathetic and he knew it. 'Promises were made to me. I did exactly as I was told!'

Something sharp pricked at the crown of his head. 'Who else knows about Zeus?' one of the men asked. His tone was bland, conversational.

'No one! I swear! Nobody knows. I did my part. So did Mara!'

A stinging line, almost like fire, ran straight down behind his ear to the back of his neck. There was a slight breeze, an air current, but it lit up the pain like acid.

'Not Adam Petoskey? Not Esther Walcott?'

'No! I mean . . . they might have figured a little out. Adam wasn't as careful at the end as he was at the beginning. But I swear to God — '

Two more cuts slashed across the front of his chest and down his abdomen. Nicholson screamed both times.

He drew in his stomach muscles as if he could somehow escape the blade even as it continued down slowly, separating skin from skin, until it stopped just at the base of his cock.

'Who else, Nicholson? Now would be a good time for you to get chatty.'

'Nobody! Jesus, God, don't do this!'

He was crying now, moaning out of control. It was all so incredibly unfair. He'd spent his adult life trading in one kind of a lie or another, and now here he was, caught in the truth.

'I don't know what it is you want,' he blubbered at them. 'I don't know anything anymore . . . '

Somewhere behind him, a third voice came out of the dark. It was different than the other two, with the kind of *Dukes of Hazzard* redneck twang Nicholson had looked down on ever since he came to America.

'Hey, fellas, let's move this along, all righty? I got some work of my own to attend to.'

And that's when Nicholson gave up the last piece, his *lifeline* — at least he hoped so.

'I gave a disk to the cops. Zeus was on it. Detective Alex Cross has the disk!'

93

It takes what it takes. That had always been a favorite expression of Nana's — one part stubbornness, one part optimism — and it kept running through my head these days. I wasn't giving up on this case, any more than I was giving up on her.

The entire intensive-care unit at St. Anthony's, Five West, was more than a little familiar by now. I knew all the nurses and some of the patients' family members. In fact, I was in the hall that night, chatting with a new acquaintance about her father's brain injury, when the alarm went off in Nana's room.

Alarms weren't always a reason to panic on Five West. They rang all the time, for slipped finger clips and some electronic glitch or another. The rule of thumb was that the higher and more obnoxious the sound got, the more you needed to be concerned.

This one started low, but by the time I got inside Nana's room, it was up to a hard wail. One of the nurses, Zadie Mitchell, was already in there.

'What is it?' I asked Zadie. 'Anything?'

She was adjusting Nana's O$_2$ clip and watching a wave pattern on the monitor, so she didn't answer right away.

Another nurse, Jayne Spahn, came in behind me. 'Bad pleth?' she asked.

'No,' Zadie said. 'It's accurate. Page Donald Hesch.' She hit the hundred-percent-oxygen button on the ventilator and started suctioning Nana right away.

My heart was pounding now. 'Zadie, what's happening?'

'She's desaturating, Alex. Don't worry yet.'

I wasn't so sure. Even with the ventilator, all the excess fluid in Nana's system made it a constant struggle for her heart to circulate enough oxygen. For all I knew, she was drowning in front of my eyes.

Dr. Hesch came in a couple minutes later, with Jayne and one of the staff respiratory therapists. They squeezed between the machines to work on Nana. All I could do was stand by, listen in, and try to keep up.

'She was bolused this morning for MAPs in the forties. I've been suctioning blood-tinged sputum since we paged you.'

'Did she get a gas today?'

'No. She's a hard stick; her last gas was two days ago.'

'Okay, go up to ten and try to get a reading in an hour. Let's see what dialysis does in the morning. I'll check her X-ray in the meantime.'

Hesch rushed back out without another word, and Jayne took me by the elbow into the hall.

'She's having a rough night, Alex, but she's going to get through this okay.'

I watched Nana through the door, where Zadie and the RT were still working on her. It was such a helpless feeling, not being able to give her what she needed, even something as basic as oxygen. Especially something like that.

'Alex, did you hear me?' Jayne was still talking, I realized. 'There won't be any more to know until tomorrow morning. Someone can call and check in around seven — '

'No,' I said. 'I'm going to stay tonight.'

She put a hand on my shoulder. 'That's really not necessary,' she said.

'I understand.'

But it wasn't about necessary anymore. It was about what I could and couldn't control here. For the past ten minutes, I hadn't just been thinking about losing Nana. I'd been wondering, *What if I wasn't here?* What if she died and no one was with her when it happened?

I'd never forgive myself, I thought. So if it meant going back onto the night shift for a while, then that's what I was going to do.

Whatever it took — I was going to be there for Nana.

94

Senator Marshall Yarrow was pulling a bag of golf clubs out of the back of his Navigator when he saw me and Sampson coming across the parking lot of the Washington Golf and Country Club. He looked like I'd just ruined his perfectly good Saturday morning. Imagine that. What a damn shame.

'What in hell's name are you doing here?' he asked as we came up to his vehicle.

'Three appointments, three cancellations,' I told him. 'Call me crazy, Senator, but I'd say you're avoiding me. You *were*, anyway.'

'And who's this?' He looked John over — more up than down, given Sampson's height.

'This is my partner, Detective Sampson. You can just pretend he's not here. He fits right in, doesn't he? We both do. Maybe as caddies.'

Yarrow snorted at me and waved to someone waiting under the porte cochere in front of the club. 'Mike, I'll see you inside. Order me an espresso, would you?'

I realized after the fact that the other man had been Michael Hart, a senator from North Carolina, and a Democrat to Yarrow's Republican.

'Would you rather talk in my car?' I asked him. 'Or maybe in yours?'

'Do I look like I want to get in a car with you, Detective Cross?' I was surprised he remembered my name.

He stepped back out of sight then, between his own SUV and the other giant boat parked next to it, a brand-new Hummer H3T. With the likely hundred-thousand-dollar joining fee at this place, I guess no one was too worried about gas prices.

'I won't keep you long, Senator,' I said, 'but I thought you'd want to know, we're a little short on leads here. The only next step I can see is to start releasing the recordings from Tony Nicholson's club.'

Yarrow's eyes flitted over to Sampson; I think he was wondering if both of us had seen him in action, or just me. His hands tightened over the head cover of the TaylorMade driver in his bag.

'So unless you've got some other meaningful direction we might go in — '

'Why would I?' he said, still cool.

'Just a gut feeling I had. Something about all those missed appointments.'

He took a deep breath and ran a hand over the weekend stubble around his chin. 'Well, obviously I've got to run all this by my attorney.'

'That's probably a good idea,' I said. 'But just so you know, this is a working Saturday for us. We need to get one thing or another done today.'

I almost felt bad for Yarrow, he looked so uncomfortable. There were no good options left, and he knew it. When I'm lucky, that brings people right to the truth.

'Just for the sake of argument,' he said, 'what could you offer me by way of immunity?'

'Nothing right now. That's up to the DA.'

'Right, 'cause you people never wheel and deal, is that it?'

'Here's what I can offer you,' I said. 'You tell us what you know, and then when the Secret Service comes looking for you, and they will, it won't be about obstruction of justice and conspiracy to cover up a string of murders.'

I could only imagine how much Yarrow was hating me right now. Without ever taking his eyes off mine, he said, 'Tell me something, Detective Sampson. Would you say your partner here is a vindictive man?'

Sampson laid a big hand on the roof of Yarrow's car. 'Vindictive? Nah, that's not Alex. I'd say more like *realistic*. Might be a good word for you to consider about now.'

At first, I thought Senator Yarrow was going to walk, or maybe even go postal with one of those TaylorMade irons of his. Instead, he reached into his pocket, and the doors on the Lincoln chirped open.

'Just get in the car.'

95

Yarrow's car's leather interior reeked of coffee and cigarettes. I would have pegged him more as a cigar smoker.

'Let me get a few things out of the way,' I said first. 'You were a paying client of that club, yes or no?'

'Next question.'

'You were aware that escorts connected to the club had died.'

'No. That's not true,' he said. 'I'd just started to suspect something was wrong before all this fuss happened.'

'And what did you plan to do with that information? Your suspicions.'

Yarrow turned suddenly and pointed a finger in my face. 'Don't interrogate me, Cross. I'm a goddamn US senator, not some worthless thug in Southeast DC.'

'Exactly my point, Mr. Yarrow. You're a US senator and you're supposed to have a conscience. Now, do you have something for us or not?'

He took a beat, long enough to pull a pack of Marlboro Reds out of the console. I noticed that the flame on his gold Senate lighter shook when he used it.

After a couple long consecutive drags, Yarrow started to talk again, facing the windshield.

'There's a man you should check out. His name's . . . Remy Williams. If I had to guess, I'd say he's in this thing deep.'

'Who is he?' I asked.

'That's a good question, actually. I believe that he used to be in the Secret Service.'

Those last two words went off in my mind like a Roman candle. 'Secret Service? What division?' I asked him.

'Protective Services.'

'At the White House?'

Yarrow smoked almost continuously while the knuckles on his free hand went white gripping the wheel. 'Yeah,' he said with an exhale. 'At the White House.'

Sampson was staring over the headrest at me, and I'm sure we were wondering the same thing. Was this the White House connection we'd already heard about? Or the kind of coincidence that gums up investigations all the time?

Senator Yarrow went on without any more prodding from me. 'Last I heard, Remy was living in some godawful shack, way out in Louisa County, like one of those survivalists with the bottled water and the shotguns and all. *Into the Wild* kind of lifestyle.'

'What's your association with him?' Sampson asked.

'He was the one who told me about the club in the first place.'

'That doesn't really answer the question,' I said. 'Look, Senator, I'm not recording any of this. Not yet anyway.'

Yarrow opened the window and twisted the last of his cigarette onto the pavement, then put the butt in his ashtray. I could sense him starting to circle the wagons again.

'He's my ex-wife's brother, okay? I haven't seen the bastard in over a year, and it doesn't matter. The whole point is, you take a drive out there, you might just have something more to do with your Saturday than harassing public servants.'

96

It was just over two hours' drive to the western edge of Louisa County, which was also about an hour south of Nicholson's club. Those two locations triangulated easily with the spot on I-95 where Johnny Tucci from Philly had been pulled over carrying my niece's remains in the trunk. Maybe we were actually getting somewhere with all this.

Yarrow's vague sense of the cabin sent us down a handful of wrong turns before we eventually found the right gravel road off Route 33. Several miles back through the woods, it came to a makeshift dead end, with a row of rocks blocking the way. They'd obviously been moved there by hand, and it didn't take us long to clear them.

Beyond that were two dirt tracks retreating into the brush, and another half hour of slow going before we saw anything man-made. Remy Williams's nearest neighbor seemed to be Lake Anna State Park to the east.

The driveway, such as it was, came up on the back of a rudimentary single-story building surrounded closely by fir trees. It looked unfinished from here, with a galvanized standing-seam roof but just warped and silvered plywood over Tyvek on the walls.

'Very nice,' Sampson muttered, or maybe growled. 'Unabomber east, anyone?'

It was bigger than Ted Kaczynski's famous shack,

287

which I'd been to once before, but the general feeling was about the same: madman in residence.

Around front, the two small windows under a covered porch looked dark. There was a dirt yard big enough for several cars, but no sign of any vehicle. The place seemed completely deserted, and part of me hoped it was.

It wasn't until I'd driven around nearly full circle that I saw the wood chipper at the side of the house.

'Sampson?'

'I see it.'

It was an old industrial unit, with two tires and a rusted trailer hitch balanced on a cinder block. Most of the paint was long gone, just a few impressionistic flecks of John Deere green and yellow on the frame. Next to it, a blue tarp was folded on the ground, weighted down with a two-gallon gas can.

I kept the car running as we got out, and I pulled my Glock.

'Anyone home?' I called halfheartedly.

There was no answer. All I heard was the wind, a few birds chattering in the trees, and my idling car.

Sampson and I took the porch from opposite sides to check the windows first, then the door.

When I looked in, it took a few seconds for my eyes to adjust. Then I saw a man, sitting in a chair against the far wall. It was too dark for details; I couldn't even tell if he was alive or dead. Not for certain. Not yet.

'Fuck,' Sampson muttered,

Exactly right. My thoughts exactly.

97

The shack's front door had no lock, just a hammered-iron latch, and as soon as I swung it open, the smell hit us.

It was that combination of sweet and putrid that's so distinct and so hard to take. Like fruit and meat rotting for days in the same barrel.

The place was mostly empty, with just a few pieces of furniture — a metal cot, a woodstove, a long farm table.

The only chair in the place was occupied, and Remy Williams had apparently died in it.

He looked graphic-novel-style slack jawed where part of his face had been blown off. A Remington shotgun was still half-clutched in his left hand, barrel pointed down at the soft pine floor.

The other hand hung loose at his side, and it looked like there was some kind of writing on his forearm. *Writing? Was that it?*

'What the hell?' Sampson covered his mouth and nose with his arm and bent down for a closer look. 'Oh no, he didn't.'

When I put my Maglite on it, I saw that the arm had been *carved*, not written on.

A six-inch hunting knife was on the ground at Williams's feet, streaked the same reddish brown as his skin. The letters were still easy enough to read:

SORRY

98

A lot happened really fast after we found Williams. Within a few hours, we had new versions of all the old players on the scene — Virginia State Police out of Richmond and the FBI team from Charlottesville. There was no one I knew here, which was maybe a good thing and maybe not. I'd find out which pretty soon.

The Bureau's Evidence Response Team included serious-looking folks from serology, trace analysis, firearms, photography, and finger-printing. They set up a tent and spread long sheets of butcher paper over plywood-and-sawhorse tables.

The ground around the wood chipper was sectioned into eight-inch squares, and they started right in, meticulously sifting one square at a time, separating potential evidence from dirt and debris.

The chipper itself would be disassembled in a lab in Richmond, but blood-enhancement agents had already shown trace amounts of serum. A visual inspection also turned up some likely bone fragments in the mechanism's blades.

Everything was duly photographed, documented, and either set out to dry or put into manila envelopes for transport.

The faster job turned out to be a search of the woods. A lieutenant colonel with the state police called in two K-9 units, and within the first hours, they'd sniffed out a freshly turned patch of earth half a mile east of the cabin.

Some careful digging brought up two plastic bags of 'remains' from about five feet down. Everyone on the site was carrying around a hangdog face. No one is ever ready for this kind of murder scene.

The new remains looked exactly like Caroline's had, and the consensus was that they hadn't been in the ground for more than three days. Right away, I thought of Tony Nicholson and Mara Kelly, who were still officially MIA.

'It adds up, on paper anyway,' I said to Sampson. 'Get them out of jail, and you can make them disappear once and for all. We were supposed to think they fled the country.'

'Hell of a way to cover your tracks,' Sampson said. 'But I have to admit, effective.'

We were sitting on the edge of the porch around one a.m., watching an agent tag what was left of the newly deceased as evidence, before they went into body bags. John couldn't take his eyes off it, but I'd seen enough. It depressed me to know that my own niece's case was becoming the single grisliest piece of work I'd ever investigated.

But that fact kept me moving too. For the fourth time in as many hours, I dialed Dan Cormorant's phone number.

This time the Secret Service agent actually picked up.

'Where the hell are you guys?' I asked him. 'Are you even tracking this?'

'You're obviously not watching TV right now,'

he said. 'It looks like they've got everyone but ESPN out there in those woods.'

'Cormorant, listen to me. Remy Williams wasn't Zeus, any more than Tony Nicholson or Johnny Tucci was. Williams may be a stone-cold killer, but he's not the one we're looking for.'

'I agree with you,' Cormorant said, 'and you know why? 'Cause we've got Zeus pinned down. *Right now.* You want to be part of the sideshow, you stay where you are. But if you want to be here when we finish this thing once and for all, I'd suggest you get your ass back to the city. Pronto, Detective Cross. This case is about to close. You should be there.'

99

Sad to say, I was operating on nothing but adrenaline and caffeine by the time we got to the Eisenhower Executive Office Building across from the West Wing. It was nearly four a.m. at this point, but the Joint Operations Center was buzzing like midday.

The mood in the briefing room was tense to say the least. They had CNN on one of a dozen flat screens arrayed on the wall, with an overhead shot of Remy Williams's cabin and the subhead *Secret Service Agent Found Dead.*

At the front of the room, a fiftyish agent in shirtsleeves was shouting on the phone, loudly enough to be heard over everyone else.

'I don't give a shit who you need to speak to; he's not a member of the Secret Service. Now change the damn graphic!'

I had already spotted several people I knew, including Emma Cornish, who was MPD's liaison to the Service's High Intensity Violent Crimes Task Force; and Barry Farmer, one of two Secret Service agents assigned to Metro's Homicide Unit. It was as if the two departments had suddenly been knitted together, right there in the middle of the night.

For show, maybe?

I wasn't ready to say yet.

We all gathered around a long oval table for the first briefing. The man with the big voice in front turned out to be Silo Ridge, deputy special agent in charge. He was the whip on this one, and he stood up with Agent Cormorant.

'I'm sending around a fact sheet,' Ridge said, handing half a stack in each direction. 'The subject's name is Constantine Bowie, aka Connie Bowie, aka Zeus. Most of you know this already, but Bowie was an agent with the Service from 1988 to 2002.'

Nobody flinched but me — and maybe Sampson. It was like a whole new map of this thing had just been unfolded in front of us.

I put up my hand. 'Alex Cross, MPD. I'm just catching up here, but what's the known relationship, if any, with Remy Williams? Other than the fact that they're both supposed to be former agents.'

'Detective Cross, glad to have you here,' Ridge said, and a few more heads turned my way. 'The focus of this operation is former agent Bowie. Everything else is on a need-to-know basis for the time being.'

'I'm only asking because — '

'We appreciate MPD's participation, as always. This is all obviously a little sensitive, but we're not going to start unpacking it here. Moving on.'

I gave Ridge the benefit of the doubt, for the moment at least. It wasn't a bridge I had to cross yet. Or burn.

An image of Bowie's 2002 credentials came up on one of the screens. He looked like a million other agents to me — waspy, square jaw, brown hair combed back. Everything but the dark shades.

'Bowie's been implicated in the murder of at least three women,' Ridge went on, 'all of them known employees of the so-called gentlemen's club in Culpeper County. Those women are Caroline Cross, Katherine Tennancour, Renata Cruz . . . ' Surveillance photos that I'd seen before went by in a slide show. 'And this is Sally Anne Perry.'

A video started up, and right away I recognized the recording I'd handed over to Cormorant just the other day. Like Ridge had said, *the Secret Service appreciated MPD's participation.*

'There's nothing pleasant about having to watch this,' Ridge said, 'but you should know who we're going after. The man about to come into the bedroom is Constantine Bowie. And he is about to commit murder.'

100

Everyone held their professional cool as the video played out, and Agent Ridge kept talking as it did.

'A little history here. Bowie was recruited from Philadelphia PD into the Service in 1988. For thirteen years, there's not much to tell, but shortly after 9/11, his performance started to slip.

'Then in February of 2002, after an improper firearm discharge, which I'm not going to detail this morning, Bowie was removed from the Service without benefits.'

Cormorant took it from there and brought up a slide of a generic-looking office building.

'In 2005, he opened Galveston Security here in DC — '

'Galveston?' someone asked.

'His hometown,' Cormorant said. 'Today, he's got satellite offices in Philadelphia and Dallas, with a personal net worth of seven million, give or take. The Philly ties don't prove anything, but it's worth noting that at least some contract work with the Martino crime family out of Philadelphia has been part of this whole picture as well.'

Cormorant's eyes traveled over to me before he went on. 'One other thing we can tell you is that phone records show two calls from Bowie's cell phone to the one found in Remy Williams's cabin today. One of those calls was made two months ago, and the other was four days ago.'

'Where's Bowie now?' one of the agents asked.

'Surveillance puts him at home, as of twenty-three hundred hours last night. We have half a dozen agents watching his house.'

'How soon can we move on this?' someone else asked. You could feel the impatience in the room. No one wanted to tackle the operation, I think, so much as they wanted to get it over with.

Agent Ridge looked at his watch. 'We go as soon as you're ready,' he said, and everyone started to stand up.

101

It was eerily quiet when we pulled up to a row of flat-topped brick town houses on Winfield Lane in Northwest. One pair of tennis players was at it on the Georgetown courts across the road, and the playing fields were still wet. If Nana were home, I thought, she'd just be getting up and ready for church.

We had four SWAT officers posted in back, with MPD cruisers at either end of the block and EMS on standby. The rest of us emerged onto the street several doors away from Bowie's place, where a single white van was just coming to a stop.

Once Ridge gave the go, an entry team of five men in ballistic gear exited the van and snaked up the front steps of Bowie's town house in a line. It was a silent operation; they pried the door and then disappeared inside.

After that, it was ten long minutes of waiting while they leapfrogged through the house, clearing one space after another. Ridge kept his head down and a hand over his earpiece as the SWAT commander whispered their progress to him. He held up two fingers to indicate they'd reached the second floor, and a few minutes later, three fingers.

Then he straightened up suddenly. I could hear shouting coming from the house.

'They've got him!' Ridge said — but then, 'Wait.'

There was some fast back-and-forth now, with Ridge blurting communications. 'Yes? I hear you. Do not stand down.' Eventually he said, 'Okay, give me one second,' and turned to address the rest of us.

'We've got a standoff situation inside,' he said. 'Bowie's armed and belligerent. Says he won't talk to Secret Service.'

I didn't have to think about this. 'Let me talk to him,' I said.

Ridge held up a finger and went back to the mic in his cuff. 'Peters, I'm going to send in a throw phone — '

'No,' I said. 'Face-to-face. All he's looking at in there is five armed officers. We're not window dressing, Ridge. You brought us here for a reason, and now we know what it is.'

There was another long stretch of back-and-forth after that, relayed between Ridge, SWAT, and Constantine Bowie inside. Eventually, an agreement was reached. Bowie would let them check the rest of the house to make sure no one else was there, and then I'd go in. All of a sudden, someone was handing me a vest and Ridge was giving me the rundown.

'Keep SWAT between you and Bowie at all times. If you can get him to stand down, do it, and if not, leave. Don't drag it out.' He checked his watch again. 'Fifteen minutes. That's it. Then I'm going to pull you out myself.'

102

The profiler in me was working overtime as I entered the alcove of Bowie's town house by myself. The place was airy and well appointed inside. A large amount of cash had gone into Early American antiques and art. It was also extremely neat; not a loose magazine, newspaper, or stray knickknack in sight. I saw a lot of control at work in this house. *Was this where Zeus lived? Had he murdered here as well?*

The master bedroom was at the top of the stairs on the third floor.

Two SWAT officers in the hall nodded at me as I came up, but they didn't say anything. I could also see two of the three who were inside the bedroom, covering Bowie from different angles with their MP5s. I called out to Bowie.

'Bowie, my name's Alex Cross. I'm with MPD and I'm coming in, okay?'

There was a pause, and then a strained voice. 'Come in. Let me see a shield.'

He was sitting flat on the floor, wearing just boxers, sweating profusely. The king-size bed had obviously been slept in, and the nightstand drawer was hanging open.

He'd cornered himself under a window, between the bed and one of the two closets. His arms were locked out in front of him, with a .357 SIG Sauer pointed at the nearest officer.

The other thing I noticed was the signet ring

on his right hand — gold with a red stone, just like the one in the video we'd all seen by now. *Man, he was making this too easy. Why? Was he Zeus?*

I kept my own hands in front of me with my badge showing, and only came as far as the doorway. Everyone else stayed still as statues.

'Nice house,' I said right off. 'How long have you lived here?'

'*What?*' Bowie's eyes took me in for half a second, then went back to his target.

'I was wondering how long you've lived here. That's all. Breaking the ice.'

He scoffed. 'Checking my mental acuity?'

'That's right.'

'I've been here two years. The president of the United States is Margaret Vance. Seven times eight is fifty-six, okay?'

'So I guess you understand the gravity of what you're doing,' I told him.

'That's where you're wrong,' he said. 'I have no fucking clue what's going on here.'

'Well then, I'll tell you. I'll try to anyway. Technically, you're under arrest for the murder of Sally Anne Perry.'

His eyes flashed anger without actually moving. 'Fuck that! They've been gunning for me ever since I got pushed out.'

'Who has?'

'The Service. The Feds. Goddamn President Vance for all I know.'

I stopped and took a breath, hoping he'd do the same. 'You're giving me mixed signals here, Bowie,' I said. 'One second you seem lucid and the next — '

'Yeah, well, just 'cause I'm paranoid doesn't mean they're not out to get me, right?'

Oddly enough, I couldn't argue with that, so I moved on.

'Why don't you tell me what you need to hear before you lower that weapon?'

He chinned at the officer closest to him. 'They put theirs down first.'

'Come on, Constantine. That's not going to happen, and you know it isn't. Work with me here. If you really are innocent, then I'm on your side. Where did you get that ring?'

'Stop with the questions. Just stop.'

'Okay.'

His arms were all muscle, but after at least twenty minutes outstretched, they were starting to shake. And in fact, he moved to adjust himself, up onto one knee with the shooting arm resting on top.

'Bowie, I — '

A tinkle of glass sounded. That was all it was. One of the small windowpanes behind him split into shards, and Bowie fell facedown onto the carpet, a small dark hole in the back of his head.

I couldn't believe it. Didn't want to believe it. Immediately SWAT flew into action. Someone pulled me backward into the hall while the rest closed in around Bowie.

'One round fired — subject is down! We need medical up here right away!'

A few seconds later, I'd pushed my way back into the room. My body was shaking with rage. Why had they fired on him? Why now? I had him talking. Bowie was splayed on the ground, arms

302

out at his sides. Through the broken window, I could see another officer on the opposite roof, standing down with his rifle.

'Scratch that, medical,' the commander was saying. 'We'll meet you downstairs and bring you up.'

And then two of them were walking me out the door and down the stairs, in no uncertain terms. My usefulness had obviously played itself out here.

When we got to the front stoop, the EMTs were waiting. It was protocol to call them in, but at this point, that's all it was. I'd already seen enough to know that Constantine Bowie was as dead as he was going to get.

And that I'd just been bait in the whole damn thing. They had meant to kill him all along.

Whoever *they* were.

103

It all seemed too neat, too easy, but that didn't mean Constantine Bowie wasn't the killer, did it? The next few days were all about paperwork, lots and lots of it. I don't think most people have any idea how much ink it takes to put a murder case in the drawer, especially one of this magnitude.

Not even when the FBI and the Secret Service are both arguing that justice has been done.

There were endless meetings to come, and after that, public hearings. A full congressional investigation had already been promised, amid all kinds of unchecked speculation on the Hill and in the media. The country was buzzing: about Tony Nicholson's client list, about the involvement of Secret Service, and even about who else might still be out there as part of Bowie's murder spree.

Once the paperwork was behind me, I put in for the rest of the week off. I left the office late on Wednesday and went straight to the hospital. Nana was looking a lot more peaceful these days, like an angel, which was kind of nice and also hard to take. I stayed awake most of that night, just watching her.

Then Aunt Tia spelled me early on Thursday, and I managed to catch Bree still in bed when I finally, finally got home. She was just starting to stir as I spooned up next to her.

'Do whatever you want,' she whispered softly.

'Just don't wake me up.'

But then she laughed and turned over to kiss me good morning. Her feet and legs stayed tangled up with mine under the covers.

'All right, then, just do whatever you want to me,' she said.

'This is nice. Remember this?' I said.

She nodded with her forehead against mine, and I was thinking maybe I never had to be anywhere else but here. Ever again.

Then the bedroom door opened. *Of course it did.* 'Daddy, you home?' Ali poked his head around the corner and jumped up onto the bed before we could tell him to go away.

'Little man, how many times have I told you to knock first?' I asked him.

'About a million,' he said, and he laughed and wormed in between us anyway.

Not to be outdone, Jannie was there soon enough, and the two of them started chattering at us like maybe it wasn't six thirty in the morning. Even so, it was kind of nice to be all together again.

By seven, I was frying up a batch of bacon, egg, and tomato sandwiches while Bree made coffee and poured the orange juice. Jannie and Ali were scanning the morning paper for my name, and I even had a little Gershwin playing in the living room. Not the bedroom with Bree, but not too shabby either.

Just as I was flipping my breakfast creations out of the pan, a phone chirped from upstairs, loud enough to be heard over the music.

Everyone stopped what they were doing and

looked at me, standing there with my greasy spatula in hand.

'What?' I said, all wide-eyed and innocent. 'I don't hear anything.'

That got me a chorus of cheers all around the table, and even a little pat on the butt from Bree.

Whoever it was, they had the good sense not to call again.

104

A few hours later, Bree and I were back from walking the kids to school and running a few necessary errands to the drug- and food stores. 'Upstairs,' I told her before the front door had even closed behind us. 'We've got some unfinished business, you and I.'

She took the grocery bag out of my hands with a kiss. 'I'll be right there. Don't start without me.'

I was halfway up the stairs, when she called me back from the kitchen.

'Alex!' Her voice was tense. What was it now? '*Company.*'

When I came down, she was standing at the pass-through to the sunporch, looking out.

'Guess who's here?' she said.

I stepped up next to her and saw Ned Mahoney sitting in our backyard, drumming his fingers on the picnic table.

'God *damn* it,' I said.

He stayed where he was as I came out onto the porch and then down into the yard to see what was happening.

'Was that you who called earlier?' I asked. Ned nodded, and before he even said a word, I realized the case wasn't over. 'You want to come in?'

'Let's talk out here,' he said.

I grabbed a jacket and two cups of coffee from

inside, and then came back out to the picnic table.

Ned gulped the coffee as I sat down. He looked exhausted. All his usual effusiveness seemed to be gone — or at least depleted.

'You okay?' I asked him.

'Just a little tired,' he said. 'I haven't let go of this thing, Alex. I've used up all my personal days, all my vacation. Kathy's ready to kill me.'

I nodded. 'So is Bree. And she has a gun.'

'Still, it's paid off. Boy, has it ever. I've got somebody I want you to meet. His name is Aubrey Lee Johnson. He lives down in Alabama, but he's got a custom fly reel business that brings him up to Virginia a lot.'

Ned downed the last of his coffee, and I slid mine over to his side of the table. Some of the usual rev was coming back into him already. 'This guy's got a story he thinks might be important. And guess what, Alex? *It is.*'

105

There was no way Mahoney could get travel status for this. Even if it were his case, which it wasn't, the Bureau watches out for our tax dollars by requiring agents to use the local field offices for out-of-state interviews. Ned had already traded a few electronic communications with the Mobile office, but in the end, we decided to fly to Alabama on our own nickel.

We arrived at Mobile Regional Airport late the next morning and rented a car from there.

Aubrey Johnson lived on Dauphin Island, about an hour south. It was a sleepy little village, at least this time of year, and we had no trouble finding his store — Big Daddy's Fishing Tackle, on Cadillac Avenue.

'This is why we're here? Big Daddy's Fishing Tackle?' I said to Ned.

'Odd as it may seem, this is it, the end of the road. The conspiracy gets tripped up here. If we're lucky, that is.'

'So let's start getting lucky.'

Johnson was a tall, gregarious guy in his mid-fifties, and he ushered us in like a couple of old friends, just before he double-locked up behind us.

Ned had already questioned him on the phone, but Johnson repeated his story for me — how he'd been driving late one night on Route 33 in Virginia about a month ago, when a beautiful girl in a negligee stumbled out of the woods in front of his truck.

'Truth be told, I thought it was my lucky night,' he said, 'until I saw what kind of terrible shape she was in. Any bigger caliber on that slug in her back and she would have been dead.'

Even so, the girl had insisted that Johnson keep driving, at least until they were across the state line. He finally got her to an ER just outside Winston-Salem.

'Still, Annie wasn't hanging around for any cops to show up,' he went on. 'She told me she was either leaving there on foot or in my truck, so I drove her. Probably shouldn't have, but what's done is done. My wife and I have been looking after her ever since.'

'Her name is Annie?' I asked.

'I'll get to that part,' Johnson said.

'Why did she come forward when she did?' I asked them. All I knew was that the contact between Mr. Johnson and Mahoney had started before the names Constantine Bowie and Zeus had ever made it into the headlines.

'That's a little complicated,' he said. 'She still hasn't told us everything. We don't even know her real name; we just call her Annie to keep things simple. When I tried putting out some feelers, there wasn't much I could say, so I don't think people took me too seriously. At least, not until Agent Mahoney here called me back. He was following up on a call I'd made to the FBI field office in Mobile.'

'And where is she now, Aubrey?' Ned asked.

'Not far.' Johnson took a set of keys off the counter. 'I'll let her speak for herself, but I will tell you this much. That fellow they're calling Zeus on the news? She says you all got the wrong man. She isn't Annie, and he isn't Zeus.'

106

Johnson led us back through the village in his truck, almost to the mainland bridge.

Then he turned off and parked at the Dauphin Island Marina. Fewer than half of the slips were occupied, and the office and snack shack on the waterfront both looked closed and shuttered for the season.

We followed him up one of the three long docks to a sport fishing boat called the *May*. A heavyset woman, presumably Mrs. Johnson, was waiting on the deck. She looked at us a lot more skeptically than her husband had.

'This them?' she said.

'You know it is, May. Let's go.'

She didn't move. 'This girl's been through a living hell, do you understand me? You need to go easy with her.'

I had no quarrel with the attitude; actually, I was grateful for it. We assured Mrs. Johnson that we'd be good with the girl, and then followed her down to the little cabin below deck.

'Annie' was sitting in the crook of the dining banquette, looking drawn and nervous. Even so, she was an obviously beautiful girl, with the kind of china doll features that Tony Nicholson seemed to have favored for Blacksmith Farms. Her cargo pants and baggy pink sweatshirt were either borrowed or thrift shop specials, and she had a gray canvas sling on her right arm. She was huddled over, and when she moved, I could see that her back, where she'd been shot, still hurt quite a bit.

Mahoney started with introductions and asked if she was willing to give us her name.

'It's Hannah,' she said, tentatively at first. 'Hannah Willis. Is that something you can help me with? Becoming somebody else? Witness protection, or whatever it is you use these days.'

Ned explained that the US Attorney's office would decide if she even needed to testify, but if so, then yes, she was a perfect candidate for WitSec. In the meantime, he assured her, we wouldn't record anything that she had to tell us.

'Let's start with what happened to you,' I said. 'The night Aubrey picked you up in his truck.'

She nodded slowly, mustering the memory, or maybe just the will to tell it. May Johnson sat next to her, holding her hand the whole time.

'It was supposed to be some kind of private party at Blacksmith,' Hannah said. 'We didn't know anything except the client code name. Zeus. You think maybe he has a high opinion of himself? Code name is a god?'

'Was this party held in the apartment over the carriage barn?' I asked.

'That's right.' She seemed surprised that I already knew. 'I'd never been up there before. I knew the pay was better.'

'When you say 'we,'' Ned asked, 'how many of you were there with Zeus?'

'Just me and one other girl, Nicole,' she said. 'Although I doubt that was her real name.'

It also wasn't the first time I'd heard it used in

a conversation like this. I could feel my heart thumping as I reached into my pocket and took out the picture of Caroline that I'd been carrying with me from the start of this terrible, unholy mess.

'Is this her, Hannah?' I asked.

She nodded, and the tears started to come.

'Yes, sir. That's the girl who died. That's Nicole.'

107

I listened carefully, filtering my rage away from the information Hannah was giving us about Caroline's murder and her own terrible ordeal at Blacksmith Farms.

She described how Zeus had handcuffed them to the bed, then used his fists and his teeth, focusing more on Caroline than on her, for reasons she couldn't explain, even now. By the time he had raped both women, she said, 'Nicole was barely conscious, and the mattress cover on the bed was slick with blood.'

He left soon after that, and Hannah had begun to hope the worst of it might be over, until two men came in to take them away. One was tall and blond, the other Hispanic and stocky. That's when she understood what was coming next — on account of what had happened with Zeus, *on account of what she and Caroline knew about him*.

'They worked quickly, like they'd done it before. Cleaned up his mess,' Hannah said. 'I can still see the two of them. The bored look on their faces.'

Both girls were then carried down and put in the trunk of a car. Hannah told us how she held Caroline's hand there in the dark and tried to keep her talking for as long as possible. Eventually, though, Caroline stopped answering. By the time they got where they were going and the trunk opened again, she was dead.

They were in the woods, at a cabin of some kind. A third man was there, and he seemed to take over for the other two. The only light on them was his lantern, and he held it up to Hannah's face, examining her as though she were a piece of meat. Then he set it on the ground to have a closer look at Caroline, to make sure she was dead.

That's when Hannah decided she had nothing left to lose, since they would surely kill her too. She kicked the lantern over and ran for the woods.

The three men came after her, of course, and there were gunshots, including the one that lodged in her back. Somehow, she managed to keep going. It was nothing she could explain at this point, or even remember very clearly, right up until she came out on the road and saw the oncoming headlights of Aubrey Johnson's pickup truck.

Everything about the story lined up with what I already knew — the indications of bite marks on Caroline's remains, the cabin in the woods, the description of the two men with the car. There was only one question still hanging.

The question.

'Who was he, Hannah? Who was Zeus? How did you know who he was?'

'We knew because he showed us his face. He lifted his terrible mask and said it didn't matter if Caroline and I saw him.'

'Hannah,' I said next. 'Who is he? Who is Zeus?'

And even then, with everything else I knew about this case, her answer still floored me.

108

The Kennedy Center's Grand Foyer was lit up like a Macy's Christmas window for the spectacle that was the annual Honors reception. Medals had been awarded to five of the entertainment industry's best and brightest tonight, and half of LA seemed to be here, rubbing elbows with half of DC. In Washington terms, there was no other night quite like this one. No night was more star filled.

For Teddy, it was definitely a night to celebrate. Ask any of these glitterati about the week's headlines, and nine out of ten would have told the same story. Zeus was dead. A very bad man had done terrible things, and he'd paid the ultimate price for his indiscretions. It was the stuff of classics.

And like any good fairy tale, it was a lie only loosely based on truth. In fact, Zeus was right here among them, enjoying the lobster cocktail and champagne just like anyone else. *Well, not exactly like anyone else.* Teddy's was a world where even the power elite kissed his butt on a regular basis, and people paid good money just to be in the same room with him. If that wasn't a privilege worth preserving, he didn't know what was.

Still, there was the matter of 'the urges.' To screw beautiful girls. To see them in pain. To kill. Whether or not he could keep 'the urges' in check now was yet to be seen, but the timing, and the opportunity to leave it all behind, could not have been better. He was in the clear now. He'd been given a second chance.

So Teddy pushed all those hot thoughts way to the back of his mind, where they belonged for now, and resumed working the room as only he could. This was pure Teddy, Teddy at his best, Teddy in his element.

He chatted briefly with Meryl Streep and John McLaughlin at the bar. Complimented the House Speaker on his recent *Meet the Press* slam dunk interview. Congratulated Patti LuPone, one of the night's honorees, for all of her stunning achievements — whatever they might have been. And he kept moving, kept moving, kept moving, never staying too long in the same place, never wearing out a welcome, never revealing a thing about himself. That was the beauty and allure of the cocktail hour.

Eventually, he came upon Maggie in the Hall of Nations, schmoozing the new Democratic governor from Georgia and his greyhound-faced wife, whose name Teddy could never remember.

'Speak of the devil.' Maggie hooked her arm into his. 'Hello, darling. We were just talking about you. Douglas, Charlotte, and I.'

'Hello Doug, Charlotte. All good things, I hope,' he said, and the others laughed as though it were expected of them, which it was.

'Your wife was just telling us you're quite the equestrian,' the governor said.

'Ah,' Teddy answered. 'My little-known secret. I have so few these days. I don't like those to get out.'

318

'We'll have to have you down to the farm sometime. We've got some beautiful trails around our summer place.'

'That sounds absolutely terrific — the farm,' he said, telling the kind of lie that never hurt anyone. 'And the president and I will have to have you overnight at the White House one of these days.' He looked over at Maggie, smiling placidly. 'Isn't that right, sweetheart?'

109

Driving in from the airport that night, Ned Mahoney and I were part of an emergency conference call that had been pulled together while we were still in the air. Theodore 'Teddy' Vance was known to be with his wife, the president of the United States, at the Kennedy Center Honors. We had him. The question on the table was how to proceed.

Most of the resistance was from Secret Service, who ironically had the least say in this decision, except maybe for me. Their deputy director of investigations, Angela Riordan, was doing most of the talking.

'We're certainly not going to put up with any of this habeas grabbus crap, understand? This is the First Gentleman of the United States we're talking about. If the Bureau even thinks about crossing our security line, he'll be gone before anyone gets inside the building. Do I need to repeat myself?'

'We have no issue with that, Angela.' This was Luke Hamel, the Bureau's assistant director in charge on the case before it got moved to Charlottesville. We also had the FBI director himself, Ron Burns, listening in with a few of their people from legal. 'No one's talking arrest yet,' Hamel went on. 'We just want to speak with him. He's a person of interest at this point.'

'Then there's no reason it can't wait until

tomorrow.' I recognized the slight accent of Vance's personal attorney, Raj Doshi, who was driving in from Maryland as we spoke.

'Actually, there's a very good reason,' I said. 'People have already died under this cover-up. Not doing anything tonight means risking more lives, and the fact that we're having this conversation only increases that risk.'

'Excuse me — Detective Cross, was it?' Riordan asked. 'We're not going to make tactical decisions here based on your gut feelings or your paranoia.'

'With all due respect, you have no idea if I'm being paranoid or not,' I said. I didn't want to put too fine a point on it, but Ned Mahoney and I were holding more cards here than anyone else on the call.

Ultimately, I think Riordan recognized her lack of options, and she agreed to pull Vance in for questioning.

When Doshi insisted the interview take place off site, the FBI had no objection to the demand. They quickly settled on the Eisenhower Building.

'This is Cross again,' I said into the speaker. 'Can I assume Dan Cormorant is already on duty at the Kennedy Center?'

'Why do you want to know?' It was Agent Silo Ridge this time; I hadn't even realized he was on the line.

'Cormorant's been my Secret Service contact on Zeus,' I said. 'I'd be surprised if he *didn't* have information we could use.'

The full truth was that I had some questions

of my own for Cormorant, and I wanted to see him face-to-face before I said anything I might regret later.

They never answered me, but it didn't matter. I'd find out soon enough. I could see the Kennedy Center looming straight ahead.

110

There had probably never been a takedown like this one, not in the annals of police history, definitely not in my police history.

We convened on the Kennedy Center's River Terrace just outside the Grand Foyer, where the party was in full swing. I'd already seen a handful of movie stars floating by the sixty-foot-high windows, but as yet there was no sign of Teddy Vance. *No sign of Zeus?*

Luke Hamel from the Bureau had brought another senior agent with him, James Walsh, whom I didn't recognize and didn't think I'd met before. My old boss Ron Burns was keeping his distance on this one, but he'd also made sure there was a place here for me and Mahoney. I'd return the favor someday if I could.

From Secret Service, we had Riordan and Ridge in addition to the operational team already on site. That meant agents in tuxes paired up on all the doors, a heavy MPD presence down at street level, and a chopper and EMTs on standby, all standard for any presidential event.

Other than the White House, there wasn't a more secure building in Washington tonight. I could feel the tension spreading everywhere in my body.

Once we were in place, Riordan put the center on a temporary 'crash condition' — no one in or out until the First Gentleman was away. Next,

323

traffic was routed away from the building. A lot of drivers were about to be seriously inconvenienced, but that was the least of our problems right now.

The First Gentleman was in all probability a murderer.

Less than a minute passed before Dan Cormorant stepped outside in his tux. He reported straight to Angela Riordan and ignored everyone else.

'Ma'am. We're good to go inside.'

'All right. I want a nice, quiet exit on this, understood, Dan? Montana will come out this way, and we'll proceed to the EEOB.'

'Yes, ma'am.'

He caught me staring at him as he turned to go. I didn't know how much Cormorant had already been told, but my presence spoke for itself. He'd have to know what this was about. Still, I couldn't get a read on him, and he was already headed back in, radioing orders into his cuff.

'This is Cormorant. I need Montana detail ready to move, on my lead. Command, we're going to need full transport from the North Plaza. *Immediately.*'

On instinct, I leaned over and spoke quietly to Agent Ridge.

'You should go in with him,' I said.

He didn't look at me. 'Thanks for the tip, Detective.'

'I'm serious,' I told him, but he put a hand out to keep me back, more like a straight-arm.

'Cross, someday you're going to be king of the

world, but in the meantime, just keep your damn shirt on.'

I was finding that hard to do. I didn't like this scenario one bit — not if Theodore Vance really was our killer.

111

Something was wrong. Teddy could feel the tension coming off Cormorant before the Secret Service agent even spoke into his ear. 'Excuse me, sir. Would you come with me, please? It's kind of important.'

Maggie saw it too, and knew exactly how to respond. She smiled her best Big Party smile. 'Don't keep him long now, Dan, okay?'

'Yes, ma'am.'

'Governor, hold that thought,' Teddy told his and Maggie's guest. 'I'll be right back.'

Then, not knowing quite why, he leaned in and kissed his wife on the cheek. 'I love you, darling,' he whispered, and she winked back.

Sweet Maggie. The world would probably never know how good this woman could be. Not that he really loved her, exactly, or could even tell himself what that was supposed to feel like. But it worked. *They* worked. However much about him she would never know, it couldn't erase what was true between them. Sum of the parts and all that. Complicated, like all relationships.

He double-stepped to come alongside the agent as they moved across the foyer.

'What's going on, Dan?'

'Sir, I need you to stay calm,' Cormorant said. 'The FBI have a few questions for you. They're waiting outside to follow us to the EEOB.'

Teddy stopped short. 'Hang on a second. Are you trying — ' He cocked his head to one side and smiled at a couple of passing gawkers. Then he turned his back to the room. 'Are you trying to give me a fucking heart attack here?'

'Sir, I know what I'm doing. I really do. I need you to trust me.'

'Trust you? You're walking me right into them!'

Cormorant shoved his radio hand into his pocket, and his voice dropped to a fierce whisper. 'Haven't I proven anything to you by now? For God's sake, Teddy, get it together. They just want to ask you some questions.'

'Why don't I believe that, Dan? This is bad. This is very bad, isn't it?'

'Listen to me.' The agent's eyes traveled to the farthest exit and back again. 'The only viable way out of this is straight through those doors. We either keep moving or they're coming in after you. There's nowhere to run, Teddy. If they come in here, it will be an embarrassment for the president.'

He could see them now, a collection of dark suits out on the River Terrace — including that MPD detective who had been dogging him. Alex Cross. The one who should have been dead and disposed of a long time ago.

'Sir, we have to go.'

'*Don't rush me*, goddamnit! Are you forgetting? I'm Teddy Vance.'

Teddy straightened his tie and took a fluted glass off a passing waiter's tray. It was a struggle not to down it all at once. Just a swallow for now, and another casual smile for the room, while the blood pounded in his ears.

'All right,' he said. 'Let's do this. I can certainly answer a few of their questions.'

112

Dan Cormorant was smooth and efficient, I'll give him that much. He disappeared into the Grand Foyer and reappeared about forty-five seconds later with Theodore Vance at his side. Everything seemed to be right on track so far.

Then Vance stopped before they actually reached the door. He turned to say something to the Secret Service agent. Cormorant pocketed his mic. This wasn't good, not good at all.

Next to me, Angela Riordan cupped a palm over her earpiece, trying to hear. 'Dan, what are you doing?'

He didn't respond.

'Cormorant, keep it moving. Dan! Get Montana out of there now,' said Riordan.

She motioned to Agent Ridge that he should go in, but then pulled him back when Vance turned on his own and started to come our way. He was looking right at us now.

Was he Zeus? According to Hannah Willis he was. And I believed her.

Cormorant followed a step behind, with three other members of the spousal detail just ahead and on either side of the First Gentleman. An agent at the door pushed it open and stepped out first, then held it for Vance to come through.

The next happened in a blink. One of those instants that comes and goes but is photographed in the mind, then never, ever forgotten.

Cormorant was mostly obscured behind Vance, and I just saw the back of his jacket flip up.

My Glock came out an instant later, but already it was too late.

The .357 rose in Cormorant's hand, and he fired into the back of Theodore Vance's head. Vance flew forward and landed hard on the cement outside.

Chaos followed. Incomprehension. Terror. Disbelief. Almost immediately, Cormorant took some number of simultaneous shots from the agents around him. Within seconds, he was down too and the place had erupted into sheer madness.

Hundreds of people were screaming and trying to run for the exits. Right away, the foyer drapes started to close, cutting off the scene of the shootings.

As they did, I spotted a tight cluster of Secret Service agents, running with what I assumed was the president toward whatever nearest hard room they had set up. I wondered if she knew her husband had been shot.

Riordan was shouting into her radio, trying to be heard over the other noise. 'Shots fired! Montana is down; I repeat, Montana is down! We need an advanced life support team to the River Terrace. North side. *Now!*'

Teddy Vance's detail had formed two circles around him, one close on the ground and the other facing out, weapons drawn. Mahoney and I spread out as part of a wider perimeter.

Already, the press corps was pushing in at the

330

edges, frantic to get their stories, to get *anything*. Cops were everywhere, sirens were blaring in the street, and there was deafening shouting coming from all sides, all at once.

It was too early for official theories, but I thought I knew what we'd just witnessed. Cormorant was a veteran agent, a patriot, at least in his own mind. He'd waited for Teddy Vance to clear the building, then fired one lethal bullet, knowing he'd take kill shots in return. It was a suicide as much as an assassination — the last act in a bloody cover-up and, in Agent Cormorant's own way, the last piece of damage control he could offer his president.

113

Shaken and exhausted, I got home around four thirty that morning, maybe the last of my vampire hours for a while. If Bree wasn't already up, I was going to wake her and tell her what had happened —

But she wasn't even there. Bree wasn't anywhere in the house.

I realized this as soon as I saw Aunt Tia's big knitting bag on the floor by the kitchen table. Tia had come to stay with the kids, and Saint Bree had gone to cover my overnight at the hospital. Of course she had. She wouldn't have wanted Nana to be alone any more than I did.

I almost got back in the car, but it made more sense to spell Bree first thing in the morning and let Tia go home then. We were stretched thin as it was.

So I went upstairs and lay on top of the covers, wide awake and buzzing with everything that had happened, not just tonight but in the past few weeks. The scope of it all was going to reverberate for months, even years, I was sure. We still didn't know how many others like Caroline there had been, and maybe never would. Nor did we know the extent of the cover-up for Zeus, or who had been doing the covering. Theodore Vance had been a successful and very rich businessman on his own. He'd had the resources to do whatever he wished or fantasized about. Apparently that's exactly what he had done.

Later in the day, I'd have to call my sister-in-law, Michelle. I'd also have to decide how much of her daughter's story I was going to tell her. Some of the details had no place in a mother's memory. Sometimes I wonder about the place they have in mine.

It hadn't been half an hour since I'd gotten home, if that, when the phone rang out in the hall.

I jumped up to catch it before a third ring. Considering the events of the past twenty-four hours, it might have been any number of people looking for me.

'Alex Cross,' I answered in a whisper.

And just like that, life changed again.

'Alex, it's Zadie Mitchell calling from the hospital. How soon can you get over here?'

114

I ran.

I ran out to the car in the driveway.

I ran my siren all the way to St. Anthony's, and I ran up four flights of stairs to Nana's room.

When I came in, Bree was there with tears streaming down her face. And next to her, in the bed, with eyes like slits — but *open* — was Nana Mama.

Regina Hope Cross, the toughest person I've ever known in my life, wasn't done with us yet.

Her voice was just a crackle, static almost, but it nearly bowled me over. 'What took you so long?' she said. 'I'm back.'

'Yes, you are.' I was beaming when I knelt down to kiss her as gently as I could. She still had two IVs and the A-V line to her heart, but the vent and feeding tubes were off, and it was like seeing someone I hadn't laid eyes on for weeks and weeks.

'What did I miss?' she asked.

'Nothing much. Hardly a thing. The world stopped spinning without you.'

'Very funny,' she said, although I was kind of serious. Everything else could wait.

Zadie and one of the cardiologists, Dr. Steig, were in the room monitoring Nana's condition. 'Regina's going to need what we call an LVAD,' the doctor said. 'A left ventricular assist device.

It's the next best thing to a transplant, and it'll help get her home sooner rather than later.' He put a hand on Nana's shoulder and spoke up a little. 'Looking forward to anything in particular, Regina?'

She nodded groggily. 'To not being dead yet,' she said, and I laughed with everyone else.

Her eyes fluttered closed again.

'She'll be in and out for at least a few days,' Steig said. 'Nothing to worry about.'

He took a few more minutes to go over the care plan with Bree and me, and then gave us some time alone in the room.

As we sat together by the bed, Bree told me she'd seen the overnight news. All the major channels were broadcasting live from the Kennedy Center, the White House, and the Vances' home in Philadelphia. Already, a kind of awkward mourning had begun and was spreading around the country.

'So, is that really it?' Bree asked. 'Is it over?'

'Yeah,' I said, thinking more about Nana than about Teddy Vance. 'As much as anything ever is. Zeus is dead. That much we know for sure.'

Epilogue

PHOENIX RISING

115

The holiday season flew by this year, and I'm not kidding. Damon came home for Christmas break, and by New Year's Eve, Nana was mobile enough to do a whole crown roast for the family, with a little help from her friends. It was a perfect way to say good-bye to the year, just the six of us — even if Ali and Nana didn't quite make it to midnight.

New Year's Day started quietly too. I listened to a few chapters of Ha Jin's *A Free Life* with Nana in her room, made brunch for the kids, and then asked Bree if she'd take a drive with me in the afternoon.

'A drive in the country would be perfect,' she said. 'Good idea. I'm in.'

It was just below freezing out, but perfectly climate controlled inside the car. I put on some John Legend, pointed north, and watched the world sail by for an hour or so.

Bree didn't even notice where we were headed until I got off 270 in Maryland.

'Oh, goody.'

'Oh, *goody?*'

'You heard me. Oh, goody. Goody, goody gumdrops. I love this place!'

Catoctin Mountain Park is something of a sentimental favorite for us. It was the first place Bree and I ever went away together, and we'd gone camping there a few times since, with the kids and just the two of us. It's beautiful year round — and closed on New Year's Day, as it turned out.

'No big deal, Alex,' Bree said. 'It's a beautiful drive here, anyway.'

I pulled over at the big stone gate outside the main entrance and turned off the car's engine.

'Let's go for our walk. What are they going to do, arrest us?

116

A few minutes later, Bree and I had the Cunningham Falls trail all to ourselves, as alone as we were going to get in the course of an afternoon. The snow was fresh; the sky was bright blue — one of nature's perfect days.

'Got any resolutions?' I asked her.

'Sure,' she said. 'Work too much, stop going to the gym, and eat until I'm fat. How about you?'

'I'm going to stop recycling.'

'Good plan.'

'Maybe spend a little less time with the kids.'

'Definitely that. Great idea.'

'And I want to see if I can't get the woman I love to marry me.'

Bree stopped short — I would have hoped for no less. I took advantage of the moment and pulled the ring out of my pocket.

'It was Nana's,' I said. 'She'd like you to have it too.'

'Oh, my God.' Bree was smiling and shaking her head; I couldn't quite read the expression. 'Alex, so much has just gone down in your life. Are you sure this is the right time for you?'

If this were some other woman, I might have thought it was code for letting me down easy. But this was Bree, and she doesn't do code.

'Bree, do you remember the night of my birthday?' I asked her.

'Sure,' she said, a little confused. 'When

341

everything started. All the gunk. That's the night you first heard about Caroline.'

'And up until that phone call from Davies, it was supposed to be the night I asked you to marry me. So if we can't have that back, I'd say right now is just about perfect. Will you marry me, Bree? I love you so much I can't stand it.'

The wind kicked up, and she reached inside my coat to put her arms around me. Then we kissed for a long time. 'I love you too,' Bree whispered.

'Then yes, Alex,' she finally said. 'I do love you so much. Yes to you. Yes to your amazing family — '

'Our amazing family,' I said, and kissed her again.

She nodded, close in against me, shutting out the cold. 'Yes to all of it.'

117

We celebrated again that night, Szechuan takeout this time, and then a bottle of champagne with Sampson and Billie over at the house to hear the big news. No one could have been more excited than I was, but Sampson and Billie came pretty close. I didn't hear a single crack about how crazy Bree was for marrying me.

Much later, we were lying in bed — just Bree and me, that is — and already talking about a summer wedding, when my cell phone rang in the nightstand.

'No, no, no.' I pulled a pillow over my head. '*This* is my New Year's resolution. No more phones. Maybe ever.'

We were both due back at work the next morning — but that wasn't for another eight hours.

'Sweetie' — Bree climbed over me to take the phone out of the drawer — 'I'm marrying a cop. Cops answer their calls. Get over it.' She handed it to me with another kiss and rolled off again.

'Alex Cross,' I said.

'I wanted to be among the first to congratulate you, Alex. You and Bree. What a happy ending this is.'

I sat up. The voice wasn't just familiar. It was a stone-cold *live* nightmare.

Most of the world knew Kyle Craig as the Mastermind. I knew him as an old friend who was now my worst enemy.

'Kyle, why are you really calling me?'

'I'm bored, Alex. Nobody plays with me the way you do. Nobody knows me like you do. Might be a good time for some more fun. Just the two of us.'

'I don't think we define that word in the same way,' I said.

He laughed softly. 'I'm sure you're right. Besides, even I can see you need a little break after Zeus. Consider it my wedding present to you. Just don't get too comfortable, my friend. Nothing lasts forever. But then, you already knew that, didn't you? All my best wishes to Bree, to Nana, and of course the kids. And Alex — *here's to fun.*'

THE WOMEN'S MURDER CLUB SERIES:
3RD DEGREE (*with Andrew Gross*)
4TH OF JULY (*with Maxine Paetro*)
THE 5TH HORSEMAN (*with Maxine Paetro*)
THE 6TH TARGET (*with Maxine Paetro*)
7TH HEAVEN (*with Maxine Paetro*)
9TH JUDGEMENT (*with Maxine Paetro*)
10TH ANNIVERSARY (*with Maxine Paetro*)

We do hope that you have enjoyed reading this large print book.

Did you know that all of our titles are available for purchase?

We publish a wide range of high quality large print books including:
Romances, Mysteries, Classics
General Fiction
Non Fiction and Westerns

Special interest titles available in large print are:
The Little Oxford Dictionary
Music Book
Song Book
Hymn Book
Service Book

Also available from us courtesy of Oxford University Press:
Young Readers' Dictionary
(large print edition)
Young Readers' Thesaurus
(large print edition)

For further information or a free brochure, please contact us at:
Ulverscroft Large Print Books Ltd.,
The Green, Bradgate Road, Anstey,
Leicester, LE7 7FU, England.
Tel: (00 44) 0116 236 4325
Fax: (00 44) 0116 234 0205

10TH ANNIVERSARY

James Patterson and Maxine Paetro

Detective Lindsay Boxer's wedding celebration becomes a distant memory when she is called to investigate a horrendous crime: a badly injured teenage girl is left for dead, and her newborn baby is nowhere to be found. She finds that the victim may be keeping secrets. Meanwhile, Assistant District Attorney Yuki Castellano is prosecuting a woman accused of murdering her husband in front of her two young children. Yuki's career rests on a guilty verdict. So when Lindsay finds evidence that could save the defendant, should she trust her best friend or follow her instinct? And while the pressure to find the baby begins to interfere with her new marriage to Joe, Lindsay wonders if she'll ever be able to start a family of her own.

9TH JUDGEMENT

James Patterson and Maxine Paetro

A young mother and her infant child are ruthlessly gunned down while returning to their car in the garage of a shopping mall. There are no witnesses, and the only evidence for Detective Lindsay Boxer is a cryptic message scrawled across the windshield in blood-red lipstick. The same night, the wife of A-list actor Marcus Dowling walks in on a cat burglar who is about to steal millions of dollars' worth of precious jewels. In seconds there is an empty safe, a lifeless body, and another mystery that throws San Francisco into hysteria. Before Lindsay and her friends can piece together either case, one of the killers forces Lindsay to put her own life on the line — but is it enough to save the city?

WORST CASE

James Patterson and Michael Ledwidge

The son of one of New York's wealthiest families is snatched off the street and held hostage. But this kidnapper isn't demanding money: he quizzes his prisoner's family on the price others pay for his life of luxury — wrong answers are fatal. Detective Michael Bennett leads the investigation, and as another student disappears, powerful, well-connected families pressurise all possible agencies to stop this killer. Eventually, the FBI sends their top Abduction Specialist, Agent Emily Parker. Bennett's work life — and love life — suddenly get more complicated. And Bennett is unable to protest against the FBI's intrusion on his case, when, suddenly, the mastermind changes his routine. His plan involves the most shocking demonstration yet — one that could bring cataclysmic devastation to every inch of New York.

SWIMSUIT

James Patterson and Maxine Paetro

A breathtakingly beautiful supermodel disappears from a swimsuit photo shoot at a glamorous hotel in Hawaii. Just hours later, Kim McDaniels' parents receive a horrifying phone call. Fearing the worst, they board the first flight to Maui and begin the hunt for their daughter. Ex-cop Ben Hawkins, now a reporter for the *LA Times*, gets the McDaniels assignment. The local police are so inept that Ben has to start his own investigation for Kim McDaniels to have a prayer. And for Ben to have the story of his life. Meanwhile, the killer sets the stage for his next production. His audience expects the best — and they won't be disappointed . . .

THE MURDER OF KING TUT

James Patterson and Martin Dugard

Since 1922, when Howard Carter discovered Tut's 3,000-year-old tomb, most Egyptologists have presumed that the young king died of disease, or perhaps an accident, such as a chariot fall. But what if his fate was actually much more sinister? Now, in *The Murder of King Tut*, James Patterson and Martin Dugard chronicle their epic quest to find out what happened to the boy-king. The result is a true crime tale of intrigue, betrayal, and usurpation which presents a compelling case that King Tut's death was anything but natural.